MISSION HILL

PAMELA WECHSLER

MISSION HILL

MINOTAUR BOOKS
NEW YORK

MISSION HILL. Copyright © 2016 by Pamela Wechsler. All rights reserved. Printed in the United States of America. For information, address St. Martin's Press, 175 Fifth Avenue, New York, N.Y. 10010.

www.minotaurbooks.com

The Library of Congress Cataloging-in-Publication Data is available upon request.

ISBN 978-1-250-07569-7 (hardcover)
ISBN 978-1-4668-8713-8 (e-book)

Our books may be purchased in bulk for promotional, educational, or business use. Please contact your local bookseller or the Macmillan Corporate and Premium Sales Department at 1-800-221-7945, extension 5442, or by e-mail at MacmillanSpecialMarkets@macmillan.com.

First Edition: May 2016

10 9 8 7 6 5 4 3 2 1

To my father, Henry,
and in memory of my mother, Joan

MISSION HILL

Chapter One

I'm in bed, silently reciting their names. Number one, Lester Beale, stabbed his girlfriend twenty-six times. Number two, Jeffrey Younts, shot a fifteen-year-old boy as he stepped off the school bus. Number three, Omar Monteiro, gunned down twin brothers on their thirtieth birthday. This is my nighttime ritual. I count killers, the people I've prosecuted for murder.

My list contains twenty-six names. It's arranged in chronological order and reaches back four years. It used to include victims, the people who fuel my addiction to the job and keep me coming back for more. When my homicides climbed into double digits, there were too many names to remember. Someone had to go, either predator or prey. Reluctantly, I let go of my victims, held on to my killers. I had to. That's the whole point. They remember me, so I have to remember them.

Many of my victims' names have blurred, but I'll never forget their faces. Number four, Devon Williams, smashed the life out of his son. The boy was fifteen months old. He had big brown eyes, pudgy cheeks, and weighed all of twenty-two pounds. When paramedics brought him to the morgue, there was blood spatter on the front of his Tony the Tiger onesie.

When I reach number five, Rodney Quirk, who shot his cousin at point-blank range, I feel a familiar jolt of anxiety. My heart pounds as the beginning of a panic attack takes hold. I sit up and remind myself to breathe, knowing that it will pass.

Rodney is the reason I started my list. He strapped a vest onto the chest of a ten-year-old, grabbed a fully loaded .357, and pulled the trigger. Turned out, the vest wasn't bulletproof. He was charged with first-degree murder, but my only eyewitness got cold feet, and the case fell apart.

Now Rodney is my silent stalker, part of my daily routine. Every morning he takes up his perch in the window of a coffee shop across from the courthouse. He sits, stone-faced, and watches me stride by on my way to work, hugging my Prada tote. He's never confronted me—not yet—but he wants to remind me that he's there, thinking about me.

It would be easy to avoid him. I could enter the rear of the building with the judges and prisoner vans, but that would signal defeat. I don't want him to know I'm afraid. I don't want anyone to know I'm afraid. Besides, this way, I can keep track of him. We can both know where the other one is. There's only one thing scarier than seeing Rodney in that window every morning— *not* seeing him, wondering where he is and what he's up to.

I steady my breathing and reach for the bottle of ginger ale that I keep on my bedside table. As the warm, spicy soda trickles down the back of my throat, I let go of Rodney and move on to numbers six and seven, Jimmy Franklin and Roosevelt Prince, drug deal gone bad.

The phone chirps, startling me. I grab it, catching it between the first and second rings. There's no need to check the name on the display. A phone call at 3:00 A.M. can be only one thing: someone in Boston has been murdered.

Chapter Two

I leave the warmth of my bed and draw the curtains. Outside, the moon is full, illuminating wide streaks of ice on the Charles, the river that divides Boston and Cambridge. The view stretches all the way to Winthrop House, the dorm where I lived as an undergrad at Harvard.

I put my hand over the phone and cough, trying to clear the remnants of panic from my throat.

"Abby Endicott, homicide," I say.

"You catching tonight?" Kevin says.

Boston police detective Kevin Farnsworth is not one to waste time with pleasantries. He's rough around the edges but has earned the respect of everyone he deals with, from the rank and file on the street to the judges on the bench. He's old-school, a cop who commands with competence.

We met over a decade ago, when I was a rookie assistant district attorney and he had just earned his detective's shield. Over the years, we forged an unspoken agreement; he gives me first dibs on his murder investigations, and, whenever possible, I accept.

"What do you have?" I hope he can't detect the dryness in my voice.

"You got a cold or something?" he says.

"I'm fine," I lie.

"You sound like a frog."

I used to worry that Kevin's bluntness would be off-putting to jurors, but it's the opposite. People trust him. The fact that he's six two with 0 percent body fat doesn't hurt. More than once, a female grand juror asked about his marital status. He's been happily married for sixteen years and four months. Not that I'm counting.

"I'm gonna swing by and get you," he says.

My antenna goes up. "Since when do you shuttle prosecutors to crime scenes?"

"I can be there in twelve minutes." He's all business. "I'm just leaving Doyle's."

"There was a murder at Doyle's?"

Located in Jamaica Plain, about five miles from my Back Bay condo, Doyle's is an unlikely place for a homicide. It's the bar of choice for police and prosecutors, a traditional Irish pub where you can order a pint of Guinness with your breakfast. The walls are lined with autographed black and whites of local celebrities—who, in Boston, are athletes and politicians. Distress calls are a rarity, maybe an occasional drunken brawl, but there are plenty of off-duty cops on-site to handle that type of thing.

"Doyle's is the last place the vic was seen alive," Kevin says. "They found the body a couple of blocks away."

"Thanks for the offer, but I don't need an escort. I'll meet you there."

"If you're trying to convince me that you're not high maintenance, that ship sailed three years ago when you showed up at that shooting in Roxbury wearing a ball gown and high heels."

"I told you, it was a family thing, my parents' fortieth anniversary party."

"My folks celebrated theirs at the VFW hall in Allston."

"When Chris Sarsfield is catching, I bet you don't offer him a ride."

"Suit yourself," he says. "The crime scene is behind the tow lot, off Joan Drive. Meet me at the perimeter—there's something I want to talk to you about before you jump in."

"What's going on?"

"I'll tell you when I see you."

Kevin tends to keep his own counsel, but not about cases we're working together.

"You're starting to freak me out."

"Do yourself a favor and stay off the Internet."

I grab my iPad and log on to boston.com, the best source for local news, but I can't find anything about a murder in Jamaica Plain.

"Is the victim still at the scene?"

"Yup."

If there's no hope for survival, the victim is left undisturbed until the medical examiner arrives. Otherwise, he's rushed to a hospital—usually Boston Medical Center—where emergency room doctors work miracles these days. Many insiders believe the real reason for the decline in the murder rate isn't community policing or social engineering—it's improved urgent care.

My mind races. "Are there any suspects?"

"Not yet," he says. "I'm onto you—you're trying to keep me on the horn long enough to drag something out of me, but it's not going to work."

Kevin knows my Achilles' heels, the cases that upset me most, and he's protecting me from something. I imagine the worst. Maybe the victim was burned or decapitated. Maybe there are two victims, or three. Or maybe the victim is a baby.

He reels off directions, and I jot down the street names. After I hang up, I check Twitter and a couple of local TV websites but come up empty. Trying to stave off a full-blown anxiety attack, I go into the bathroom and focus on my routine. Brush my teeth. Apply blush, mascara, and lip color. Not too much—it's bad form to arrive at a crime scene looking like I wasted time with makeup.

I rush back into the bedroom and slip into my standard homicide response outfit, a black sweater and black pants. It's both reverential and stylish, suitable for any funereal occasion. Homicide prosecutors never have to worry about making a good impression on clients—they're all dead. But there are survivors—friends and family. Our first meeting is important. We'll spend the next year together. They'll tell me about their loved one's life, and I'll tell them about his death.

My boyfriend, Ty Clarke, is in the living room, sprawled out on the beige leather sofa, wrapped in the burgundy mohair throw that my parents picked up on their recent trip to Scotland. The sofa can barely contain Ty's muscular six-foot frame. His sinewy forearm dangles over the edge. His deep-brown complexion is flawless, the softest skin I've ever touched. Open-mouthed, he's breathing deeply, pretending to be asleep.

The skunky smell of marijuana fills the room. Ty must have been smoking a joint and stubbed it out when he heard the phone ring. Usually, he goes out on the terrace to get high, and I pretend not to notice. It's one of the games we play.

Ty and I have been together for a little less than a year. He's unlike anyone I've ever been with before: unpretentious, undemanding, and lighthearted. For our first date, he took me to Anchovies, a hole-in-the-wall not far from my Back Bay apartment. We quickly discovered that we both like mussels fra diavolo, full-bodied red wine, and early Miles Davis. Besides that, we have almost nothing in common. I waited the obligatory three dates before taking him home and screwing him on the living room couch, the one he's fake snoring on now.

What began as a string of one-night stands has slowly evolved into a relationship, and recently, he's been spending most nights here. His apartment is a few miles away, across the river in Somerville. It's not uninhabitable, just bare bones. He has a couch and a bed, but nothing frivolous like a kitchen table. Even though my apartment is over two thousand square feet, with plenty of closet space, I haven't offered him a place to store more than a toothbrush and a change of clothes. He never pushes, which is one of the reasons we've lasted this long.

Committing to a partner is not my strong suit. I came close with one man, and it was devastating when he chose someone else. Heartbreak is a predictable part of my workday, and I do everything I can to avoid it at home. It's easier to commit to dead strangers than to risk pain with living, breathing human beings.

The bottom of my coat closet is lined with an assortment of shoes: stilettos, wedges, sneakers, flats. I rummage around and select a pair of sensible black pumps. There's no predicting how far I'll have to walk or what I'll be stepping on. Mud, gravel, viscera.

Ty starts to stir. "Is that you, babe?"

"Sorry, I didn't mean to wake you."

He sits up and wipes invisible sleep from his eyes. "Where are you off to?"

"Jamaica Plain." I put on my coat and double-wrap a scarf around my neck.

"I'll walk you to your car."

"That's okay, I'm in a hurry. Don't get up."

Ty stands, steps into a pair of cowboy boots, and throws on a leather jacket. I grab my tote, and we head out the door.

Chapter Three

Manny Lewis, the night doorman, is in the lobby of my building. He stands when he hears our shoes scuffle across the marble floor. Manny knows the drill, is accustomed to my crazy hours. He nods and adjusts the name tag on his lapel. The condo board insists that he wear an identification badge even though he's been working here for twenty-five years.

My last apartment was in a charming brownstone on quiet, tree-lined Marlborough Street, where there was no doorman, no security. That was before Rodney Quirk entered my life. Now it's all about being anonymous and vigilant. Living in a high-rise building, walking a different route to and from work every day, reciting my list.

I untwist a key from my silver circle ring and hand it to Manny. "Can you get this to Lilia?"

"Didn't you used to keep a spare for your housekeeper here at the front desk?" Manny says.

Ty flashes a smile and dangles the key that I gave him last month. "I'll go down to the hardware store on Charles Street and have another one made," he says. "I'll drop it off later."

I hadn't intended to surrender permanent access to my apartment to Ty, but my upstairs neighbor flooded my bathroom last month, and Ty volunteered to oversee the renovations.

9

Temporary convenience, not long-term commitment, was the impetus for our arrangement, but it works. I used to dread coming home late to an empty apartment. He's easy company, willing to tolerate my neuroses, and, as much as I try to resist, he's filling a space in my heart.

"Are you headed to that murder in JP?" Manny says.

His tablet is on the reception counter, streaming the news. The crawler at the bottom of the screen has a special alert. *Breaking News . . . Sixth Murder of the Year . . . Homicide in Jamaica Plain . . . Boston Police Officer Believed to Be Victim . . . Name Not Yet Released.*

"Oh, God, it's a police officer." My stomach drops. "I've got to go."

"Careful—there's black ice out there," Manny says.

The automatic glass doors slide open, and a blast of cold air hits my face, causing my eyes to tear up. Ty and I walk two blocks, up Beacon Street, to where my Prius is parked. I use the remote to unlock the car. Ty opens the trunk and pulls out my Kevlar vest.

"This thing weighs more than you do," he says, helping me slip it on.

The armor feels long and bulky under my cashmere coat.

"Why don't you take an unmarked Taurus like the rest of your squad? You'd have the lights and siren."

"I like my hybrid. I want to do my part, help save the planet."

Ty looks at me and raises his eyebrows, not buying it.

"Okay, I want to fly under the radar," I say. "Navigating the underbelly of the city in the middle of the night is dangerous enough without being mistaken for a cop."

"Then you should've kept the Audi your parents gave you for your birthday."

"Audis are magnets for carjackers. I don't know any self-respecting criminal who would jack a Prius."

Ty moves to kiss me good-bye, but I've already turned my

head away. His lips land on my ear. I open the door, toss my tote on the passenger seat, and turn back to kiss him.

"Stay safe," he says.

I close the door and press the ignition. Idling in neutral, I turn on the radio and scan the stations for news of the murder, desperate to learn the victim's identity. All the reports are the same: *Name withheld pending notification of next of kin.*

The mall that runs the length of Commonwealth Avenue is festive; thousands of white lightbulbs are twisted around the branches of the leafless trees. Barreling through the darkness, I pass familiar landmarks. The stately brownstone on Dartmouth Street where an investment banker bludgeoned his wife to death with a nine iron. The nightclub on Tremont Street where a French au pair was snatched off the street, eviscerated, and tossed in the garbage. The corner of West Dedham Street where a Tufts medical student was mugged, knifed, and left to bleed out on the sidewalk.

A couple of miles from my apartment, the landscape shifts from artisan bakeries and yoga studios to liquor stores and bail bondsmen. The GPS instructs me to take a left, but Kevin mentioned a shortcut. I reach over to the passenger seat and feel around for the paper with his directions. I must've hit a patch of ice—I skid and regain control of the car.

A group of gang kids watches me drive by, one spits on the sidewalk—a sign of disrespect, aimed at me. He's made me, in spite of the Prius. I want to tell him that I'm a lawyer, not a cop. I can't arrest him. I don't carry a gun. I'm lost. And I'm scared.

Chapter Four

The area around the tow lot is controlled chaos. A swarm of uniforms and plainclothes detectives hold flashlights as they scour for evidence. Technicians roll measuring wheels and use white chalk to mark distances. The crime scene unit erects a white tent, affording investigators privacy, shielding the victim from view. Lookie-loos gather, assess, speculate. A pack of reporters and cameramen prepare to set up live shots. A young aide in a rumpled suit sets up a podium with the city seal, a sign that there's going to be a press conference.

My boss, District Attorney Max Lombardo, is standing on the sidelines, talking to Mayor Ray Harris. Lately, Max has been putting out feelers, toying with the idea of running for mayor, and Ray knows it. The two men are political rivals, vying for attention, usually taking swipes at each other in the press. Tonight they seem to have set aside their differences. They look united in their solemnity and purpose.

Max catches my eye and holds up a finger, signaling that he'll be with me in a minute. I nod in recognition and duck under the yellow crime scene tape.

"Evening, ADA Endicott," Officer Santos Muniz says. "Kevin Farnsworth has been looking for you. I'll let him know you're here."

Santos is holding a clipboard, and he writes down my name. Everyone who crosses the perimeter must be accounted for.

"Thanks, Santos," I say. "Booties?"

He offers up a cardboard dispenser filled with blue paper shoe covers, and I take two.

"If I was you, I wouldn't be in a rush to get over there," he says.

"I appreciate the heads-up, but at this point, I've pretty much seen it all."

"Yeah, me too. But this one is really bad. I wish there was a way to un-see what I just seen."

The sight of a dead body repulses me. I know that it's important to view the decedent firsthand, that every corpse tells a story, but I prefer to get the information secondhand from the medical examiner. When I was new to the homicide unit, I forced myself to attend every autopsy. Once I made my bones, had several convictions under my belt, I begged off.

Memories of those procedures still haunt me. The bodies of my victims, splayed out on a cold, hard slab. The medical examiner holding a scalpel, slicing into the torso, making a Y-shaped incision, and prying open the flaps of skin. The lab assistant plopping the rubbery, reddish-brown liver onto a scale, and dumping the stomach contents into a plastic container. And there's the smell, the unforgettable combination of odors, formaldehyde and freshly cut bowels. I tried all sorts of tricks to mask it. Wearing heavy perfume. Breathing only through my mouth. Drinking from a can of Coke with a smear of VapoRub under my nose. Nothing worked.

I glove up, steady myself on a hydrant and slip the booties on over my pumps. Carl Ostroff, an anchor from Channel 7, charges over. Carl has camera-ready good looks, overbleached white teeth, and perfect hair, but he's not afraid to roll around in the mud. We have about as good a relationship as a reporter and a prosecutor can have. I leak information to him when it serves my case, and he gets the exclusive. He hasn't double-crossed me yet, but chances are that he will.

Carl stops just short of the crime scene tape and pushes a microphone in my face. A klieg light flips on, blinding me. I block the glare by cupping my hands over my eyes, and stare at him. He's not dissuaded.

"I'm here behind Lattimore's Towing with Abigail Endicott, chief homicide prosecutor for the Suffolk County District Attorney's Office. Abby, I know this has to be a difficult one. What can you tell us?"

"This better not be live."

He waves off the cameraman. "I thought you'd want to go on the record, share some thoughts about the victim."

"Come on, Carl, I just got here."

"Yeah, but you know, right?" He seems genuinely confused.

Kevin is moving away from the tent, rushing toward me. His right arm is extended, palm facing me, like a traffic cop.

"Hold up, Abby. Let's talk for a minute." Kevin takes my elbow and tries to turn me in the opposite direction, but I jerk my arm away.

"Enough of this protective, paternalistic bullshit," I say. "Everyone knows what's going on but me. Who is it?"

"I wanted to tell you in person."

"Okay, I'm here. Tell me."

On the periphery of the white tent, a technician holds a magnifying glass as he meticulously dusts a Ford Taurus for prints.

"That's a detective's car," I say.

"No, the vic wasn't a detective," Kevin says.

He starts to explain, but something catches my eye, distracting me. It's ten feet away, on the pavement, encircled by a chalk outline, a few inches from an orange cone evidence marker. I stare in disbelief.

"Abby, listen," Kevin says.

"It can't be."

Everything starts to swirl in slow motion, the noise around me sharpens into a shrill hum. This is worse than anything I ever could have imagined. The reports got it wrong. It's not a cop.

"Try to breathe," Kevin says.

I take a few steps closer to get a better look. There's no mistaking what it is: his trademark blue-and-white NY Yankees baseball cap.

Plenty of people wear Yankees paraphernalia in Boston—students, tourists, my uncle Dalton. But there's only one man who has the irreverence, bravado, and sense of humor to wear a Yankees hat while tossing back a pint at Doyle's or sitting behind the wheel of an unmarked Boston police car.

I know who it is but I have to see for myself. With Kevin by my side, I inch forward and peer inside the tent. There he is—Tim Mooney—with a bullet hole in his head.

Chapter Five

Tim and I started our careers together. We shared an office in the decrepit Suffolk Superior courthouse, before it was evacuated and condemned, like one of my crime scenes. There were eleven of us crammed into a windowless room, buried between floors. Chips of paint, most likely lead, fell from the walls. It was unbearably hot in the summer and even hotter in the winter. The water dispenser was permanently out of repair and the only bathroom was public—sometimes it doubled as a shooting gallery for defendants who needed a heroin fix.

We were district court prosecutors, earning $27,000 a year, working long hours under impossible conditions. Unwilling victims berated us, sleazy defense attorneys challenged our ethics, political hack judges mocked us. And we loved every second of it.

Now we're each assigned to our own offices, windowed and carpeted, in a modern building, One Bulfinch Place. Most prosecutors at our level have plaques, commendations, citations, adorning their walls. The only decorations in Tim's office are snapshots of his wife and daughter tacked to a bulletin board. My walls are filled with pictures too—mug shots, crime scenes, and murder victims. I don't keep any family photos, birthday cards, or posters from my favorite museums. Nothing that could

17

give visitors a clue about who I spend time with or where I go outside of work.

"You're shaking." Kevin unscrews the cap from a water bottle and hands it to me. "Here, drink this."

I force the breath out of my throat. "That baseball hat—it's Tim's."

"I'm sorry. I know you guys were close."

Kevin doesn't know the half of it. No one does. People think that we're the kind of friends who would eventually realize we were meant for each other. Like Ross and Rachel or Mulder and Scully. The truth is that Tim and I dated secretly, off and on, for years. He's the only man I ever felt sure about. I was convinced that he was the one, even after he broke my heart.

Four years ago, Tim met Julia at a retirement party for her father, a Boston police sergeant. We were all introduced to one another at the same time. We got into a discussion about TV cop shows, each declaring our favorite. Mine was *Prime Suspect*—the British version. Tim's was *Law & Order*—the original version. Julia's was *Monk*. I don't think that *Monk* qualifies as a cop show, but I didn't want to seem petty, so I didn't debate the issue.

Tim was okay looking, kind of short at five eight, nondescript with his rep ties and boy's regular haircut. But there was something about his quiet self-confidence, his resolve, that was apparent upon first meeting him. He made you feel lucky to be in his presence. Julia was drawn in, just like I was.

Everything about Julia was gentle: her laugh, her smile, her flowing auburn hair. Tim was attracted to her immediately, and she to him. She's everything in a partner that I'm not: trusting, patient, nurturing, reliable. She was the perfect mother, the perfect wife. Tim, however, was not the perfect husband.

We continued our relationship after they married. If it had been up to me, I would have let our affair go on forever. Tim broke it off six months ago, after his daughter was born, but we remained close. I held out hope that he would come to regret his decision, searching for signs of affection and desire every time he smiled or touched my arm.

My head throbs. My mind races. "Who killed him?"

"I don't know," Kevin says. "We'll have to rip into every case he's ever touched."

"Maybe the guy didn't know who Tim was. It could have been a robbery gone bad."

"So far, it looks like a hit. His credit cards and cash are still in his wallet, keys in the ignition." He lowers his voice and leans in. "What do you know about his personal life? You knew him better than most."

I wonder if Kevin is signaling knowledge of our relationship. It never occurred to me that he might know, but it makes sense that he would. He's seen us together umpteen times, and he's a master at deciphering body language—maybe he picked up on our unspoken intimacy.

Embarrassed, I avert his eyes. "I don't know anything that would make him a target."

"I heard he was about to start a trial."

"He impaneled a jury yesterday and was planning to give his opening tomorrow."

"Which case?"

My mouth is dry. I guzzle some water. "Orlando Jones."

"From the North Street Posse?"

Boston doesn't have the large centralized gangs that inhabit L.A. or New York. Most of our street gangs are disorganized, scattered, with new ones popping up every few months. North Street is one of the more established neighborhood gangs. They've been around for decades and continue to have a strong criminal presence in the city.

Tim and I discussed the murder when it first came in. Over the past year, we strategized and analyzed holes in the case. Yesterday, the last time I saw him, I helped him craft his opening, the one he'll never deliver. *Orlando Jones sprayed bullets into a crowd of people sitting on a porch, drinking beer, enjoying a summer night. He shot three people: the first is dead; the second might as well be dead; and the third is living in fear.*

"Your boss is here," Kevin says, looking over at Max, who is still huddled with the mayor.

Max is my boss, but he's also my friend. He helped me learn the ropes when I began my career in Boston Municipal Court, and he mentored me after I was promoted to the homicide unit. In the courtroom, he was a prosecutor's prosecutor—sharp, steady, and fearless. Since he was elected DA three years ago, he's become more political, reluctant to make the tough calls. Some say he panders to the media and special interests. I think he's just finding his sea legs.

He lumbers toward us, looking slightly disheveled. He missed a button on his trench coat, making one side higher than the other. Clumps of black hair stick out from under his scally cap. He takes pains to ensure that he is positioned with his back to the cameras, aware that reporters are filming, capturing his every move.

"Christ, this is unfucking believable."

Max, a former basketball player at Providence College, is a foot taller than I am. Even at this distance, I can smell the booze on his breath. I wonder whether he'd been drinking before he got word of the murder or had a quick shot after he heard the news. Knowing Max, it's both.

"I've got to get out to Roslindale and talk to his wife, Julie," he says.

"Julia," I say.

"Julia. Julia." He repeats the name, attempting to improve the likelihood that he'll remember it. "Tell me, what the fuck am I going to say to Julia?"

"She doesn't know yet?"

"She knows. Owen drove over to the house when the call came in. He's staying with her until I get there."

Owen Guilfoyle is Max's chief of staff, his loyal apostle. He's a policy wonk and a numbers cruncher, but he's also got political savvy, and if you dig past a few layers of machismo, you'll find compassion. Max gets to play good cop; he dispenses the promotions and salary bumps, announces arrests and guilty verdicts. Owen is stuck playing bad cop; he doles out the discipline and pink slips, and apparently, he's the guy who has to go to your house in the middle of the night to tell you that your husband is dead.

"I never thought I'd see the day when one of my own would be killed. On my watch," Max says.

"Do you know who he was with at Doyle's?"

"Chris Sarsfield and Owen were there. They said that they saw Tim with a detective, Nestor Gomes."

"Nestor and Tim were working the Orlando Jones case together."

"Have you thought about who you want to run lead on the investigation?" Kevin says. "We should start papering potential witnesses with subpoenas and get the canvass going."

Kevin is clearheaded, two steps ahead of the rest of us. This isn't the first time he's been through this kind of crisis. Unfortunately, in the past couple decades, four Boston police officers have died in the line duty. None, however, was gunned down by an assassin.

"There's a clear conflict. As much as I hate it, I'm going to have to bring in outsiders," Max says. "I've called Middlesex."

Mayor Harris comes over and interrupts. "Sorry, Max, but we should get this presser going. We have to keep the calm. The news is leaking out, and people are going to start to panic."

The mayor leaves us to take his place, front and center, at the podium.

Max takes a deep breath and exhales. "I've got to get this over with."

I take a tin of Altoids from my pocket and offer it to him. His hands tremble as he struggles to grasp one of the tiny white mints and pop it in his mouth.

"You may want to fix your coat," I say.

He rebuttons his trench, pushes his shoulders back, and moves toward the scrum.

Chapter Six

Max usually loves to stand behind the microphone and hold court with the press, but not tonight. He joins Mayor Harris and Commissioner Paula Davies, who are already at the podium. Reporters jockey for position. Camera lights flick on. The mayor squints and leans into a tangle of microphones.

"At approximately two o'clock this morning, Timothy Francis Mooney, head of organized crime in the district attorney's office, a beloved and respected member of the law enforcement community, was gunned down. He was on his way home to his wife and child in the very city that he was sworn to serve and protect. Like the rest of you, I'm in a deep state of shock. This is a sad day for all of us."

As soon as he pauses to catch his breath, a dozen reporters hurl the same question. "Do you have any suspects?"

Commissioner Davies steps up. "Not yet. We're following every lead and asking for the public's help. If anyone saw anything, has information that could assist us, please contact our TIPS line. All calls will be strictly confidential."

"Is there any reason to believe that this was a random attack? Should residents be concerned? Does this mean it's open season on prosecutors?" *Boston Tribune* reporter Teresa Lynch calls out.

Teresa is sporting a dowdy brown suit and shiny platinum hair, kind of like a human mullet. She's always searching for the most sensational angle to a story. Max adjusts the microphone and glares at her.

"No, this is not open season on prosecutors. And it never will be. Make no mistake about that. And you're an insensitive moron for suggesting the possibility."

Max's face reddens and beads of sweat form on his forehead. He never loses control like this in public. If Owen had been here, he'd do something to reel him in. The mayor sees it as an opportunity to make Max look unstable during a time of crisis. He takes over, looks into the cameras, keeping his tone measured.

"Everyone should use their common sense. I'd urge residents to take precautions, but we don't believe this was a random incident," he says.

Carl Ostroff raises his hand but doesn't wait to be called on. "Since Mr. Mooney was assigned to prosecute organized crime, do you think this could have been a mob hit?"

Max moves back to the microphone and regains control. "We're not going to speculate—that would be irresponsible. We're obviously at a very early stage of the investigation." He pauses and looks out into the audience. "Tim Mooney's family, his friends, and the entire law enforcement community have suffered an immeasurable loss tonight. We are all grieving. I promise you that we will find the bastard who is responsible for this atrocity and hold him accountable."

Reporters shout out a few more questions, but the officials walk away from the cameras. The press conference is over.

Max returns to finish our conversation. "Tim started the trial—he's already sworn in the jury. Whether we like it or not, the clock is ticking, and we need to think about who's going to take over."

Once a jury has been sworn, the trial has officially commenced, which means jeopardy has attached. There's no do-over. The Constitution mandates that the case continue to its conclusion— otherwise, it's double jeopardy and the bad guy walks. We all know that's not an option.

"Chris Sarsfield has impressed me lately," Max says. "I'm going to tap him to finish the trial."

"Chris is good," I say, "but he's still pretty green when it comes to murder."

"We'll assign him a second chair, someone from appeals to help out with the motions and jury instructions."

"Orlando Jones was my case. I want it back. Please, let me—"

I look at Max and choke up, unable to get any more words out. He fills the silence.

"Abby, we've already been down this path."

When Orlando Jones emerged as a suspect last year, I grabbed the case, but Max took it away and reassigned it to Tim. Orlando and I have a history that few people know about. I revealed the details to Max's predecessor when I applied for my job, and I told Max last year when the case came in.

Orlando gave me my first taste of the criminal justice system. Our paths crossed seventeen years ago, when I was in high school and he was in middle school. My senior year at Winsor, I was a Latin scholar, preparing to compete in the Junior Classical League, a national geek-fest for high school students. My best friend, Crystal Park, and I were at school one afternoon, practicing our declensions. Crystal was a scholarship student, and she had to go to her babysitting job. I stayed behind to get in some more studying.

When Crystal left school, it was starting to turn dark, but there was still a lot of traffic on the Jamaica Way. She took the shortcut to the trolley, through a wooded area. Orlando jumped out of the bushes, shoved a knife in her face, and demanded her backpack. Crystal panicked, tried to flee, and ran into the busy street. A couple of motorists saw her fall in front of an oncoming car. Orlando said she stumbled and tripped, but I think he pushed her.

Orlando went to a youth detention center. Crystal went to the morgue. He was released from custody on his eighteenth birthday. Over the past decade, he's been doing life on the installment plan—he's been locked up and released seven times for shootings, robberies, assaults, threats, and witness intimidation. Most of the cases never go anywhere because his victims recant, relocate, or die. I've been ordered to stay away from him and his cases, and I've complied—not because I yielded to authority but because I was worried that my involvement would jeopardize the cases. Now all bets are off.

"I want to finish the trial. I owe it to Tim and the three victims, and to Crystal and her family."

Max shakes his head. "I have to think about what's best for the office."

"Winning is what's best for the office. All these years, we did it your way. Let's do it my way."

"You can't be objective. Think about what you'd be risking—sanctions or disbarment for overzealous prosecution. There's too much public scrutiny, too many variables."

Daylight has landed, making everything feel permanent. I face the glare of the sun and squint as I take in the scene—detectives, technicians, reporters. Max turns and we stand in silence, watching, as Tim is zipped into a body bag, hoisted onto a gurney, and slid into the back of the medical examiner's van.

"This case is more important than my bar card," I say.

"People will think you're using the office to settle a score."

"He's a cold-blooded killer with a history of violence. He needs to be locked up for good."

"It's a tough case. If you lose, you'll never forgive yourself."

"Then I won't lose."

Chapter Seven

Suffolk Superior Court is an art deco–style tower, built in the 1930s. The building has undergone extensive renovations, but it's still an eyesore—especially compared to its neoclassical granite neighbor, where the state's more august Supreme Judicial Court and Court of Appeals are housed.

I trudge across the plaza toward the courthouse, past clusters of lawyers, clerks, probation officers, stenographers. Word has already spread throughout the legal community. Some people are crying and others gossiping, but everyone is stunned.

Rodney Quirk is seated in his usual spot, the window of the coffee shop. He blends in, wearing a blue-and-white-striped shirt, the collar just high enough to cover the *Roscoe Street Boyz* tattoo that runs down the length of his spine. When our eyes meet, I take pains to avoid breaking stride. There are two things in life that I can always count on: death and Rodney Quirk.

I'm startled when John Blum, the defense attorney who represents Orlando Jones, steps in front of me and blocks my path. Blum looks even more bedraggled than usual. His mop of salt-and-pepper hair is about three weeks past due for a trim. A stain on his tie looks like he accidentally spilled coffee on himself, but it's an intentional part of his game-day uniform.

He presents as sloppy and forgetful, fooling young prosecutors into thinking he's just another ill-prepared ham-and-egger. They let down their guard, and once the trial commences, he runs circles around them in the courtroom.

"First and foremost, let me offer my deepest condolences. I know I don't have to tell you, but Tim was a good man. He was fair, reasonable, a real gentleman," Blum says.

"Yes" is all I can say.

"I called your office, and they told me you inherited Orlando. I hate to bring it up, but jeopardy has attached."

"I know." My voice cracks.

"Judge Volpe is waiting for us in his chambers."

To avoid further conversation, I fall a few steps behind Blum as we walk to the courthouse. An assortment of defendants, jurors, victims, and witnesses are assembled on the front steps, waiting to pass through security. Blum stops to confer with another lawyer while I cut the line and skirt the x-ray machine. Skipping the security check is a perk of being a prosecutor. A court officer nods to me, an expression of solidarity. I'm grateful for the gesture, even more so when he doesn't ask about Tim's murder.

Blum catches up with me in the lobby. There are eight elevators, but only five are in service. I jostle my way onto a crowded car. A man, probably a defendant, clearly strung out on heroin, squints and gives me a full-body scan. He inches a little closer, brushing up against me. I sharpen my elbow and jerk it into his chest, causing him to fall backward into Blum.

"Keep your fucking hands to yourself," I say, surprising myself and everyone else in the car.

On the ninth floor, Blum goes inside the courtroom, and I stay out in the hallway. The lead detective on the case, Nestor Gomes, is seated on a bench, dressed in a blue blazer and necktie. Nestor played football at Cornell, and last year he graduated from New England Law's night program. Since police officers can outearn prosecutors by threefold, Nestor didn't give up his shield. In a few years, once he's vested in the police pension system, he'll probably retire from the force and hang out a shingle.

"I can't believe it," Nestor says. "I left Tim at eight o'clock last night. We finished an interview and had some beers at Doyle's. He was all psyched up, ready to start the trial."

"Was he worried about anyone? Did he say anything?"

"Nothing like that. We talked about the case, Chris Sarsfield came over to say hi, and Tim bought us all a round."

I try to exude more confidence than I feel. "I'm going to file an appearance and ask the judge for a continuance."

"I admire your fortitude, Abby. You're tougher than most—" Nestor catches himself before he finishes his sentence.

"Were you about to say tougher than most *women*?" I say.

"She's tougher than most anyone—man, woman, or pit bull." Kevin rounds the corner, holding up a familiar green-and-white cup. "I figured you'd be running on fumes."

"Wow, Starbucks. You wandered outside your comfort zone."

"I was embarrassed to order it—grande latte." He hands me the coffee. "Only for you. Gotta keep your beautiful blues open and alert."

Judge Volpe's chief court officer, Sal Gambino, pokes his head out the door to the courtroom. Sal is bald, lean, and hyper-vigilant. His eyes are always moving, searching for danger.

"The judge wants to see you," Sal says.

Kevin and Nestor follow me inside the dimly lit gallery and cram into the wooden pews. The heaters hiss and clang.

The back row is lined with a half-dozen gang members. They sit shoulder to shoulder, arms crossed, baseball caps in their laps, heads leaning back against the wall. One man looks at me and smiles broadly, exposing two gold front teeth. We lock eyes for a second, and I shiver in spite of the tropical temperature in the room.

The next couple of rows of the gallery contain mostly prose-cutors and defense attorneys who have no business of their own to conduct. Scattered among the suits are five or six court watchers, men who spend their days alternating between trials in the always-busy courthouse. Court watchers have their favorite prosecutors, and we have our favorite court watchers. Harold is mine. His brown head is shaved bald, and he carries a silver-tipped walking stick and speaks with a British accent even though he grew up in nearby blue-collar Revere.

The front row is reserved for family. Relatives of the victim sit on the prosecutor's side, relatives of the defendant on the defendant's side. Like a wedding.

The Jones family is huddled together; Blum is leaning over, whispering to them. The last time I saw the Joneses was in Boston Juvenile Court seventeen years ago, when Orlando was sentenced for robbing Crystal. They glance at me briefly with-out registering any hint of recognition. They may not remember me, but I'll never forget them.

Orlando's mother, Marie, digs through her purse, pulls out a handkerchief, and dabs at her nose. She's wearing a stylish aubergine suit and her hair looks freshly coiffed, but her face is world-weary. Orlando's father, Melvin, puts his arm around her; his forearms are bigger than my thighs. Melvin has expensive loafers on his feet and thick calluses on his hands. Orlando's younger sister, June, seems well dressed and well mannered.

I pass the bar, drop my tote on the prosecutor's table, and wait outside the door to the judge's chambers. Blum joins me.

"I thought Orlando's father was a preacher," I say. "It looks like he made some dough."

"He gave up the pulpit about five years ago," Blum says.

"Construction?"

"He landed a couple of big-city contracts."

I look over at Mrs. Jones's designer suit. "I hope the taxpayers aren't footing your bill."

He shakes his head and smiles. "I've been privately retained."

"Does the family still live in Mattapan?"

"They bought a huge estate in Weston. Orlando was there for a little while, after he got out of juvie," Blum says.

In the gallery, Kevin and Nestor keep a close watch on the gang members in the back row. Mr. Jones keeps his arm wrapped around his wife, who is looking down at her lap, praying. Orlando is not just another poor kid from a bad neighborhood who joined a gang because he didn't have love and support at home. He had options, and he chose gang life.

Sal is seated at his desk on the side of the courtroom. The red light on his phone flashes. He picks up the receiver and has a brief conversation.

"The judge is all set," he says. "You ready?"

I glance into the audience. Kevin gives me a *go get 'em* nod. Nestor gives me a thumbs-up. The gold-toothed man catches my eye, tilts his head back, and smirks.

"Ready," I say.

Chapter Eight

Sal opens the door to the judge's chambers, stands aside, and gestures us in. Judge Thomas Volpe, compact in both stature and temperament, is seated behind a warped desk. His cramped office is decorated with a few lawbooks and a banker's lamp. A black robe dangles from a metal hook on the back of the door.

Judge Volpe is no-nonsense, calls them like he sees them. He's obsessed with ensuring that his verdicts are unassailable. All murder cases are automatically reviewed by appellate courts for errors of law and Judge Volpe's cases are rarely overturned.

Dotty Davidson, the judge's stenographer, sits by his side. She talks softly into a black cone, repeating everything we say. Judge Volpe can't see from where he sits, high up on the bench, but sometimes Dotty falls asleep in the middle of her transcriptions. Sal usually wakes her up before she misses more than a question or two by discreetly tapping her on the shoulder and offering her a peppermint candy.

The judge extends his arm, directing Blum and me to sit in the worn green vinyl chairs in front of his desk.

"I'm sorry, Ms. Endicott. You have what appears to be a herculean task ahead of you."

"Thank you, Your Honor. I ask the court for some leave to prepare," I say, "and to attend the funeral services."

"Yes, of course. We all want to pay our respects. I can excuse the jury for a week so you can get your ducks in order."

"It was a triple shooting—I was hoping for at least three weeks."

When I was in fifth grade, my family spent a rainy week in Bermuda, and to pass the time, my father taught me and my brothers how to play poker. We spent hours perfecting the art of the bluff, which has come in handy, whether negotiating a plea, cross-examining a witness, or asking for a continuance. I don't expect Judge Volpe to grant me a long adjournment, but I figure if I ask for three weeks, he'll give me two.

"Sorry, I can only give you a week. I conferred with my colleagues this morning," Judge Volpe says. "The consensus is, given the extraordinary circumstances, anything longer will expose us to prejudice."

I mask my disappointment and shift into default mode. "Please note my objection for the record."

"Let's bring in the jury. I'll introduce you to them and inform them that they'll have the rest of the week off."

Judge Volpe unfurls his shirtsleeves, puts on his black robe, and zips up the front.

"Your Honor, out of an abundance of caution, I am disclosing that, years ago, Mr. Jones committed a crime against one of my friends." I act as though this is a run-of-the-mill potential conflict that hardly merits mentioning—like the time a pickpocketing victim happened to be my mother's vintner.

The judge turns back around. "What type of crime was it?"

"It was a robbery."

"Were you a victim, as well?"

We were all victims—Crystal, her parents, her siblings, me. "No," I say. "I wasn't a victim."

"Were you a percipient witness?"

"No, I didn't see it happen."

"What kind of time frame are we talking about?"

I try to maintain my casual, matter-of-fact tone. "It happened almost twenty years ago."

"Wait, I know that case," Blum says. "Orlando was convicted of armed robbery, but the initial charge was manslaughter."

Judge Volpe looks at me and raises his eyebrows. "The case involved a death?"

"Yes." The back of my neck tenses.

"I move to disqualify Ms. Endicott. If her friend was a victim, she has a stake in the outcome—a clear violation of the rules of professional conduct," Blum says.

"My only interest in this, or any case, is protecting the safety of the public." I sound indignant, but I'm concerned about what Judge Volpe might do.

He pauses before speaking. "Ms. Endicott, I'll give you some leeway, but if I see a hint of misconduct on your part, I'll declare a mistrial and report you to the Board of Bar Overseers. Capeesh?"

"Got it."

"You could lose your license to practice law."

"That won't happen."

Judge Volpe moves toward the door. "Anything else we need to cover before I bring in the jury?"

I consider my next request and decide to go for it. The worst that can happen is I'll get slapped down.

"I've been up all night, and I'm not properly dressed for court. I'd ask Your Honor's indulgence in allowing me to sit in the gallery. I don't want to make a bad first impression."

"You don't want me to introduce you to the panel?"

"I'd rather wait until next week."

Blum looks at me and shakes his head. "This is an attempt to manipulate the jury and elicit sympathy."

"How's that?" Judge Volpe says.

"Ms. Endicott wants to leave an empty chair at the prosecution table. She's trying to send a message to the jurors."

"What's the message?"

"Yesterday, Mr. Mooney was seated at the prosecution table, today, his seat is empty. She wants to create a visual and drive home the point that there is a void."

"There is a void," I say. "Contrary to popular belief, we're not fungible."

"That's not what I meant."

"Your objection is noted and denied, Mr. Blum," Judge Volpe says.

Judge Volpe puts his hand on the doorknob, but stops and looks at Blum.

"Sal tells me that Mr. Jones has a propensity for extreme violence. I'm going to increase security in the courtroom."

"That's not necessary," Blum says. "He's had a few minor scrapes with the law, but nothing that requires an extra show of force."

"I'm told that he's among the top ten most dangerous felons in the state, which is an accomplishment, given the competition. We're going to have six court officers for the duration of the trial."

He opens the door and we follow him into the courtroom. Blum takes his place at the defense table, and I sit next to Kevin in the gallery. Orlando is ushered in by four burly court officers, who walk him to the defense table and unshackle his wrists and feet. Over the years, I've snuck into various courtrooms to catch quick glimpses of Orlando. I've watched him grow from a gangly teenager into brawny man. Today he has a shaved head and a trim beard, and it looks like he's made use of his year in lockup, bulking up, bench-pressing massive amounts of weight.

Orlando smiles and waves to his family. He looks at the back row and nods—his gold-toothed compatriot echoes the greeting.

Blum whispers in his ear. I can make out a few of the words. *Remember . . . Robbery . . . Jamaica Way . . . Endicott.* Orlando twists his body around to look at me. His face drops and his expression sours. *Right back at you, Orlando.*

The jurors file in. Judge Volpe lets them know what's going on and sends them home for the week. After the hearing, Nestor, Kevin, and I reconvene in the hallway to debrief and come up with a game plan.

"Volpe kind of screwed you with the continuance, don't you think?" Nestor says.

"There's nothing else he could have done."

"You should file an interlocutory appeal."

Like any recent law school graduate, Nestor knows just enough about the law to be annoying but not enough to be helpful.

"Nestor, you round up the exhibits," Kevin says. "I'll take Abby out in the field."

This was Nestor's case, and he's not happy to suddenly be taking orders from Kevin, but he knows that a power struggle will have to wait.

"You've got a full plate with your other cases," I say to Kevin after Nestor is gone. "Nestor is solid. I can work with him."

"I'm sure you can, but I want in on this one."

"You and Tim worked a lot of cases together."

"We had some fun chasing down the bad guys. He always volunteered for the toughest ones."

Orlando, flanked by court officers, shuffles toward the prisoners' elevator, his leg-irons clanking. He looks at me and sucks air through his teeth.

"*Futue te ipsum,*" I say under my breath.

"Sounds fancy," Kevin says. "Italian?"

"Latin. Roughly translated, it means, 'Fuck him.' "

"You got a way with words—must be all those Harvard degrees."

As soon as Orlando and his escorts disappear around the corner, a surge of anxiety rushes through my body.

"I can't lose this case, Kevin."

"We won't," he says, reminding me of one of the best things about being part of the law enforcement community. "We're in this together."

Cops know how to rally and take care of their own. They organize fund-raisers to support the widows of fallen comrades. They shave their heads when a colleague's child is stricken with cancer. They're always there for each other. Not because it's in their job description. Because it's in their blood.

Chapter Nine

Kevin's black SUV is parked alongside a dozen other un-marked police cars on the median strip in front of City Hall. Nearby, there are a line of press vans, their satellites extended toward the sky, ready to transmit.

"The vultures got here fast," I say, relieved that we escaped from the courthouse before the media swarm hit.

"Yesterday, no one cared about Orlando Jones or his victims. It was just another murder in the hood. Now the trial will be live-streamed," Kevin says.

I prefer the federal system, where cameras are banned and exposure is limited to courtroom sketches and reporters' articles and tweets. In state courts, judges will occasionally shield a reluctant witness's identity, but prosecutors are always considered fair game.

"Think of the upside," Kevin says. "In a short time, you'll be a household name, like Judge Judy or Lady Gaga."

"More like Lady Macbeth—when she started to unravel."

"Maybe you'll get your own show on Fox like those other lady lawyers. You pretty much fit the bill. You don't have the blond hair, but you have the blue eyes and the nice figure."

"I'll take that."

"You're a looker—but you might want to do something about those bags under your eyes."

Kevin uses the remote to unlock his car. As I buckle my seat belt, he grabs Orlando Jones's murder book from the back.

"I stopped by HQ on my way here." He hands me the black three-ring binder bursting with plastic sleeves. "This is going to be a tough one. Big stakes, with the whole case resting on a couple of shaky witnesses."

Kevin pulls a U-turn into oncoming traffic and smiles as he cuts off a Beemer. The murder book slides off my lap, and a photograph slips out of the front pocket. It's Orlando Jones's booking photo. He isn't looking into the camera, he's confronting it. A lot of killers have an empty stare, often described as dead eyes. Not Orlando—his eyes are alive, active, brimming with rancor.

"I know that you two have a past," Kevin says.

"I just disclosed it. How'd you find out so fast?"

"I've known about it for years, before I even met you."

"Who told you?"

"I did your background check when you applied to the office."

"You investigated me?"

"Yup."

"You never mentioned that. What did you find out?"

I fiddle with my cell and shift in my seat, knowing that I'll be uncomfortable with his response.

"You're loaded. You pay your taxes, or your accountant pays your taxes. You have a clean driving record. You've never been arrested." He pauses. "And your best friend died right in front of you."

I look out the window, bite my lip, and try not to cry. I've always taken Kevin's steadfast support for granted, never wondered about the genesis.

"My first year on the job, I went through the same thing," he says.

His voice catches. He stops talking, clears his throat, and coughs. In the ten years that I've known him, he's never brought up the subject of his partner's death.

"Yes, I know. I'm sorry," I say.

"Even though there was nothing I could have done to save him, I've never forgiven myself."

"Survivor's guilt." A few tears well up in the corner of my eyes, and I wipe them away with the side of my hand.

Kevin weaves in and out of traffic on Cambridge Street and takes a left onto Bowdoin, a steep side street leading up the back of Beacon Hill. We drive past rows of what were once seedy rooming houses and are now multimillion-dollar condos. There's a line in front of Saint John's, a church that serves soup to the homeless and communion to the wealthy.

A dozen tourists are gathered at the top of Mount Vernon Street, listening to a guide who is outfitted in a brown colonial-style dress, complete with an apron and puffy white bonnet. She directs their attention to the brick sidewalks, wrought iron fences, and antique gas lanterns.

"Where are we going?"

"We'll stop by and see Jasmine Reed's mother, bring her up to speed. But I want to make a quick detour."

Descending the more fashionable south slope of Beacon Hill, we pass the brick townhouse where my older brother, Charlie, lives with his fiancée.

"Must've been nice," Kevin says, "growing up here with all the muckety-mucks, spending your summers in Nantucket."

"For your information, we summered on the Vineyard. Besides, you're one to talk. You belong to the oldest, most impenetrable club of all: the OBN."

"What's that?"

"The Old Boys' Network."

When we reach the flat of the hill, Kevin parks on Charles Street in front of a Tow Zone—No Parking sign. The street is lined with an assortment of cafés, boutiques, and antique shops. Kevin helps an attractive redhead navigate her double stroller around an elm tree, its gnarled roots protruding through the sidewalk.

We stop at the Paramount, a cafeteria-style diner that caters to Brahmins and blue-collar workers alike. It's relatively cheap, and the food is good. Kevin opens the door and pulls back the thick red curtain that protects diners from the cold wind.

The room is jammed with tables. The open kitchen emits the permanent smells of breakfast: eggs, bacon, pancakes. We join the line, and I grab a tray, silverware, and paper napkins.

"Just coffee," I say when it's my turn to order.

The cashier hands me a white ceramic mug emblazoned with a picture of former mayor Kevin White, and I scope out a table.

"We're not here for a coffee break—it's lunchtime." Kevin unpacks a tray with two burgers and a tower of onion rings. "I'm not leaving until you eat something."

The burger tastes warm and juicy. Kevin smiles as I scarf down the food.

"You want me to order a brownie sundae for the road?" he says.

I take the brownie, sans ice cream and hot fudge, and devour it on the way out the door.

"I have to run a quick errand," I say.

I dash across the street to DeLuca's, a gourmet grocery store, where I find a bouquet of fuchsia gerbera daisies. I don't want to arrive at Jackie Reed's house empty-handed. She was in the office last week to meet with Tim, and she seemed like someone who cares about etiquette.

"I thought prosecutors aren't supposed to give gifts to witnesses," Kevin says when I meet him at his car with the flowers.

"Screw it. Let the judge sanction me for common courtesy."

Kevin drives us into the high-crime section of Mattapan,

where hardworking families have to contend with the gang warfare that surrounds them.

"That boyfriend of yours, is he taking care of you?" Kevin says as we idle at a traffic light on Blue Hill Avenue.

Like most of the people in my life, Kevin has never met Ty, but he knows about him. Kevin and I have spent hundreds of hours together since I started seeing Ty last year; he's heard us on the phone, talking, laughing, making plans, arguing.

"Ty doesn't take care of me. I'm a modern woman," I say.

"He's got a criminal record." He turns to look me in the eye. "But you already know that."

I tell most people that Ty and I met at a party, which is true, albeit misleading. We were in a club, but not as invited guests—we were both working. Ty, a musician, was there to perform, and I was there to authorize warrants.

There had been a stabbing on the dance floor earlier in the night, and he was a witness. It was a gruesome scene. The victim had his throat slashed and his gut ripped open. When I arrived, the first responders were slipping and sliding on the sticky, bloody dance floor.

The case took about eight months to resolve, enough time for us to get to know each other pretty well. It's hard to flirt over crime scene photos, but I always looked forward to our meetings, remembering to put on an extra coat of lipstick and spritz of perfume. Ty swears that he was initially turned on by my intelligence, but he seemed more interested in my butt. I caught him once—checking me out when I leaned over to pick up the bloody knife.

He asked me out for a drink as soon as the trial was over, but while the jury was still deliberating. I complied with the state ethics rules and waited until the guilty verdict came down before accepting the invitation.

Kevin knows that, as a matter of course, prosecutors run the criminal record of every potential witness. If he's done the math, and I'm sure he has, it's obvious that I learned about Ty's criminal past before we got involved.

"How do you know about Ty's record?" I say.

"I don't sell shoes for a living."

"You ran his record without any legitimate investigative purpose—that's a violation."

"He has a conviction for D with intent, and it's not a youthful indiscretion. It's from 2010."

"That was before my time."

"I'm just looking out for you."

"I wouldn't expect anything less."

Kevin has been my guardian angel for years, starting with my first trial. Two weeks on the job, I had a shoplifting case from Neiman Marcus. I was so nervous that I forgot to introduce the key piece of evidence: a women's suit. To add insult to injury, the suit was Chanel. Kevin was the arresting officer; he finessed my direct examination by answering a question that I had never asked.

"You spared me the humiliation of a not guilty on my first trial. I almost hope that you'll screw up one day so I can return the favor."

"Ain't gonna happen."

"I know."

"Possession with intent to distribute marijuana," he says. "You can't sell pot in this state unless you're a doctor running a licensed medical marijuana dispensary. Is your boyfriend a doctor?"

"No, Detective Farnsworth, he's not a doctor. And he doesn't sell drugs anymore."

"You're a public servant, subject to public scrutiny. Getting involved with a convicted drug dealer isn't the best road to career advancement."

"Duly noted," I say.

Chapter Ten

Jackie Reed lives in a dilapidated triple-decker on drug-infested Samoset Street. The second- and third-floor porches are slanted forward, like they're about to break off from the house and topple onto the sidewalk. We climb up the warped front stoop and look at the rusty mailboxes, hoping to learn the occupants, but the ink is faded. Kevin pulls out Jackie's form twenty-six, takes out his cell, and dials.

"This is Detective Kevin Farnsworth, Boston Police. I'm outside. I was wondering if we could talk for a minute."

There's no buzzer or entry system, so Jackie has to come downstairs to open the door and let us in. She greets us wearing a cheerful pink dress and matching hat. When she extends her hand, I'm half expecting to see white gloves like the ones I wore to Miss Pringle's ballroom dance classes in fourth grade at the Park School.

We follow her up two flights of creaky wooden stairs. The inside of her apartment is as tidy as the outside is messy. I hand her the flowers.

"These are lovely." She arranges them in a glass vase. "I was getting ready for court. Mr. Mooney said I should be there this afternoon."

"That's why we're here," I say.

"Where's Mr. Mooney?"

Worried that my voice will crack, I sit quietly and let Kevin take over.

"There was a shooting last night."

"Oh, goodness, I hope everyone is okay."

"Tim, Mr. Mooney, was the one who was shot," Kevin says. "But we don't want you to worry—you're in good hands."

"Shot? Is he okay?"

"I'm sorry to tell you, he passed away," Kevin says.

She stops and bows her head. "He was a kind soul."

I clear my throat. "Yes, he was."

Jackie crosses herself before looking back up at me. "When is the service? I'd like to pay my respects."

"We're not sure yet."

She gestures to a brown plaid sofa, still wrapped in its protective cover even though she's probably had it for years. "Please have a seat."

When Kevin sits, the stiff plastic crinkles and bends. I walk over to a table lined with photographs in a hodgepodge of frames.

"This one is from her first communion." Jackie picks up a fading black and white in an ornate gold-colored frame. "I was saving the dress for when she had a girl of her own."

She tears up. I put my hand on hers.

"This was her high school graduation. And this is when she left for her tour of duty in Afghanistan. She had nothing to do with gangs or drugs. She was outside on the porch, talking with her friends."

Every mother swears that her child was an innocent bystander, but in this case, it happens to be true.

"The jury isn't going to think Jasmine did anything wrong," I say.

"I'm not worried about the trial. My baby is gone, the Lord will take care of the rest. Mr. Mooney, he was such a nice man. I'm sorry for your loss."

Jackie Reed, a woman whose daughter was murdered two days before her twenty-sixth birthday, wraps her arms around me and rubs my back. I let my shoulders drop and accept the warmth of her hug. I want to hold on to this moment, remember it next week when I'm face-to-face with Orlando Jones.

A woman who looks eerily like Jasmine enters the room. "Mom, did you hear what happened to the prosecutor?"

She's surprised when she sees us. Kevin stands, extends his hand, and introduces us.

"You must be Jasmine's sister," he says.

"Tiffany," she says.

"Twins?"

"Yes."

Jasmine had a twin sister. My heart breaks a little more.

"I heard about your colleague. I'm sorry," she says. "We've been waiting a long time for this trial. He needs to pay for what he did."

Tiffany is not as generous as her mother. I don't blame her, but I want to warn her, tell her not to expect too much from a conviction. The verdict will only start a new phase of grief. She won't have a trial to focus on anymore. There will only be the emptiness.

Chapter Eleven

Denny Mebane is Orlando's second casualty. Before he was shot in the head with a sawed-off shotgun, Denny was a sophomore at Bunker Hill Community College, studying computer science. He lived in Mattapan with his girlfriend and their two short-haired cats. Now he lives alone in Healey House, a rehabilitation facility on a quiet residential street in West Roxbury.

My first visit to Healey House was when I was prosecuting drunk-driving cases. The victim, a seven-year-old girl, was in the backseat of her mother's minivan, en route to Chuck E. Cheese's. The mother, drunk and stoned, passed out and crashed head-on into a delivery truck. My most recent visit to Healey House was to meet an MIT student who had fallen off the roof of his fraternity during a drunken hazing ritual.

"I don't know why they call this place a rehab," I say. "Most patients never get better."

"Maybe they should call it *a place to stay, somewhere between life and death,*" Kevin says.

"That's catchy, but I think they're probably better off sticking with rehab."

Kevin pulls into the parking lot behind the building, and we get out of the car. Tim used to talk about Denny Mebane, how painful it was each time he came here to meet with him and his mother. When we get inside, I take a breath and steel myself while Kevin signs us in at the reception desk.

A nurse directs us to Denny's room, which is on the third floor.

"Let's hoof it," Kevin says. "I need to stretch my legs."

I follow him into the bile-green stairwell, where the stench of cleaning solution makes me gag. The sharp, disorienting symptoms of a migraine start to take hold.

The door to Denny's room is halfway open. Inside, his mother, Adele, is sitting on a metal folding chair by his bedside, her back to the door. She's wearing a white cardigan and black wool slacks. Denny is wearing a hospital johnny and a bib. Adele spoon-feeds him something the color and consistency of oatmeal, singing "The World Is Not My Home." We pause and listen to her soothing voice. *And I can't feel at home in this world anymore.*

Adele wipes goop from Denny's chin. Kevin looks at me to be sure I'm ready and then taps on the door. Adele turns, rises, and greets us each with a hug and a smile. She takes my hand and walks me up to the edge of the bed.

"Denny, this is the new lawyer I was telling you about, and this is the detective."

She talks to her son as though he were healthy, something I wasn't expecting and am not sure how to handle. I hesitate, then decide that the polite thing to do, the only thing to do, is to go along with it.

"I'm Abby. Nice to meet you." I start to extend my hand, but catch myself and pull it back.

Denny seems to have a permanent grin plastered on his face. He lets out some primal grunts, and his eyes shift periodically. Even though his features appear distorted, it's obvious that he was once a handsome man with big brown eyes complemented by giraffe-like eyelashes.

"What did you say, honey?" Adele pauses and waits, as though he might respond.

She's so hopeful that I'm almost convinced he's going to speak.

"Tim spoke highly of you both," I say.

"We're praying for him. Did he have a family?"

"A wife and daughter."

"Then we'll pray for them too."

I grew up Episcopalian, attending services at the Church of the Advent on the flat of Beacon Hill. As a child, I loved the formality, the weight of it all—the Victorian Gothic structure, the rhythmic sound of the bells, the somber service, the smoky incense. After Crystal died, I went there to meditate and reflect, finding solace in the music and the predictable rituals. When I joined the DA's office and my assignments took me deep into the depravity of murder, the heavily perfumed clouds of smoke pouring from the swinging thuribles began to give me a headache. The choral service of evensong became overbearing, claustrophobic.

Now the only appeal for me at the Advent, or at any church, is the passing of the peace. I enjoy looking at my neighbor, shaking hands, turning clockwise, and repeating the process. *Peace be with you. And also with you.*

"Do you still need me to testify?" Adele says.

"Yes, I'd like to call you as a witness. I know you've gone over everything with Tim. I'll ask you to tell the jury about Denny. What he is . . . was . . . like. I mean before the shooting."

"Denny never gave me a minute of trouble when he was coming up."

"Does he have siblings?" I say, hoping that Adele has other children to care for and love, and vice versa.

"No, it's just the two of us."

"The trial will be graphic at times, painful to watch. It's good to have support."

"My pastor is coming. And some people from my choir."

A young nurse wearing tie-dyed scrubs comes in. She has a long, thick braid that falls down the length of her back, reminding me of Rodney Quirk's tattoo.

"I see he ate some of his dinner." The nurse picks up his tray and sets it on a side table.

"He's trying to get his strength back," Adele says.

The nurse changes his catheter bag and checks his vitals. "How are you doing today, Denny?" she says with a smile.

I take out my iPhone. "If it's okay, I'd like to film him."

"Tim took some pictures. He said he was going to show them on a screen in the courtroom."

"Yes, but I'd like to have a video too, if you don't mind."

"Whatever you think is best," Adele says.

"Let's make him look nice." The nurse props up his pillows and starts to untie his bib.

"I'd prefer that he not look posed."

The jury needs to get the full picture, oatmeal-spattered bib and all. I film Denny amid an assortment of machines and medical devices. He shifts in his bed and grunts. Vomit percolates up the back of my throat and my migraine throbs.

Kevin sees me struggling. "How about you and I go over your statement, Ms. Mebane?" he says.

"Excuse me," I say on my way out the door.

I creep down the hallway, willing myself forward until I find a bathroom. *Staff Only.* I step inside and lock myself in. The glare of the fluorescent overhead causes the pain behind my eyes to intensify. I search for the light switch, flick it off, stand in total darkness, and try to get my bearings.

Once inside the bathroom stall, I break out in a heavy, cold sweat. I throw up, regretting the greasy onion rings I ate for lunch. I flush the toilet, flip down the lid, and sit for a minute, head in hands, waiting for the sweating to subside. My shirt is soaked through. I start to hyperventilate. Someone knocks on the door and tries to open it.

I take a deep breath. "Just a minute," I say.

Turning on the light, I move to the sink and splash cold water on my clammy face. I unbutton my sweater and pull my blouse under the hand dryer. Watching the circles of sweat slowly begin to disappear, a blanket of loneliness envelops me.

I take out my cell and dial the only person who would understand what I'm going through. After five rings, Tim's voice mail picks up. I hold the phone tightly to my ear and listen to the sweet sound of his voice. *You have reached Tim Mooney. Sorry I can't take your call right now. If you leave your name and number, I'll get right back to you.* The message ends, the beep sounds. I hang up and call again.

When I return to Denny's room, Kevin is asking questions that he already knows the answers to, allowing Adele to share pleasant memories of her son.

"Where did he go to high school?"

"Concord-Carlisle. He was a METCO student." Adele is referring to the state-funded program that gives Boston kids from low-income families the opportunity to go to public schools in more affluent suburbs.

"That bus must've come pretty early."

"He got up at five every morning. Those teachers gave him hours of homework every night, and it never seemed to bother him. He wants to invent computer games."

"He sounds like a good son, a special man," I say.

"He is," Adele says. "I hope he can still have his dreams."

I'm not sure if she means this literally or figuratively, but either way, I hope so too.

"He also had a part-time job?" Kevin says.

"Delivering Chinese food. I told him he should work inside the restaurant, waiting tables or filling orders. But he said he liked to meet new people. The lady, Jasmine, the one who got killed, she called for takeout. When she was out on her porch paying her bill, that man, Orlando Jones, started shooting at them. For no reason."

"I'm sorry this happened, Adele," I say.

"How is Jackie?" she says.

"You know Jasmine's mother?"

"I met her in court last year, at the bail hearing. That's who I feel for. I don't have it half as bad as she does. She had to bury her daughter. I still can still visit my son—he's here with me."

Yes, Adele can still visit Denny. But more than that, I'm not so sure.

Chapter Twelve

It's sleeting when we leave the rehab, and there's a coat of heavy slush on the pavement. With no choice, I slog through it. Icy water seeps into my shoes, causing a sharp pain to surge up my legs. Once inside the car, I leave the door open long enough to tip my shoes and pour the liquid out. My socks are drenched.

"You look like you've been through the wringer." Kevin turns on the headlights and cranks the heat. "Let's call it a night."

"I should go back to the office. I have a ton of things to do."

The windshield wipers move slightly and then get stuck in a mound of wet snow. Kevin blasts the defrost.

"Is your boyfriend gonna be at your place?"

I shake my head. "He has a gig tonight at Wally's."

"You shouldn't spend so much time alone. Get yourself a guy with a regular job, like in a bank."

Ty is a brilliant tenor sax player. He performs mostly locally, but he travels every other month or so to New York or San Francisco and four or five times a year to Europe. He won me over last summer at the Newport Jazz Festival with his sublimely seductive rendition of "Body and Soul." His hours are as unconventional as mine, which is one of the reasons we're compatible. Tonight, however, I agree with Kevin. I don't want to go home to an empty apartment.

"I have to look through the motions in limine and jury instructions. How about you drop me off at Bulfinch."

"It's after ten. I'm taking you home. If you want to make yourself sick, you're on your own."

We veer onto the Jamaica Way, and Kevin takes a call from his wife. As they talk, we pass the Winsor School and the spot where Crystal's body landed on the side of the road. The heat of my breath fogs the side window.

By the time we reach the Back Bay, the wet snow turns into softer, fluffier flakes. A lone cross-country skier glides down the snow-covered mall in the center of Commonwealth Avenue. He moves his arms and legs rhythmically, forward and back, leaving a narrow trail in his wake.

I remember being ten years old, bounding through knee-high snow with my brothers, Charlie and George. Wearing down parkas and L.L. Bean boots, we'd race each other up and down the mall. When we were fully exhausted, we'd fall onto our backs, moving our arms and legs in semicircles to form snow angels.

What started out as a joyful frolic in the snow would inevitably evolve into a heated competition over who could run faster or form the most perfectly symmetrical figure. Our nanny, Magdalena, was the self-appointed judge. She awarded the winner our most coveted prize—selecting that night's dessert. Charlie, her favorite, was almost always crowned the victor, whether the competition involved snow angels, swan dives, or sand castles. Even though the games were rigged, I always held out hope and gave it my all.

Kevin pulls up to my front door. I get out and climb over a pile of snow amassed between two cars. When I start to lose my footing, I lean on the hood of an Escalade, causing the alarm to blare. Gabe, a maintenance worker from my building, is nearby, holding a bucket full of green salt and sprinkling it onto the sidewalk. He hears the commotion, comes to my aid, and helps me inside.

Manny is at the reception counter. He greets me and hands me an envelope.

"Mr. Epps in 7-C asked me to be sure to get this to you. It's from the homeowners' association."

I open the envelope and unfold the letter. *Second Notice of Delinquency. Your condominium fees are 60 days past due. Failure to pay will result in the issuance of a lien, and the commencement of foreclosure proceedings.*

"The condo board has had it out for me since the day I moved in."

"Maybe they just want their money," Manny says.

I stuff the papers in my tote and press the button for the elevator.

"I've been kind of busy."

He purses his lips and blows out air. "Those condo fees pay my salary."

The elevator doors open and I step into the car. "Sorry, I'll do it tomorrow."

Manny is the last person I want to offend. He's the only one in the building I care about. It's not that I don't have the money—I have ample funds. The family trustee deposits $15,000 into my checking account every month, and if I need more, all I have to do is ask. But I've had more pressing matters. Plus, there's an element of passive aggression aimed at the condo board that I enjoy. I guess I'll have to find another way to express myself, like leaving a brick of Limburger cheese in the trash room or taking up tap dancing.

The dead bolt on my front door is unlatched; my housekeeper must have forgotten to set the lock. Opening the door slowly, I hear the swaying sound of bossa nova music. Ty is in the kitchen doing something I've never seen him do before: cooking dinner.

"I thought you were performing tonight." I fling my coat over a chair.

Ty puts down a bottle of olive oil and wipes his hands on a dish towel. "I heard about what happened."

"You canceled your gig?"

"I'd never leave you alone at a time like this." He looks me in the eye and gives me a gentle kiss. "I tried calling a bunch of times, but you didn't pick up. I was worried."

I remove my waterlogged $475 Ferragamos and toss them in the trash. They might be salvageable, but it feels good to discard something, shed some part of this horrific day.

"Are you okay?" he says.

Sapped of energy and emotion, I look at Ty and start to speak but don't know what to say. He wraps me in his arms, holds me close, and makes me feel safe. We share a moment of silent intimacy until I pull away.

In the kitchen, Ty uses a fork to lift two steaks out of a marinade and throw them on the grill. Small flames shoot up as the meat starts to sizzle.

"Smells good," I say.

"I figured all you've had to eat today is a bag of popcorn, like twelve hours ago. You need protein."

He whisks together a vinaigrette, tosses a salad, and finishes grilling the steaks. After he plates the food, we move to the dining room table. I remove my laptop and brush aside a stack of papers to make room for two place settings. He brings out a bottle of Malbec and two cloth napkins.

I slump into a chair. "I really appreciate this."

"I got you," he says.

The meat is tender and juicy, but after my second bite, I start to feel queasy. I put the fork down and sip my wine. I check my cell: nineteen missed calls, one hundred and six e-mails on my office account. I don't even want see what's in my personal account.

"Your father stopped by," Ty says.

I look up from my phone. "My father was here?"

"He seemed pretty freaked out, said he's been calling all over the place, trying to reach you."

"What time was he here?"

"A few hours ago. Looked like he was on his way home from the gym."

"He doesn't belong to one—he works out at the Harvard Club."

Ty and my father have never met. So far, it's been easy to avoid introductions since my parents are never in Boston at times when most families gather—Thanksgiving and Christmas. As an only child of divorced narcissists, Ty is used to spending holidays on tour or with friends. If he finds it odd that I haven't invited him home to meet my parents, he's kept it to himself.

I rarely talk to my family about anything personal, including boyfriends, and Ty is no exception. I don't want to subject myself to the scrutiny. I wonder if my father is shocked that I'm dating a black man. My parents are elitists, not racists, but this is still Boston. We like to think we're evolved when it comes to issues of race, but there's a deep history of division that still hasn't fully dissipated.

I have a hard time imagining Ty and my father, standing across from each other in my living room. Ty clad in jeans and a T-shirt; my father, in a dark suit, holding a briefcase and a squash racket.

"That must have been awkward," I say. "He never comes here."

"It was fine. We were going to meet this weekend anyhow."

I look at him blankly and sip my wine.

"Your brother's wedding is on Saturday, right?" he says.

"Oh, shit."

During a moment of weakness, I extended a wedding invitation to Ty and then promptly blocked it out of my consciousness.

He takes a few bites of steak, has a sip of wine. "Your father didn't seem to know anything about me. He's probably got a few questions, like, 'Why didn't you tell me that you're practically living with someone?' "

Ty deserves an explanation, but fully unraveling the reasons for my neurotic secrecy will take insight and a good therapist, and at the moment, I don't have either.

"Did he try to enlist you in his campaign to get me to quit my job?"

He refills our wineglasses and looks at me. "Everyone is worried, especially after what happened last night."

"You think I should quit too?"

"I didn't say that. I'll text your father, let him know you're okay."

"He gave you his number?"

The thought of Ty and my father engaged in a conspiratorial relationship aimed at getting me to leave the DA's office makes me feel a combination of comfort, frustration, and fear.

Ty looks at my plate. "You barely touched your dinner," he says.

I drop my head into my hands. "I don't know what I'm doing anymore."

"Baby, it's going to be okay."

Suddenly the dam breaks. My body trembles, and tears fall, slowly at first and then a flood. My breathing turns into soft hiccups that evolve into deep, chest-heaving sobs. It goes on for several minutes. I don't even try to make it stop. Ty hands me tissue, stays by my side, rubs my back.

"I'm in over my head. It's like I'm drowning."

"You've got to be exhausted."

He takes my hand, leads me into the bedroom, and helps me remove my clothes. He pulls down the covers, and I fall into bed.

"Try to sleep." He turns off the light.

"Can you leave the door open a little?"

After he's gone, I close my eyes and listen: Ty's footsteps as he walks across the living room floor. The clattering of plates as he clears the table. The clinking of silverware as he puts it in the dishwasher. The whoosh of the machine as he turns it on.

The terrace door slides open—he's gone outside to smoke a joint. I'd like to join him, escape my reality. Instead, I snuggle into the down comforter, sink my head deeper into the pillow, and recite my list. Tonight I add my newest killer: number twenty-seven, Orlando Jones, gunned down three people as they sat on a porch, enjoying a summer night.

Chapter Thirteen

Bulfinch Place is empty at six A.M.; the next person won't arrive for hours. I run my security badge over the sensor and press the elevator button for the eighth floor. The suite that houses the homicide unit is quiet, the only noise the hissing of heating vents.

The corridors are lined with scores of banker's boxes, swollen with files and stacked from floor to ceiling. About a dozen of the boxes have my name on them, my most recently closed cases. Number twenty-three, Mauricio Flores, stabbed his neighbor with a broken beer bottle. Number twenty-four, Riley Stimpson, shot a pharmacist during a stickup. Every month, a clerk inventories the contents of these boxes, transfers them into enormous plastic tubs, and transports them to our on-site storage facility in the basement.

The automatic lights kick in when I enter the threshold to my office. I search my desk drawers for a K-Cup and find a gift-wrapped box of Dunkin' Donuts coffee from last month's Yankee Swap. My coffee mug is plain black. I have cups with identifying logos—the Ogunquit Playhouse, MoMA, or the Santa Fe Opera—but I leave them at home. The milk in my minifridge expired two weeks ago. I toss the carton in the trash and check my briefcase for a stray sugar packet. In the side

pocket, I find last night's steak, wrapped in tinfoil. I smile, thinking about Ty, how thoughtful it was for him to pack my lunch.

I sip my coffee as I walk down the hallway and around the
corner to the organized crime section. Bright-yellow tape is
stretched across the doorway to Tim's office, blocking entry.
Crime Scene—Do Not Enter.

Two days ago Tim was sitting in the chair behind his desk. We
were laughing about Detective "Inch" Donovan and whether I
should demand that he stop calling me "Toots." Tim said he
thought the term was demeaning, that I should be offended. I
said I didn't mind, that it's endearing.

Tim wasn't the most organized lawyer and he had a tendency
to hoard. His desk is buried under stacks of files. Piles of papers,
exhibits, maps, diagrams line his floor. There's a spent shell
casing from an old investigation on a bookshelf. Reams of
grand jury minutes are spread on a table. Soon investigators
will review every item in this room, hoping to gain insight into
his murder.

Crossing into a crime scene without authorization is prohib-
ited, as it could compromise the integrity of the investigation. I
pry off the strip of yellow tape, careful not to tear it, and step
inside the office. There's a legitimate reason for breaking the
rule: gathering Orlando's files for my trial. There's also a personal
reason: finding and destroying evidence of our relationship.

I sink into Tim's worn leather chair, feel the permanent im-
print left by the shape of his body. A photo of him with Julia
is thumbtacked to a cork board over his desk. It looks like
Chatham, where they spent a week two summers ago. Julia either
didn't know or didn't care that Tim hated the Cape. He would
come back from their trips to the beach and complain about the
mosquitoes and traffic on the Sagamore Bridge.

The mounds of paper represent a panoply of cases, both active and resolved, a walk down memory lane. A mob hit that
went down in a North End pizzeria. A rape-murder solved by

cutting-edge DNA but complicated by the fact that the suspect had an identical twin brother. An exhaustive investigation into the Big Dig, a bazillion-dollar construction project. Work on the tunnel was plagued with problems, cost overruns and delays, and it was finally completed seven years ago. Five years later, part of the ceiling broke off and a schoolteacher was killed when a slab of concrete slammed through the roof of his car. Tim investigated allegations of negligence and corporate malfeasance against the contractor.

I pull out anything that has to do with Orlando Jones and place it in an empty banker's box. There's a small, fading photograph in the top desk drawer, taken on the night Tim and I first met. We're standing next to each other, being sworn in as new assistant district attorneys. We were both so excited to start our careers. After the ceremony, he bought me an inaugural martini, and we toasted to a future of guilty verdicts and life sentences. It's hard to believe that ten years have passed. I slip the picture into my jacket pocket.

Tim and I e-mailed and texted each other often. We never sexted, but a lot of our communication had flirtatious undertones. I log on to his computer and try a few passwords—iterations of Julia and Emma, hitting it on the third try, Emma's birthday. Tim wouldn't mind the invasion of his privacy; at the very least, he'd want to protect Julia from scandal.

Tim was undisciplined when it came to official record keeping, and he was reckless when it came to personal communications. There is a jumble of e-mails; none have been sorted, archived, or deleted. I search for anything to or from me, deleting the more personal ones, saving those that relate to cases and investigations.

I find a message that he sent shortly after he and Julia got engaged, one of the many times that he decided we shouldn't see each other anymore. *Please, Abby, you have to stop calling my house. Julia isn't stupid. She's going to figure us out.* Or the one he sent two months later. *I miss you. Let's meet at your place tonight, after work.* My heart races. I move the e-mails to the trash folder and empty it, but it's a temporary fix. I've overseen enough computer searches to know that nothing can ever be fully erased.

A recent message from Josh McNamara catches my eye. *Subject: Our Meeting.* Josh is a special agent assigned to the FBI's public corruption unit. He's one of the young, energetic up-and-comers, dispatched to Boston in the aftermath of the Whitey Bulger fiasco.

The e-mail was sent two nights ago, and it looks like Tim never opened it. He must have received it shortly before he was killed. It's odd that he never mentioned working an investigation with Josh. Sometimes we work cases with the feds—the FBI, the DEA, the U.S. attorneys' office—but it's not a common occurrence. Tim and I talked five times a day about far less interesting matters, and a case with the feds is something we definitely would have talked about, or so I'd thought.

Josh's message is terse, unrevealing: *Tim, I need to postpone. I'll touch base tomorrow to reschedule.*

Most federal investigators and assistant U.S. attorneys look down on us locals. I was one of the few from my law school class who applied to, and received offers from, both the DA's office and the U.S. attorneys' office. None of my Harvard classmates had any interest in becoming a local prosecutor, though a handful became feds.

Assistant United States attorneys play in a bigger sandbox. Federal cases have a national interest. A multimillion-dollar bank fraud. An international terrorism ring. A billion-dollar drug cartel. ADAs conduct some proactive, long-term investigations, particularly in organized crime and political corruption, but mostly we're reactive. Our bread and butter is street crime. Not very glamorous, but unlike the feds, we have a strong connection to the community that we serve.

Tim's computer files don't reveal any details about the meeting. Maybe they wanted to keep their communications off-line. It could involve a confidential informant.

At a little past seven, the elevator dings. Footsteps in the hallway grow louder. I take a gulp of cold coffee and start to dump the rest of the liquid into a trash can but remember that investigators will want to sort through every scrap of paper, including what's in the rubbish. I finish the coffee, put the rest of Orlando's files in the box, and stick the crime scene tape back across the door.

Balancing my empty mug on top of the box, I head to my office. As I round the corner, Max nearly crashes into me head-on.

"Whoa," he says.

"Morning," I say.

"How are you doing?"

The box is heavy. I start to walk. "I'm okay. You?"

"Hard to believe it's real." He eyes the bundle that I'm carrying. "What are you doing?"

"Collecting Orlando's files. I probably shouldn't have crossed the barricade, but there's only six days until trial."

Max follows me down the hallway.

"Make sure you keep an inventory of everything you took, give it to Dermot Michaels," he says.

"Middlesex assigned it to Michaels?"

"I take it you're not a fan."

"He's got a chip on his shoulder about Suffolk, like he's jealous that we get more murders than they do. It's demented."

"Well, he's coming by with some troopers this morning to start digging in, so play nice," Max says.

As we pass the archive stacks, I notice that among the boxes is one marked *Jones*.

I stop and use my foot to point. "Could you grab that? It's a long shot, but maybe it has to do with this case."

He inspects the label and picks up the box. As soon as we

reach my office, I plop my box on a table and start to unpack it. Max turns to go, still carrying the Jones file.

"Can you leave that here?"

"Oh, sure."

He hesitates before putting it down. Something about him is a little off—maybe he's hungover, or maybe he's already started drinking.

"Carmen Eggleston called me last night," he says. "She knows about the incident between Orlando and your friend."

"It wasn't an incident. It was a murder."

"The Public Defenders' office wants you off the case."

I study Max's face, trying to determine whether or not he's in my corner. He gives a neutral shrug.

"They're sticking their nose where it doesn't belong," I say. "Orlando doesn't qualify for public counsel—his father hired Blum to represent him."

"Carmen said she's speaking on behalf of the entire defense bar, not just the public defenders."

"They want to conflict me out of the case because they're worried that I'm going to win." Accustomed to whiny defense attorneys making idle threats and unreasonable demands, I turn my attention to more pressing matters. I open one of the files. "Tell them to take it up with the BBO."

"They've already filed a complaint," Max says. "You sure you don't want me to give the case to Sarsfield?"

"I'm sure," I say. "If I mess up and Orlando gets acquitted, they can go ahead and disbar me. I won't want to practice law anymore."

Chapter Fourteen

Kevin texts to let me know he's out front, and I meet him curbside. He grabs the bundles of folders from my arms and drops them on the backseat of his car.

"You brought along some light reading?"

"They're from Tim's office."

We get in the car, and he pulls onto Cambridge Street.

"What's your pleasure?"

"Let's go see Ezekiel Hogan."

When we reach the traffic light at Park Street, he takes a right up the hill instead of going straight toward the South End.

"Why are you taking this route?"

"I want you to see something." He pulls in front of the State-house and nods, directing me to follow his eyes. The flag is lowered to half-staff. "In honor of Tim," he says.

Watching the flag flap in the wind takes my breath away. We sit in silence for a minute until my phone vibrates, breaking my trance.

"Don't expect Ezekiel to roll out the welcome mat," Nestor says. "I've tried calling a few times, but he never picks up."

"The North Street Posse probably got to him," I say.

North Street gang members, particularly the man with the

gold teeth, have asserted their presence in the courtroom. No doubt, they're more menacing out on the street.

I get off the phone and take another look at the flag before Kevin pulls back into the flow of traffic.

"Did Ezekiel testify in the grand jury?" he says.

"He blew it off at first and ignored the subpoenas. Tim played hardball and had Nestor haul him to court in the back of the cruiser. Even then, he took the Fifth. Tim had to force immunity down his throat."

"Did he give it up in the grand jury?"

"He refused to answer questions—until Tim brought him to a judge who threatened to lock him up for contempt."

"But he came around?"

"Finally, he ID'd Orlando as the shooter. Then he came charging out of the grand jury room and told Tim to go screw himself."

"I don't suppose he's mellowed with time."

"Can't blame him. He took a bullet to the chest."

Traffic on Mass Avenue is at a standstill. We inch our way up to a green light, but it turns red before we can get through the intersection. To my left is the morgue—where Tim's body will be autopsied later today. The thought of him lying on that slab, having his insides exposed, makes my hands tremble and my eyes well with tears.

A man taps on my window and holds up a sign. *Homeless veteran. Please help.* My wallet is empty since I haven't had time to stop at an ATM in days. As I feel around the bottom of my tote for spare change, I find the leftover steak that Ty packed for my lunch. I open my window and pass the foil package to the man.

"You don't have money?" he says.

"Sorry," I say.

He inspects the packet, peels back the foil, and takes a bite.

"This is pretty good. Thanks."

When we reach the Mobil station where Ezekiel works, I grab the murder book and turn to a photo. He's lying in a hospital bed, eyes half-closed, a tube in his mouth.

"It's a miracle he survived," I say.

"He's had three surgeries and a boatload of physical therapy. He used to be a mechanic, but now he can't even work the gas pumps."

A door sensor dings twice as we enter the store. Ezekiel is behind the cash register, walled in by bulletproof glass. Kevin presses his tin up to the grimy, scratched plexiglass and makes the introductions. Ezekiel is not pleased to make our acquaintance.

"You got a warrant?"

"We want to talk about Orlando Jones," I say.

"Talk all you want, but do it someplace else." He turns away.

A teenage boy steps up to the counter, holding a bottle of grape soda and a Mounds bar. He puts his cash into the metal tray and slides it under the plexiglass. Ezekiel accepts the bills, and we watch the boy leave.

"You're going to have to testify. We might as well prepare," I say.

"Fuck that. I went in the grand jury, the DA told me not to worry, everything was secret. A few days later, I came home from the doctor's and the grand jury papers were stuck to my front door. Everything I said in the room was typed up, hanging by a nail. *Rat* was written, in red, all over the papers."

An elderly man comes in the store and we step aside. He asks for a pack of Newports, and then goes outside and lights up, inches from the gas pumps.

"Grand jury testimony is secret," I say, "but everything is transcribed."

"No shit. You gave the papers to Orlando's boys."

"Prosecutors have to turn them over to defense attorneys as part of discovery."

"Then the lawyer gave them to Orlando, same difference."

"We could prosecute him for intimidation."

"You don't get it, lady. Orlando Jones would kill his own sister if she got in his way." I start to talk, but he cuts me off. "Or he'd get someone else to kill her." Done with me, he turns to Kevin. "Look, I don't want Five-O coming around to my place of employment. That's gonna get me noticed even more."

I'm not ready to accept defeat. "We can get you safe transportation to and from the courthouse. We can put you up in a hotel," I say.

Ezekiel turns his back to us and starts to unpack a carton of Camel Lights.

I keep pressing, hoping I'll hit a nerve. "Someone died, and we need your help. If you don't do it for us, do it for Jasmine. Her mother is grieving. You know, she had a twin sister."

He stops what he's doing and looks at me. "I got family too."

"If you don't show up, you'll be arrested," Kevin says.

Ezekiel lifts his shirt, exposing a thick, knotty scar that runs the length of his torso. "I'm the victim, and you want to arrest me. Okay, go ahead. Lock me up," he says.

I take in the wound—it's healed, but I think about the pain and fear that preceded it.

"I know that Tim talked to you about witness protection," I say. "It's not too late. We can help you find a new place to live, a new job."

"I'm staying right here. You go into witness protection."

It's tempting. A one-way ticket to sunny Arizona. A different identity. A new career. I could be a tour guide at the Grand Canyon. Or a psychic healer in Sedona.

A woman enters the shop, grabs a couple of bags of potato chips, and stands behind me as though there's a line. I turn to her and she smiles.

"Are you next?" she says.

"No, they're just leaving," Ezekiel says.

I slide a subpoena under the plexiglass and we return to the car.

I sink into the seat and buckle up. "I don't know how I'm going to pull this off."

"He'll break. Let's give him time to think about it."

Kevin drives to the crime scene so we can get a firsthand look. Photographs don't capture how close everyone was to each other—the houses, the street, the car. Kevin measures distances and jots down notes. I position myself on the front stoop of the double-decker, where Jasmine and Ezekiel drank their beer, laughed, listened to music.

I move to the bottom step, where Denny passed Jasmine the brown paper bag containing egg rolls and pork lo mein. I picture Orlando, holding his shotgun, blasting off rounds. I try to imagine the panic that Jasmine, Ezekiel, and Denny experienced when they saw him. Then I think about Crystal and her terror when Orlando emerged from the bushes, brandishing a blade.

My cell vibrates. I take it out of my pocket and see that it's the medical examiner.

"I finished Tim's autopsy," she says. "Don't tell Middlesex that I called you first."

"What's the cause of death?"

"Single gunshot wound, entered through the front of his skull and lodged in his brain."

The news isn't unexpected, but it's still shocking.

"Sounds like an execution," I say.

"The size of the hole and stippling on Tim's forehead indicate that he was shot from close range, two to three feet away."

"Defensive wounds?"

"None—not a scratch. No bruises or broken fingernails," she says.

If there's any good news, this is it: Tim didn't suffer.

"We'll have to wait for the crime lab to weigh in on the rest," she says. "There's still a shot that they'll find trace evidence, something that'll give us DNA."

I hang up and tell Kevin what I've learned.

"Why do you think Tim went over to that tow lot?" I say.

"The doer could have been in the backseat, lying in wait. Shoved a gun in his face, forced him to drive somewhere isolated," he says.

"Or it could have been a setup."

"Maybe."

Kevin and I are silent, but we're both thinking the same thing: I hope Tim wasn't involved in something bad with someone shady who lured him to someplace remote and put a bullet in his head.

Chapter Fifteen

Six MBTA buses idle outside my office on New Sudbury Street. I choose the first one and grip the railing as I climb the steps. It's stifling inside, the rows filled with somber faces, seated in pairs. Lawyers, victim witness advocates, paralegals, and secretaries. I make my way down the aisle and take a seat next to Chris Sarsfield, a prosecutor assigned to the gang unit. As soon as I'm settled, the musky smell of his aftershave makes me wish I'd chosen a different seatmate.

"My wife thinks we're all gonna get killed," Chris says. "She's freaking out. My father said they don't pay us enough to put our lives on the line. I mean, cops are trained for dangerous situations—we're just lawyers. Don't you think?"

"Oh," I say, looking straight ahead, hoping that he'll stop yammering.

"I'm thinking about getting a license to carry, maybe go to target practice at the academy. I might abandon ship, throw in an application at City Hall. I heard the corporation counsel is looking to hire."

I take out my phone and reread old e-mails, but he keeps talking.

"Who do you think did it? You think it was someone he prosecuted?"

I shrug and gaze out the window. Chris turns around and repeats his questions to the IT specialist, seated in the row behind us.

The bus driver pulls a lever, and the front door wheezes closed. A police escort guides the buses through the busy downtown streets, zipping through red lights and stop signs like a presidential motorcade. We drive through Kenmore Square, past Fenway's Green Monster, and I think about Tim's passion for the Yankees. I never asked him about why he rooted for the team, with no personal connection to New York; I suppose it was more about rebellion than fandom.

We park on Tremont Street, near Mission Church, a Romanesque basilica made of Roxbury pudding stone. When we get outside, black ribbons are distributed among the hundreds of mourners and everyone pins one onto their lapels. The temperature is in the thirties, but most of us have left our overcoats in the bus. The silence of anticipation looms.

Church bells chime twelve times, announcing high noon. An organizer speaks into an amplifier, his voice cutting in and out.

"Attention . . . every . . . please . . . groups, according to . . . office. Suffolk first . . . the ten other district . . . attorney general . . . United States attorney."

Everyone falls into line. Max positions himself up front, ready to lead the procession. Owen is by his side. Owen is hypersensitive to Max's drinking, having given up booze after the birth of his oldest daughter eight years ago. He attends AA meetings daily, always during his lunch hour. Once I overheard him encouraging Max to go with him, an invitation that Max declined.

We march single file in silence, along Mission Hill, toward Leary's Funeral Home. Over a thousand strong, the line stretches back for what seems like a mile. State troopers in full dress, including boots and leather cross straps, form a long barrier along the curb, offering both pomp and protection. Cars slow to see the spectacle. Reporters document the pageantry from their designated area across the street.

Outside the funeral home, a kilted bagpiper serenades us with "Amazing Grace." Inside, wooden tripods prop up poster boards that are covered with yellowing photographs. A hodge-podge of the various stages of Tim's life. Age six, in red plaid pajamas, unwrapping a yellow Tonka truck. Age twelve, in swim trunks, being knocked over by a wave at Nantasket Beach. Age thirty-three, in a tuxedo, in front of a wedding cake, kissing Julia. Her dress was rayon, her pearls were glass, but I have to admit, she was a beautiful bride.

Included in the collage is a picture of me and Tim at J.J. Foley's, a cop bar in the South End. We're mugging it up for the camera, arms slung around each other, trying just a little too hard to act like buddies. Chris Sarsfield, standing behind me in line, looks at the photograph, looks at me, and then quickly looks away. Chris knows. Everyone must know. My heart drops into my stomach, and my face heats up.

I fell in love with Tim long before we slept together. We were in the emergency room at Boston Medical Center. I had gone there to meet my first rape victim, and I was so nervous that I'd forgotten to take my badge. The nurses didn't know me yet; they wouldn't grant me access without proper identification. I called Tim, and he stopped what he was doing to drive over and deliver my ID. When I came out of the interview, he was in the waiting room pacing like an expectant father. It was a moment full of promise and romance, in spite of the gunshot victim swearing at us as he was wheeled by on a gurney.

When I reach Tim's casket, I pause for a split second and start to look inside. This isn't how I want to remember him. I turn away and focus on the tallest member of the Honor Guard, who stands next to the casket, expressionless, staring straight ahead. He reminds me of a member of the Queen's Guard at

Buckingham Palace, which I'd visited with my ninth-grade class at Winsor. I imagine the man wearing a tall black fur hat with a strap under his chin.

A walk-by is just that. No talking. No stopping. No praying. No kneeling. Just walking. It's a show of support for the family and a show of respect for the deceased. Tim's family is bookended by two flags. His parents, his siblings, their spouses and children are all there. Julia looks exhausted as she desperately searches the faces of everyone, as though pleading for an explanation. She looks at me without offering recognition, just another sad face in the crowd. I'm grateful that I have to keep pace with the line.

Tim's mother and I exchange looks of shared sorrow. I touch her arm as I pass by. Up until Julia came into the picture, I enjoyed countless holiday meals with Tim's family; his mother was always so welcoming.

Outside Leary's, the cold air feels refreshing. I take in the Mission Church spires, reaching up toward the sun. We march back to the buses, still in line, retracing our steps. An endless stream of solemn faces continues to make its way to the funeral home.

A text from Kevin makes my phone vibrate. *I'm behind you, on your left.*

Carl Ostroff, reporter's notebook in hand, tries to intercept me as I cross the street. I wave him off.

"Not now, Carl."

"Off the record?"

"Have some respect."

As soon as I slam Kevin's car door closed, he hands me a silver flask.

"Can't have an Irish wake without Irish whiskey," he says.

I take a swig. The liquid burns the back of my throat, and I cough. We sit and watch the line of mourners still making their way to Leary's.

"It's intense," I say.

"The department is going to do ours tonight."

The second sip of whiskey goes down easier.

"Where are we headed?"

"Ladies' choice: we can go to the Mission Bar for a few pints, or out to Logan to see Warren Winters."

I hand him back the flask. "I need to occupy my mind. Let's go see Warren."

The trial is days away, and we have only two eyewitnesses—Ezekiel Hogan, who may not cooperate, and Warren Winters, who has been cooperative in the past, but it's been a year since he testified in the grand jury.

We set out to East Boston, where Warren works as a baggage handler at the airport. It's three o'clock, I haven't had anything to eat yet today, and the alcohol is starting to make me feel woozy. I reach into my tote and pull out a small tinfoil package. I unfurl the wrapping to find burrata, tomato, and basil on a baguette. A glob of tomatoey cheese spills out onto Warren's form twenty-six, making a mess. I wipe tomato off my coat and take a bite. The cheese is soft, smooth, and delicate.

We drive into the mouth of the Ted Williams Tunnel, the subject of Tim's Big Dig investigation, where the teacher died when the slab of concrete came loose and crashed through the roof of his car.

"I hate this tunnel," I say. "It reminds me of death."

"Occupational hazard," he says. "Everything reminds me of death."

"This one creeps me out even more. It's like driving into a coffin."

He flips on his siren, zipping past frustrated commuters.

"I'm not sure tunnel phobia would qualify as a blue-light emergency."

"If the ceiling caves and puts us out of commission, the unsolved homicide rate will quadruple."

Cars pull over, allowing us to pass.

"The Big Dig was Tim's case, right?" Kevin says.

"He spent over a year on it."

It was a cluster. The U.S. attorney, the attorney general, and the DA all claimed jurisdiction and launched their own parallel investigations. Max appointed Tim to lead the probe in our office. He looked into the potential for an involuntary manslaughter charge, searched thousands of documents, issued hundreds of subpoenas, interviewed dozens of witnesses. He impaneled a special grand jury to consider the case.

"They turned up bubkes, right?" Kevin says.

"Tim was pushing to indict the company that installed the cement. Max didn't think there was enough to make a case. It drove a permanent wedge between them."

Kevin navigates around a double line of cars, taxis, and buses, and pulls up to the curb, outside Terminal B. A state trooper blows her whistle and approaches the car, ready to shoo us away. State police has jurisdiction over airport roads, and she can order us to put the car in short-term parking like everyone else. But Kevin makes a compelling case.

He flashes his badge and his smile. "I promise we'll be quick."

"Do you mind pulling up a little?" she says as though Kevin is doing her the favor.

We find Warren's boss, Lou Fenton, in his basement office, feet on the desk, sucking on a Marlboro. Kevin taps on the door.

"Boston police, can we talk to you for a minute?"

Lou exhales a cloud of smoke and bolts upright. His feet land on the floor so hard that it sounds like he might be wearing cement shoes. He stubs out the cigarette and bats at the smoke.

"Don't worry. We're homicide, not inspectional services," Kevin says.

"How can I help youse?"

"We're looking for Warren Winters."

"He didn't show up to work today."

Kevin and I exchange looks. "Is he sick?" I say.

"Beats me. He didn't call."

"Is that unusual?"

He nods. "Warren isn't exactly employee of the year, but he always lets me know when he's not coming in."

Kevin and I thank Lou, hand him our business cards, and ask him to call if he sees or hears from Warren. When we return to the car, the trooper looks like she applied a fresh coat of scarlet lipstick.

"Hope you found what you were looking for," she says.

Kevin uses his remote to unlock the car doors. "Thanks," he says. "I owe you one."

Her face falls as we get in and drive off.

"Seems like she was expecting something more than your heartfelt gratitude," I say.

"Like what?"

"A date."

"My wife might have something to say about that."

I try Warren's cell. After the second ring, a recording comes on. *The number you have reached is no longer in service.* When we get out of the tunnel, my cell beeps—a missed call from Nestor. I hit redial, and he picks up.

"Hey, Nestor, we're on our way to Warren Winters's house."

"Don't bother. I just got off the phone with his girlfriend. She hasn't seen him since yesterday."

Kevin is approaching the Southeast Expressway. I signal him to pull over before he gets on the ramp.

"Why did she wait so long to call you?" I say to Nestor.

"She thought she had to give it twenty-four hours before filing a missing persons," Nestor says.

"Not when you're a witness to a murder."

"Tell me about it."

"We'll meet you back at HQ." I look over at Kevin, who nods in agreement.

"You'll sign my overtime?" Nestor says.

"See you in a few." I hang up.

"Where is Warren?" Kevin says.

"In the wind—someone got to him before we did."

Chapter Sixteen

Boston police headquarters is on Tremont Street in Roxbury, less than a mile from the lot where Tim's body was discovered. The building's official address is One Schroeder Plaza, named after Officer Walter Schroeder, who was gunned down when he responded to a bank robbery thirty-five years ago. The sleek, high-tech building offers one-stop shopping; it houses the homicide unit, the crime lab, the ballistics lab, the identification unit, and the fugitive squad. It's kind of like a Neiman Marcus for prosecutors.

We set up shop inside, using the cafeteria on the first floor as our makeshift war room. Kevin orders a bowl of beef stew, and I opt for a turkey dinner with all the fixings.

"At least you're getting your three squares." He sets down his tray.

"My body isn't used to all this—"

"Nutrition?"

I dig my fork into a heap of creamy mashed potatoes. "I'm going to get fat, and when I do, I'm holding you personally responsible."

"There's this thing you might want to look into—it's called exercise. I saw some top-of-the-line ellipticals in your building.

Can't you get that boyfriend of yours to teach you how to use them?"

"I get enough of a workout on the job. If I continue to eat like this, I may have to reconsider."

We each grab a banker's box and flip through files as we eat dinner, careful not to spill food on the reports. Nestor comes out of the kitchen area with a bowl of American chop suey and joins us. He opens the Jones box that I rescued from the archive stacks.

"These files aren't for Orlando," Nestor says. "This is Melvin Jones's file."

Kevin doesn't like to be out of the loop. "Who's Melvin Jones?" he says.

"Why does Melvin Jones have a file?" I say.

Nestor takes a couple of bites of macaroni and chews slowly. "It's an old investigation."

"What kind of investigation?" I say.

"Can someone tell me—who is Melvin Jones?" Kevin puts down his fork and exhales loudly, about to boil over.

"Melvin is Orlando's father," I say.

Kevin looks at Nestor. "Why didn't you tell us he was the subject of an investigation?"

"You guys ran off on your secret squirrel mission," Nestor says. "The information highway is a two-way street."

"Look, this isn't the time for a turf war," I say.

We eat in silence for a couple of minutes. I finish my last bite of stuffing and push the carrots and peas around on my plate. We clear our trays, and I grab a slice of Boston cream pie on my way back to the table.

"So, what's the deal with Melvin?" I say.

"He was part of that Big Dig cluster," Nestor says. "He owned Zelco, the company that installed the cheap cement in the tunnel."

"I didn't know Melvin was being looked at during the Big Dig invest."

"He was an unnamed target. Tim wanted to charge him with negligent manslaughter, but Max put the kibosh on it."

"Tim never mentioned anything about a tie-in with Orlando's family," I say.

"Seems like Tim had all sorts of secrets," Kevin says.

I ignore the comment and take a forkful of pie. Even though Kevin is disappointed or angry, Tim isn't here to explain or defend himself. Much of what I've learned has taken me by surprise, but I'm not going to throw him under the bus. I love him as much as ever, secrets and all.

"Why wasn't Melvin charged? His negligence cost a decent, hardworking family man his life," Kevin says.

"Politics. There was plenty of evidence, but Max wouldn't authorize the indictments because he didn't want to go out on a limb and piss people off," Nestor says.

"He's one lucky son of a bitch," Kevin says.

"They're one lucky family," Nestor says.

"Meaning what?" I take a sip of water, unsure of where this is going.

"Orlando dodged some bullets too."

Kevin looks at me. "We know he had a juvenile conviction, but he did time on that."

"After he got out of juvie, he had a lot of cases dismissed," Nestor says.

"Yeah, we know about that too," I say. "Those cases were dropped because the victims refused to cooperate."

"Did you know about the gun case he picked up about eighteen months ago?"

My chest tightens. "Orlando was arrested on a gun case? Eighteen months ago?"

"It was a total bag job—like someone waved a magic wand and made the charges disappear."

"The victim probably got cold feet," Kevin says.

"Nope, no civilians were involved."

I put down my glass to avoid spilling water on myself and clasp my hands in my lap.

"Then why was the case dismissed? Did you talk to the arresting officer?"

"The detective told me that when she showed up in court for the motion hearing, the case had already been broomed. The fix was in."

There's no way Tim knew about this case—he would have told me about it.

"Which ADA stood up on it?" I say.

"Chris Sarsfield, from your gang unit."

I call Chris, let it ring about five times, call again. He finally picks up. There's an announcer talking and a lot of drunks yelling at each other in the background. *Get him. Hit him. Kill him.* Sounds like he's at a Bruins game.

"Do you know if Orlando Jones ever worked as an informant?" I say.

"Doesn't sound familiar. Hum me a few bars," Chris says.

"Tim's murder case, the one that I'm trying right now. It looks like the defendant had an earlier gun case out of Dorchester."

"Oh, yeah, I remember. Tim asked me to get rid of that case."

Kevin and Nestor are looking at me. I cup my hand over my mouth and look at the floor.

"Did he tell you why?" My voice is trembling.

"Nope, and I didn't ask." Chris is barely audible through the screaming fans. "The score is tied up, and there's a power play—I gotta go."

I hang up and look at Kevin. "Tim was the one who wanted to get the charges dismissed."

"Then Tim wanted something from Orlando," Kevin says.

I want to give him the benefit of the doubt. If he was in bed with Orlando Jones, I want to believe it was for a good reason. I just have to figure out what that reason could be.

Chapter Seventeen

Ty doesn't seem to hear me when I open the door to my apartment, step inside, and take off my coat. I find him in the living room, drinking a beer and typing on his laptop. When he looks up and sees me, he immediately switches to his home screen, the *Rolling Stone* website. Clearly, he doesn't want me to know what he's up to, which surprises me because he's never been shy about his Internet interests. The few times I walked in on him when he was surfing for porn, he didn't flinch.

"Hey, babe," he says.

I pour myself a glass of Merlot and sit across from him. Trying not to come off as overly prosecutorial, I lean back and sip my wine.

"What have you been up to?" I say in the most casual tone I can muster up.

He looks at me and hesitates.

I don't wait for a response. "Are you chatting with women online? Is that what you do when I'm not around—find Internet hookups?"

"Babe, chill."

"Were you on Tinder checking out the local talent?"

My use of the phrase *local talent* is proof that I've been spending too much time with Kevin.

"Come on," Ty says. "Don't interrogate me."

If he were a suspect, I'd sit silently and try to maintain eye contact long enough to make him uncomfortable—often an effective way to elicit a confession. So that's what I do. He breaks in less than a minute.

"I've been reading old obituaries."

That's not what I was expecting to hear. "Why?"

"When your father was here, he mentioned someone named George—that he died. I wanted to know who he was."

Hearing George's name knocks the wind out of me. "What did he say?"

"That you suffered more than your share of loss. I thought maybe you'd been married and were a widow or something." He searches my face for a reaction.

"George was my younger brother." I sip my wine and then busy myself by refilling the glass, even though it doesn't need a refill.

Ty sees me struggling. "I'm sorry, babe," he says.

"Why all the espionage? You could have just asked."

"I didn't think you'd be straight with me. I know you love your secrets."

"I don't have secrets."

He gets out of his chair, moves next to me on the sofa, and takes my hand. "What happened? How did he die?"

I take a breath and consider whether to be truthful or to toe the family line and say that George died of heart failure.

"My brother was a junkie."

"He died of a drug overdose?"

I nod. "Six years ago."

I get up and look out the window. Webs of ice have formed in the corners of the glass. The park below, with a slide, jungle gym, and climbing rocks, is deserted and desolate. I remember being with George at the Dartmouth Street playground. I picture him—five years old, on a swing, pumping his legs back and forth, trying to gain momentum. *Push me, Abby. Push. Again. One more time.* George always wanted more.

"He was an addict since high school, maybe earlier. He'd show up at family dinners high as a kite. When he nodded off at the table, we'd all keep eating, chatting about current events and the stock market."

Ty stands and picks up a photo from the mantel: George, Charlie, Crystal, and me. We're all wearing swimsuits at the Coral Beach Club in Bermuda. Crystal's mother had to work during our school vacations—my parents invited her to join us and paid her fare.

"This him?"

"That's George."

"Who is this girl with you?"

"A friend." I turn and look out the window at a cluster of birds, flying across the river in a V formation.

"From high school?"

"Uh-huh."

"You two must have been tight if she went with you on vacation. When's the last time you hung out?"

My phone rings. I check the screen. "I have to answer this," I say. "It's Kevin."

"Can't you two take a break for one night?"

I'm taken aback by his response. I don't think Ty's ever snapped at me before. I consider sending Kevin to voice mail, but press the call-accept button and walk into the bedroom.

"We found Warren Winters," Kevin says.

I sit on the bed, relieved. "Great. Will he talk?"

He hesitates. "That's not going to be possible."

I clear my throat. "Where is he?"

"Floating in the harbor."

Chapter Eighteen

Kevin navigates us through the narrow streets of Chinatown, where a woman, wearing fishnets and four-inch platforms, leans in the passenger-side window of a Lincoln. Kevin blasts a quick blip from his siren. When she turns to look at us, the car speeds off. Kevin waves at her. *Keep moving.* She steps onto the sidewalk and gives us the finger.

We sit in silence at a red light.

"You doing okay?" Kevin says. "You're pretty quiet."

"Do you think I did right by George, getting his drug case dismissed?"

Kevin doesn't blink at the non sequitur. "You did what anyone would do for family. He got busted, you had the juice to help him out, and you did."

At the next block, the woman is negotiating with another potential customer. This time when Kevin blasts the siren, she retreats and walks away.

"Maybe things would have turned out differently if I'd let him go through the system," I say.

"He'd have wound up in Bridgewater. You know what that place is like."

I look out the window; a couple of students, backpacks slung over their shoulders, leave a restaurant. They chat and look at their cells as they cross the busy street, oblivious to the on-coming traffic. The man nearly gets plowed over by a taxi.

"If he was locked up, they'd have kept him alive."

At the next traffic light, Kevin turns and touches my arm.

"For a little while, maybe. And then what? Don't second-guess yourself."

"I don't think I ever thanked you properly."

"It was no big deal on my part. The drug cops would've dropped the charges if you'd have asked them yourself."

"You spared me the humiliation. I appreciate it."

"You come through for me in all sorts of ways."

He looks at me. We lock eyes for a few seconds until I look away.

I force a laugh, trying to deflect. "Signing your overtime slip hardly compares."

"I'm serious. You've never lost one of my cases. You've never let my evidence get suppressed. You've never refused my late-night phone calls."

"That's what I signed up for when I took this job."

The light turns green, but Kevin idles at the intersection.

"Tell that to the rest of your colleagues. This is about more than work. You believe in what you're doing. You're the real McCoy."

We look at each other again, but this time I don't look away. Admittedly, I'm conflicted about Ty and grieving over Tim, but there's no denying it: our attraction has been building. The sexual tension is palpable. I wonder how he'd react if I asked him to pull the car over and rip off my clothes.

A car behind us beeps, and the driver yells out the window, "Wake up, buddy! The light is green!" Kevin waves at the driver and moves through the intersection.

The valet in front of the Boston Harbor Hotel lets us park out front on Atlantic Avenue. I can see my breath as we walk under the towering archway that leads us behind the luxury hotel and office complex that make up Rowes Wharf.

Unis and technicians have gathered on the dock where, during the day, commuters board water taxis that shuttle them to and from the South Shore. The terminal is closed for the night, illuminated by portable police kliegs.

Businessmen, tourists, and wedding guests are standing in the windows of the high-rises, looking down on us. They are in offices, hotel rooms, and banquet halls, pulling back the drapes, craning their necks, trying to figure out what the activity is all about. They've paid a hefty price for their panoramic views of the waterfront, and they probably didn't expect the cost to include the sight of Warren Winters's bloated, waterlogged corpse.

A few minutes after we arrive, members of the Boston police dive team, wearing masks and wet suits, hoist his lifeless body onto the wooden pier. People snap pictures with their cell phones. They'll Instagram the images to their friends back home in Cleveland or Kansas City. A memento of their trip to Boston.

A small but rowdy group of twentysomethings spill out of a bar and assemble on the cement walkway that runs the length of the hotel and office complex. In varying degrees of drunkenness, they elbow each other, hankering to get a better look. They should turn away before it's too late. A murder victim is not someone you want to see up close, especially after he's been dragged out of the harbor. I consider warning them, but they won't listen. They never do. They'll have to learn the hard way.

Warren is splayed out on a plastic tarp. The on-call medical examiner, Dr. Lisa Frongello, is leaning over him. A gold cross dangles from her neck.

She gloves up, kneels down, and takes Warren's face in her hands. She twists his head and moves his wet hair, exposing a small hole in his scalp.

"He was shot before he was dumped."

I stand in a low crouch and take shallow breaths. "Is that the entry wound?"

"Looks like it. Judging by the size and shape of the opening, it's probably a small-caliber, maybe a .22."

"How long do you think he's been in the water?"

"I'd guesstimate at least five hours." She points at bite marks on his face and arms. "He's been gnawed at by marine life."

His hands are gray, his feet unshod. I avoid looking directly into his eyes.

"Any other wounds?"

"I'll check when I get him out of these clothes."

The air is frigid, and my feet start to feel numb. I stand, shifting back and forth in place to keep my circulation going.

"They did a piss-poor job of dumping him," she says. "Sign of amateurs. Pros would have weighed him down with bricks or something."

"They wanted us to find him," Kevin says. "They're sending a message."

When Lisa is done with her preliminary assessment, her assistants zip Warren into a body bag and lift him onto an awaiting gurney. The spectators continue to watch, but the party atmosphere has quieted. They stand, frozen in place. Their faces are ashen, their expressions grim. They'll never be able to wipe Warren from their memories.

The ME's assistants slide the gurney into the back of the coroner's van and slam the doors.

Warren Winters is no more.

"This is on me," I say to Kevin.

"No, it's not. You had the case for about a minute. Nestor told me Warren was offered protection, but he turned it down."

"It was an empty offer, and we both know it. We can't even protect our own."

Chapter Nineteen

Max requested a briefing on Tim's murder investigation, and Middlesex ADA Dermot Michaels is here to give an update. Dermot sits across from me in Max's conference room, fidgeting with his golf ball cuff links and tapping his pen against the side of the table.

"He's almost a half hour late," he says. "I've got a lot on my plate today."

Technically, Dermot and I are colleagues, but he feels more like an adversary. There's a history of competitive condescension between Middlesex and Suffolk County prosecutors; Middlesex thinks we're a posse of reckless cowboys, and we think they're a bunch of pampered suburbanites. We're both more than a little bit right.

"Max is the elected. He sets the schedule," I say.

"He's your boss, not mine."

If Dermot weren't so annoying, I'd let him know that he's planted himself in Max's seat, and he might want to move his ass. We sit in silence, both checking our cell phones. I've got about ten texts and e-mails. Ty: *I rented a tux for the wedding.* The condo board: *Received your check for January, but you still owe for November and December.* The medical examiner: *Warren Winters COD is a single gunshot wound to the head.*

Max breezes in, his eyes a little bloodshot. "Sorry we're late."

"It's my fault," Owen says. "Patsy's parent-teacher conference ran long."

It's hard to know if Owen is telling the truth or if he's covering for Max. I suspect the latter.

"Dermot, do you mind moving? You're sitting in Max's chair," Owen says.

"Oh, I'm sorry." Dermot gets up. "I didn't see a seating chart."

Max shrugs off the remark. "Let's get started. What's going on with the invesh-tigation?"

Owen quickly takes the reins, hoping Dermot doesn't notice Max's slurred speech. "What can you tell us?"

"We're making progress—everyone agrees that it was a murder for hire."

"Who do you think is behind it?" Owen says.

"It looks like Orlando Jones ordered the hit."

Even though Dermot is just articulating what everyone already believes, my chest tightens with a flood of emotions. Rage, sadness, fear.

"Any ideas about who pulled the trigger?" Owen says.

"It's safe to assume it was someone from North Street," Dermot says."

I picture the man with the gold teeth, sitting in the back of the courtroom, smiling at Orlando.

"What's your working theory on motive?" I say.

"Orlando wanted to threaten Warren Winters and convince him not to testify or, if that didn't work, kill him. Orlando's crew was having trouble locating Warren, and time was growing short. Orlando figured that if he got someone to kill the prosecutor, that would buy him at least a week."

Max looks at Dermot and then at me. "You think Orlando Jones is that callous, that he did a murder to buy himself an extra seven days?"

"Yes," I say. "I know he's that callous."

"People have killed for a lot less," Dermot says.

"What's your evidence?" Max says.

"The proof is in the pudding. Tim is dead, Orlando got his continuance, and your star witness was found floating in the harbor," Dermot says. "Now that Warren is dead, your case against Orlando is going down the toilet."

"That doesn't sound like evidence," Max says. "It sounds like conjecture."

"The simplest answer is usually the best one," Dermot says. "You'll see."

Dermot clicks his pen and closes his leather-bound note-book, preparing to wrap up the meeting. I swivel my chair to face him.

"Did you run Orlando's BOP?" I say.

"I haven't had a chance to go through it yet."

I slide a copy of Orlando's criminal record across the table. "It looks like he could have been working as an informant."

Owen tries to play it off as though he's not particularly inter-ested, but he flips through the papers, scanning every word. "Who was his handler?"

"He's not registered with the Boston PD. He might have been working for Tim," I say.

Max grabs Orlando's BOP from Dermot. "No way. I don't buy it. I would know if Tim was using him as an informant."

"I opened a grand jury and plan to start presenting tomor-row," Dermot says. "I'll explore it."

"You should also take a look at Orlando's father, Melvin," I say. "He has a closed investigation that could have a tie-in."

Max slams his hand on the table, startling me. "If you're talking about the construction project, forget it. Don't waste your time."

"There's an obvious connection," I say. "Tim had involvement with both father and son. It's worth checking out."

Max puts his palm up. "Stop. Melvin Jones was a bad

businessman. Period. He's not one to get involved in premeditated murder."

"He could have had something personal against Tim."

"That's crap. I don't want to reopen the Big Dig invest." Max's face reddens. "You'll never solve this case if you're running around, chasing shadows."

Owen throws me a look. *Enough.* Best to let it drop.

When the meeting breaks up, I take the stairs back to my office. As I swipe my badge to unlock the door, Max approaches me from behind, frightening me, and follows me into the stairwell. The door slams behind us. I turn to face him, and he moves toward me, backing me up against the wall. He leans in, close enough for me to smell his breath, minty fresh, with mouthwash to cover the odor of alcohol.

"Don't ever contradict me in front of outsiders."

Having crossed the invisible line into my personal space, he is gesticulating wildly. His voice echoes up and down the stairwell.

"Got it, sorry," I say.

"Middlesex is like a sieve. I don't need Dermot Michaels spreading our confidential information all over town. Next thing, *The Globe* will have another scope up my ass about the Big Dig. I don't want to reopen those wounds on top of everything else we have going on right now."

"Understood."

The stairwell door lock clicks open, and I'm relieved to see Owen. He can be overprotective—or, as Kevin calls him, a *buttinsky*—but that comes in handy at times like this.

"Everything okay in here?" Owen looks at me, knowing that it's not.

Max keeps his angry focus on me. "Abby and I are reviewing the office org chart. I was reminding her that I sit at the top, and she's somewhere below that."

Owen takes Max's forearm and moves him backward. "We're

all under a lot of pressure. Let's keep in mind that we have the same end game."

Max relaxes a little and retreats. "Get me the Melvin Jones file, in case the press office starts getting calls about it."

Max pushes on the door, fumbles for his pass key. Owen takes out his and swipes it; the lock clicks open and Max exits into the hallway.

"Inch tells me that you showed up on the security video in Tim's office last week for over an hour," Owen says.

"It's not exactly a state secret that there are cameras in the hallways. I wasn't trying to hide anything." I try not to sound too defensive.

"You shouldn't have disturbed the scene without prior approval. We're going to have to disclose it to Middlesex."

I'm not sure what he's intimating. "What's the problem? Am I being looked at for something?"

He frowns and shakes his head slightly. "Let me offer a piece of friendly advice: own up to the relationship. We all know that the cover-up can be worse than the offense."

Owen sounds judgmental, but I'm pretty sure he's trying to help. I want to ask him how long he's known. How long everyone has known.

I consider my words and speak slowly. "I admit it, I was involved with Tim."

Feeling flustered, I drop my ID. When I bend to pick it up, Owen swipes his badge over the sensor and the lock clicks open.

"They tell us in the program—you're only as sick as your secrets," he says.

I step into the hallway and turn back to him. "That's all, I don't have any more secrets."

Chapter Twenty

Yesterday the polar vortex blasted cold air into Boston, and the temperature never got out of single digits. Today it's upwards of fifty degrees. I take advantage of the disintegration of the ozone layer and go for a walk to clear my head.

I stroll up Cambridge Street to Panera, order a latte, resist the cranberry muffins, and head back to the office. Noticing that FBI agent Josh McNamara is about a half a block in front of me, I pick up the pace and try to catch up with him. Josh looks squeaky clean, with his close-cropped hair and spit-shined shoes, but he's still a fed, not to be trusted.

I want to run into him but don't want to appear too eager, so I chase after him until I'm a few steps behind and then slow down, acting as though our encounter is pure happenstance. I expend so much effort trying to appear casual that I catch my heel in a crack in the sidewalk, lose my footing, and spill coffee on my white blouse.

I mutter to myself in frustration, "Nice move."

Josh hears me and turns around as though he knows I was secretly chasing after him. "Abby, hi. You okay?"

"Oh, hey." I try to sound surprised.

"I'm sorry to hear about Tim. How are you guys holding up over there?"

"We're doing okay."

"We're all thinking about you. Let me know if I can do anything."

He starts to walk away. I try to keep pace.

"Actually, since we've run into each other, I was wondering, were you and Tim working on something together?"

He assumes an expressionless G-man look. "Why do you ask?"

"I know you worked the Big Dig case together last year."

"That case was closed out."

"Tim mentioned something about meeting with you. I'm not sure if it was connected to the Big Dig. I thought you might need someone to pick up the ball."

"Come on, Abby, don't bullshit me. We've known each other a long time. I've always admired the fact that you're a straight shooter. If you want to ask me something, then ask."

I pause, look around, shrug. "Okay, what were you and Tim working on?"

"Sorry, can't talk about it." Josh grins. "Classified."

He disappears inside his Center Plaza office building. I struggle to hold on to my belief that Tim wasn't dirty, that he didn't contribute to his own death, that he won't be the cause of mine.

At the intersection of Cambridge and New Sudbury Streets, waiting for the pedestrian light, I get the creepy sensation that someone is staring at me. I glance to my right, and there he is. Rodney Quirk. My stomach drops. I'm not used to seeing him out on the street in the middle of the afternoon, away from his perch in the coffee shop.

I should have handled this a long time ago. I've got to stop it from getting worse. He hasn't done anything to me or made any overt threats, but he wants something. I'm in as safe a place as I can be, in a crowd of people, in front of the FBI building, across from the DA's office, and half a block from a Boston police station.

I clench my jaw and look him in the eye. "You're taking your show on the road?" I say.

He looks at me blankly.

"What do you want, Rodney?"

"Ma'am?" he says.

His voice surprises me. It's quiet; there's no rasp or edge to it like I had imagined. In all the time I've known Rodney, I've never heard him speak. His public defender always served as his mouthpiece. Rodney would whisper something in his lawyer's ear, and the lawyer would repeat it for the court. *Yes, Your Honor. Not guilty, Your Honor.*

A horn blasts. Rodney and I both spin around to see a man who was texting and walking almost get sideswiped by a Tahoe. As the man jerks sideways, his phone falls from his hands onto the street and is crushed by a bus. He stumbles backward. Rodney breaks his fall and helps him to his feet.

"You okay?" Rodney says.

"Thanks," the man says. "I almost got killed."

The white pedestrian light flashes, directing me to walk. I cross the street, leaving Rodney behind.

Chapter Twenty-one

My brother's wedding is being held at the Gardner Club, a couple of blocks from the Statehouse, across from Boston Common. The club was founded in the 1800s and hasn't changed much in either attitude or décor. Membership fees are steep, but you can't buy your way in, because it's not about money. It's about ancestry. It's a dated and elitist institution. My parents dine there at least once a week.

I've been at the morgue all day, doing trial prep with the medical examiner, and I'm running late. I retrieve my floor-length black velvet Armani from the trunk of my car and change in an unoccupied autopsy room, which has more space and better lighting than the bathroom.

I slip into the dress, step into a pair of black Jimmy Choos, and throw on a strand of my great-grandmother's pearls. As I start to sweep my hair up into a chignon, two coroner's assistants come charging through the doors, pushing a gurney with a fresh body on top. I dab a drop of Chanel No. 5 behind my ear and decide to finish my makeup in the car.

When I'm done primping, I call Ty and let him know that I'm on the way. He's waiting on the sidewalk in front of my building, deep in thought, probably composing music in his head. He gets in the car and leans over to give me a kiss, and the knot in the back of my neck relaxes.

"You clean up nice," I say.

"You look beautiful, babe," he says, "but you smell like disinfectant."

"It's formaldehyde."

It's a straight shot up Beacon Street to the Gardner Club. We leave the car with a valet, arriving a few minutes ahead of the ceremony. The club's maître d', Caz Munro, greets us at the door, offering flutes of champagne atop a silver tray. He's wearing black tie, but you'd never mistake him for a guest.

"Greetings, Ms. Endicott," he says, smiling brightly. "It's a wonderful night for a celebration."

Caz always welcomes me and my family as though he spent the whole day eagerly awaiting our arrival. I think he spits on our food when we're not looking.

Inside, the club reeks of old Boston. There are a couple of hundred people chatting, milling around, and drinking champagne. Ty takes in the tattered Persian carpets and dusty leather-bound books. I take in the women, decked out in their elegant yet understated dresses. Some of the guests take in me and Ty, their eyes darting back and forth between the two of us. Looks of curiosity, disapproval, and, from my former high school rival Minnie Dorset, jealousy. Ty cuts a handsome figure, even in a rented tux.

"I've passed this place a million times," Ty says. "I always thought it was some rich guy's private house. Seems like there's a lot of history here."

"Once, I was waiting for my grandfather to finish his card game, I killed time by reading the club charter. Beware, there's a rule against whistling."

"Got it."

"Seriously, no whistling on the premises."

"I'll do my best to refrain."

Caz announces it's time for the ceremony and directs people into the designated room. As expected, it's lovely, with rows of gold chairs facing the bowed floor-to-ceiling windows. A white lattice arch, capped with a garland of white roses, will serve as the wedding altar.

I've avoided talking to Ty about the seating situation. When I told my mother that I planned to bring a date, she made it clear that she would prefer that he not sit with the family in the front row. She said it would send the wrong message and I'm ashamed that I didn't challenge her. I haven't had the heart to share her sentiments with Ty.

"Where should I sit?" he says.

"With me," I say as though there's no question about it.

I'm not going to let my mother's inane rules and arcane protocol hurt Ty's feelings. I slip my arm through his and walk with him down the aisle.

"Hello, Abigail," my mother says. "We were concerned you weren't going to be here for the family photos."

She gives me an air kiss and inspects my dress with raised eyebrows. She looks chic with her sleek blond bob and her simple teal gown. As I introduce her to Ty, her smile looks frozen. I can tell that she is not pleased, even with the Botox injections. My father gives me a hug and Ty a handshake.

The location of the service was the subject of great controversy. My parents wanted Charlie and Missy to take their vows at the Advent, our Episcopalian church on Mount Vernon Street. Missy's mother wanted to host the ceremony at Saint Cecelia's, her Catholic church in Providence. My brother and his bride aren't particularly religious, but they are snobs, so they decided to say their I do's here, at the Church of the Brahmins.

The ceremony is tasteful and efficient, just like the couple. Charlie looks boyish in black tie, as though all he did to get ready was run a comb through his thick, dark hair and throw on a tuxedo. He spends hours on the squash court maintaining his lean physique and competitive edge. Missy looks like an effortless beauty—her brown hair is long and loose under my mother's delicate lace veil; her cheeks are pink, glowing. She spent much of the day in the makeup chair to achieve this natural look.

After Charlie and Missy exchange vows, everyone moves to a large reception room for cocktails and hors d'oeuvres, emphasis on the cocktails. My parents stand in the receiving line with the newlyweds. I lead Ty as far away from them as possible, to the other side of the bar.

"The bride looks like she's gonna fit right in with your folks," Ty says.

"Missy comes off as a Main Line preppie, but she's far from it."

"Meaning her parents had to work for a living?"

"Her parents were fifteen when they had her. Her mother was homeless and gave up parental rights to her father, who abandoned her when she turned seven. She lived in foster homes until she turned sixteen. Then she was adopted by an elderly woman in Cranston."

I admire Missy. Somewhere along the line, she decided that she wanted more for herself, and she figured out how to get it. She was valedictorian of her high school class and put herself through the University of Rhode Island. She got good grades, great recommendations and, according to Charlie, perfect scores on the GMAT.

A waiter comes by with a tray of crab cakes. We each take one and I devour mine in one bite. I can't remember if I've eaten anything today.

"Where'd Missy and Charlie meet?"

"At Harvard Business School, or *The* Business School, as my parents call it, as though there's only one."

"They're both in finance?"

"Charlie is positioned to take over the family business—

buying up American companies and shipping the jobs overseas. Missy is a portfolio manager at Fidelity."

Ty intercepts a waiter who is passing around a platter of boiled seafood. I grab a shrimp by the tail and dip it into cocktail sauce.

"How did your mother take to her?"

"Initially, she did everything she could to discourage the relationship. But she softened once she came to learn how much they have in common. Missy hosts great dinner parties, always wears white on the tennis court, and is a member of the Junior League."

"Sounds perfect."

I look over at Missy, who is smiling awkwardly as lecherous Freddie Finch hugs her and cops a feel. She has a good heart. I know that her affectations come from a place of deep insecurity, but sometimes I have the urge to fling her copy of *The Social Register* into their marble fireplace and watch it burn.

Ty heads to the bar to get us drinks while I pose for family pictures. The newlyweds, my parents, Missy's mother, and I smile for the camera. After a few shots, the three women move to the dining room to inspect the floral centerpieces. My father excuses himself and goes over to backslap a client. The photographer takes a couple of candids of me and Charlie.

"I wish George could have been here," Charlie says. "I would have liked to have had him as best man."

"I keep expecting him to walk into the room," I say. "It feels like he just went outside for a smoke."

"He would have liked Missy."

"He'd be happy for you." I scan the room. "But he'd have given you a ration of shit for your choice of wedding venue. He hated this place."

"Almost as much as you do." Charlie's smile turns serious. "Abs, I'm worried about you."

"This is your night—enjoy it."

"Why did you take that case? Orlando Jones made your life a living hell. Did you forget how devastated you were?"

"I haven't forgotten," I say. "And I know you haven't either. You came through for me."

Growing up, Charlie and I were inseparable. We spent summers on Martha's Vineyard, bodysurfing in Chilmark, eating fried clams in Edgartown, stealing penny candy in Tisbury. The day after Crystal died, Charlie flew in from Hong Kong. He sat with me at the funeral and accompanied me to Orlando's arraignment. He persuaded me not to drop out of the Latin competition, used flash cards to test me on the declensions, traveled with me to Sacramento for the convention. He even helped me stitch together a toga for the after-party.

"You ought to reconsider some of your decisions. Your judgment is compromised, professionally and personally." He looks over at Ty.

"Don't be too quick to judge. He's a good guy."

Ty is standing at the bar, nodding and listening intently to Dickie Lodge, who is probably regaling him with tired stories about how he crewed at Oxford and competed at Henley like a hundred years ago. Ty surveys Dickie as he would an exotic animal at the Franklin Park Zoo. Before I can excuse myself and make my way over to rescue him, I'm hijacked.

"You're wearing black to a wedding?" my mother says in a stage whisper.

"It's Armani. That should account for something."

"Armani makes other colors." She grabs Charlie's arm. "Come say hello to the Coolidges." She whisks Charlie away.

Ty returns with a bottle of Heineken and a glass of Malbec.

"If social climbing were an Olympic sport, my mother would medal. She's always been a social butterfly, but it's gotten worse lately."

My mother made her millions the old-fashioned way—by landing a multimillionaire. Her family was far from destitute,

but she's not old money like my father. She grew up in Bronx-
ville, and her father owned a chain of grocery stores. She went to
Miss Porter's School and Smith College, and has never worked
a day in her life.

"Maybe it's the pressure of the wedding," Ty says.

Suki Stevens, Beacon Hill's most insufferable gossip, nears. I
try to grab Ty and make for the library, but it's too late.

"Abigail, darling. I haven't seen you in eons," Suki says.

She gives me a triple air kiss and looks me up and down.
Touching the ends of my hair with the palms of her hands, she
lets out a mournful sigh.

"Let me give you the name of my stylist," she says.

I didn't have time to get to Newbury Street for hair and
makeup with the rest of the wedding party, but I look fine. My
hair was cut and colored three weeks ago. I ignore her remark
and introduce her to Ty, who extends his hand to shake. She
smiles tightly.

"I never see you anymore. Whatever are you up to these
days?" she says.

"I'm still with the DA's office."

I look at Ty, wishing we had established the cocktail party
equivalent of a safe word, like a sneeze or a snort.

"You and all your murderers. I don't know how you do it,"
she says. "Or, frankly, why you do it."

Screw her. I take Ty's arm, and we move away. My father sees
us, waves, and comes over.

"Glad you could join us, Tyson," he says. "We've been worried
about you, muffin."

Ty throws me a look and raises his eyebrows. *Muffin?*

"I know, and I appreciate it, Daddy. But I'm fine."

"I don't think it's safe for you to work there anymore. Tad
Gleason would love to have you at his firm. Why don't you give
him a call?"

"Stop."

He turns to plead his case to Ty. "Maybe you can talk some sense into her."

Knowing better than to get involved, Ty smiles and shrugs. My father gives up and moves on to greet some guests.

Caz uses a small mallet to sound the chimes—dinner is served. We all move to the main dining room and take seats. There are two dozen round tables, decorated with beige linen cloths and lush bouquets of flowers—soft-pink ranunculus, white hyacinths, and cream-colored tulips.

Missy took charge of the seating chart and put me in between Ty and my uncle Chippy, who is already two sheets to the wind. Chippy takes a gulp from his glass of single malt as he yammers on about his fourth ex-wife and how she took him to the cleaners. He should have learned his lesson about the division of assets and alimony three divorces ago. I nod, pretending to care, as I cut into my overcooked filet mignon.

"I hear you're a fan of the symphony, Mrs. Endicott," Ty says to my mother, trying to find common ground.

"We're on the board," she says.

"I'm a big fan of Andris Nelsons," he says, but it's too late. My mother has already turned away and is now feigning interest in Lottie Thayer's unremarkable antique cameo.

"I understand you're a musician," my father says, trying to make up for my mother's rudeness.

"That's right," Ty says.

"Tenor sax?"

Ty and I exchange looks. My father's question has caught us both off guard, since we've never mentioned what Ty does for a living. I should have known that my father would get his own intel.

"You've done your homework," Ty says.

"You'd better believe it."

Ty nervously tries to assess whether my father is friend or foe. "What else did you find out?"

"I know you've played with some of the greats—Cecil Taylor, McCoy Tyner."

"Sounds like you know a lot about jazz."

"I played trumpet in college."

"You did?" Ty and I say at the same time.

"I think I still have it in the attic somewhere."

"Don't even think about taking that thing out of storage," my mother says, turning away from Lottie.

"I didn't know you were listening, dear." My father smiles. "I do have to admit, I'm no Dizzy Gillespie."

"That's the understatement of the century. If you go anywhere near that instrument, I'll file for divorce."

My father ignores her. "I'd like to hear you play sometime, Tyson."

Ty's parents are the opposite of meddlers or snobs, which isn't necessarily better. They're divorced, aging hippies who met at Woodstock, fell in love, stoned, stomping around in the mud, listening to Joan Baez. Their marriage lasted about two years.

Last summer, Ty introduced me to his father, Jasper, who is white, at a gig in Saratoga. He showed up with his then partner, Ronald, and said that he was a documentary filmmaker, living in New York. He talked a great game, but when I probed, he had all sorts of ideas but had never actually completed a project. And he didn't really live in New York; he was subletting a studio apartment in Jersey City.

I met Ty's mother, Melody, who is black, at the Regattabar in Cambridge. She was passing through Boston on her way to a yoga retreat in Lenox. She lives in Vermont and claims to own a bed-and-breakfast. She's invited us to stay, but every time Ty tries to take her up on the offer, she can't accommodate us. I'm pretty sure she just works there as a reservation clerk and isn't allowed guests.

I whisper in Ty's ear, "Meet me in the library on the second floor."

I excuse myself from the table, pretending that I have to go to the ladies' room, and slip upstairs. I sink into a worn, dark leather sofa. The tables around me are littered with empty glasses, toothpicks, and cocktail napkins. The sounds of glass clinking drift up from the dining room, signaling that toasts are about to begin.

Ty sneaks into the room, loosens his tie, and slides next to me on the couch. I stand and put a finger to my lips, signaling him to stay quiet, and lock the door. We kiss until we hear a knock, and someone rattles the doorknob.

Ty smiles and whistles softly.

"Was that a whistle?" I suppress a laugh.

He does it again.

"You're going to get us thrown out of here."

Whoever is at the door decides to give up, allowing Ty and me to return to the business at hand.

Chapter Twenty-two

After a night of too much wine and not enough sleep, I drag myself out of bed and drive to police headquarters, where I meet with Kevin and Nestor. We divvy up the tasks. Kevin goes out in the field to shore up witnesses and serve subpoenas. Nestor and I stay behind; he tackles the boxes of official reports, and I slog through batches of the first responders' handwritten notes.

Our workspace is warm and windowless, and there's an overwhelming stench of bacon from Nestor's breakfast. Mounds of court filings, crime lab reports, and witness statements are scattered around the table. Claustrophobia could hit at any minute. The only upside to being here is that I get to skip the postwedding brunch at the Taj.

The notes are difficult to decipher; they're tattered and smudged, filled with doodles and scribbles. I pick through bits of information about the weather and road conditions, random thoughts about suspects, and unattributed quotes. I'd like to throw most of it in the trash but Blum has reviewed it all, and I need to know everything he knows.

I drink coffee and take a few laps around the table so I don't doze off. After a couple hours of reading, I come across a sheet of notes with an unfamiliar name.

"Who is Jemald Clements?"

"I interviewed him last year." Nestor rolls his eyes. "He was a clown."

"It sounds like he got a look at the shooter. I hope we're not playing another round of hide the ball."

Nestor stops what he's doing, finds Jemald's form twenty-six, and hands it to me. I read the statement to myself. *I heard four or five shots. I looked up and saw a man in a beige Toyota. I believe he was the shooter. He was a light-skinned black or Hispanic man in his forties with a scar on his cheek and short, cropped hair. He stopped and leaned out the front passenger-side window and started firing. I think that he was the only one in the car. Signed, Jemald Clements.*

I look up at Nestor. "Am I missing something here? This guy was an eyewitness to the murder. Why hasn't anyone mentioned him?"

"We should have prosecuted him for obstruction. He gave a bogus description of the shooter. Orlando is younger, has dark skin, and had a shaved head at the time."

"Still, he knew about the car, the location of the shooter, and the number of shots—before it was made public."

Nestor isn't backing down. "It was an intentional misdirect. He hurts more than he helps."

I'm tired and growing impatient. "That's my call, not yours." Nestor may be in law school, but he's not a lawyer, and he's not in charge of the case.

"He's going to come off as a liar."

"Most of our witnesses tell a story that is part true, part lie. The trick is figuring out which is which," I say.

"Jemald Clements was full of shit, plain and simple."

"I'm not asking you to invite him home for dinner."

I take a breath and check myself. I want to pull rank and demand that Nestor follow up with Jemald, but we're a team and ordering a cop around isn't the best way to get results.

I go outside to get some air, and take a ten-minute drive to the Buttery, a café in the South End. When I return, I bring a peace offering of fresh coffee, grilled cheese sandwiches, and red velvet cupcakes. Nestor appreciates the gesture and the treats.

"Let's explore Jemald," I say.

Nestor bites into his sandwich and nods. "Okay."

"Are he and Orlando buddies?"

"We found FIOs of the two of them, hanging out."

The police gang unit keeps an inventory of field interrogation operation reports—documents that list sightings of known gang members. Nestor shows me several FIOs of Jemald and Orlando together, and it becomes obvious that they're friends. Jemald planted bad information hoping to send us in the wrong direction.

"Told you," Nestor says.

"Do you have Jemald's BOP?"

Nestor checks his computer and searches Jemald's criminal history.

"He was pinched for selling crack, and about eighteen months ago, he picked up a gun charge."

"Did he do time on it?"

"A year in the house."

This is starting to sound familiar. "Was Orlando his codefendant?"

Nestor sees where I'm going. "Yup. They were arrested together. Orlando got his case dismissed and walked. Jemald did time."

I take a bite of the cupcake and smile. "Sounds like Jemald got the short end of the stick. Maybe he resents it—let's see if he wants to vent."

Chapter Twenty-three

Jemald Clements's apartment building looks like a crack house. The front porch is unlit, a few junkies are milling around in the driveway, and someone is scavenging through a metal trash can. As soon as we park the car, I regret my decision to come along. I've had all the sadness I can take for one week.

A woman wearing one shoe approaches our car. "You got a twenty?" She sniffs and wipes her nose with her sleeve.

"Get lost, Tawny," Nestor says.

Tawny starts to limp away, trying to keep pressure off her bare foot. The ground is frozen, and the tip of her big toe is black with frostbite.

"You should go to the BMC," I say, "and have your foot looked at."

She doesn't respond, keeps hobbling away.

"I've offered her a ride to the ER a half-dozen times," Nestor says as we get out of the car. "The nurses are onto her. They refuse to give her pain meds, so she's not interested."

Nestor kicks a hypodermic needle out of our path, and we climb up the front steps.

"Sure you want to come in?" he says.

"It's better than waiting in the car alone."

Jemald Clements's girlfriend answers the door in her pajamas, cleaning the wax out of her ear with a Q-tip. A baby screeches in the background.

"Boston police," Nestor says. "We need to talk to Jemald."

She doesn't invite us inside. Nonetheless, Nestor walks past her, into the apartment, and I follow. He flips on a light, exposing the grim interior. Cockroaches scurry across the mildewed linoleum, up the wall, and onto a counter, where a hot pot and a bunch of dirty dishes are piled. I stand still, trying not to touch or lean on anything.

Jemald emerges from the bedroom with a scowl. The baby continues to wail from behind the door.

"What you want?"

"Is someone looking after that baby?" I say.

The girlfriend disappears into the bedroom, and the baby quiets down.

"Jemald, this is the DA," Nestor says.

He crosses his arms. "I got nothing to say."

A bug crawls up and into what must be Jemald's steel-toed work boot. I watch another one circle the sole.

"You witnessed a murder, and I need to know what you saw," I say.

"Read the reports," Jemald says.

"I did. They don't make a whole lot of sense."

"That's because you're going after the wrong guy. Orlando didn't do it. Why are you trying to frame him?" He lights a cigarette and blows smoke in my direction.

I don't flinch. "Didn't you and Orlando have a gun case together a while back? How come he got a deal and you served time?"

"We both should have got off. We was both innocent. He got justice, I got railroaded."

"It looks to me like he knew how to work the system, and you didn't."

"Fuck off." He drops the cigarette on the floor and stomps it out.

Clearly, Jemald and I aren't going to be besties, and that's fine with me.

I hand him a subpoena. "Be in court tomorrow."

"Can't—I got to work. I have a baby girl to take care of."

"I'll call your boss or write a letter, but you can't ignore a subpoena."

"Get out of my house."

On the way back to the car, I place a call to social services and ask them to check on Jemald's daughter. Prosecutors are considered mandated reporters, required to notify authorities if we believe that a child's safety may be in jeopardy.

Social services is all over the news these days for negligence, bungling cases, putting children at risk. Kids placed in their care have gone missing, been abused and even killed. Whether this child ends up in state custody or with Jemald and his girlfriend, the cards are stacked against her.

As we drive away, I see Tawny limping down Morton Street. She has a piece of cardboard wrapped around her unshod foot.

"Pull over for a second," I say.

Nestor stops the car. I lower my window and call out to Tawny. She stops and turns, smiling as though she doesn't have a care in the world. She found her fix.

"Take these." I hand her my favorite Stuart Weitzmans.

She takes the shoes and struggles to put one on her swollen, discolored foot. Without saying a word, she walks off.

"You're welcome," Nestor says as we drive off. "I hope they weren't expensive. She's going to trade them for a dime bag."

"I know," I say. "I don't care."

Chapter Twenty-four

Last week, Tim and Blum spent a couple of days carefully selecting the jury that will decide Orlando Jones's fate. As in all trials, once the jurors were impaneled, a court officer collected their questionnaires and shredded them. Tim wasn't a notetaker, so I have no idea why he chose this panel. I don't know anything about them—not their ages, addresses, or occupations. I don't even know their names. They are complete wild cards and whatever they decide—guilty or not—we'll all have to live with it.

Judge Volpe delivers his preliminary instructions, and I pretend to listen. It's always the same. *You will have to reach a unanimous verdict. The defendant is presumed innocent. The prosecutor carries the burden of proof.* Background noise, like Charlie Brown's teacher yammering on. *WHAA WHAA WHAA.*

Juror number five is leaning forward in her chair, her hands cupped over her ears. Either she's hard of hearing or she doesn't understand English. She'll probably wait until the second day of deliberations before telling us that she didn't follow any of what happened during the trial and asking to be excused. Number two looks at his watch and lets out a gaping yawn, as though this is the most boring thing he's ever had to endure. Number seven looks stoned.

Reporters, lawyers, court watchers, and the families of both sides are crammed into the gallery. A dozen people from my office are here; most nod and smile in support, while a few wear the bitter look of schadenfreude.

My favorite court watcher, Harold, is in the second row, hands resting on his walking stick, listening intently. He knows that, at some point, I'll ask him for his thoughts, and he takes his charge seriously.

Judge Volpe wraps up and commands Sal to distribute notebooks and pens to the jurors. They immediately start jotting things down. Some are probably copying Judge Volpe's instructions; others are likely sketching out grocery lists. They have to leave their notebooks in the courthouse when they go home for the night, and I'm always tempted to peek inside.

"Ms. Endicott, is the Commonwealth prepared to make an opening statement?" Judge Volpe says.

No, I need time, like a few months. "The Commonwealth is ready," I say.

"You may proceed."

I rise and position myself a couple of feet from the jury box. I have to own this courtroom, let everyone know I'm in charge, they can trust me, feel safe in my hands. My body language, my voice, my carefully choreographed presentation must all project resolve, sincerity, and fearlessness. My knees start to knock against each other.

There is a podium, but I don't use it. I have notes, but I set them aside. Nothing should come between me and my jurors.

I clear my throat and look each juror in the eye. "Good morning, members of the jury," I say.

About three-quarters of them respond in unison. "Good morning."

Always a positive sign.

Orlando Jones is seated at the defense table, glaring at me. My voice quivers slightly as I point at him and deliver the words that Tim had prepared.

"This man, Orlando Jones, sprayed bullets into a crowd of people sitting on a porch, drinking beer, enjoying a summer night. He shot three people: the first is dead; the second might as well be dead; the third is living in constant fear."

I return to the jury box, where I plant myself firmly and try not to fidget or pace. A camera clicks. The door slams open, and for a split second, I think it might be Tim, here to rescue me. If only we could all pick up where we'd left off, before it all went so wrong. But it's not Tim—it's Max and Owen. A few lawyers squeeze closer together, allowing room for them in the pews.

"This case is about the deliberate and brutal murder and attempted murders committed by Orlando Jones. It's about gang warfare and the carnage that results, destroying lives and shattering communities.

"The defendant believes that the streets of Mattapan belong to him and his North Street confederates. So when a rival gang began encroaching on his territory, started selling drugs on what he considered to be his sidewalks and street corners, Orlando Jones decided to do something about it—to send a message. And he chose to convey this message not with a text or a phone call but with a sawed-off shotgun.

"He didn't have specific targets in mind. Anyone out on Belmont Street, enemy territory, would do. No matter that they were innocents, hardworking residents of our city. No matter that they weren't involved in gang life. No matter that they didn't know or care about his turf war.

"Much of this case will be difficult for you to endure. I apologize in advance for what you are going to experience. But these are the facts of the case. This is the brutal reality of murder."

When I'm done, juror number five looks at Orlando and shakes his head in outrage. Number three crosses her arms and glowers at him. A couple of jurors are so disgusted that they can't even look in his direction. Mission accomplished. As I move to take my seat, I glance into the gallery and see Kevin, nodding in approval and support.

The most frustrating part of most trials is that there are so many things that the jury will never learn. I can't give a complete picture of who Orlando is and what he's done in the past. I can't tell them that he is responsible for Crystal's death. That he shot four people and threatened them until they were too scared to testify. That he beat a gun case and was possibly acting as a government informant. That he probably ordered the hit on Warren Winters. That he may be involved in Tim's murder. And that he might go after me.

"Mr. Blum, you may present your opening statement," Judge Volpe says.

"I don't intend to give an opening at this time, Your Honor," Blum says, surprising me and most of the seasoned court watchers in the room.

"Members of the jury, please gather your coats. We are about to embark on our view," Judge Volpe says. "This will be your opportunity to see firsthand where the alleged crimes took place."

Sal and two other court officers, holding tall white poles, escort the sixteen jurors outside, down the steep, icy hill behind the courthouse. Everyone boards the bus that is parked on Cambridge Street. Sal directs the jurors to the last eight rows. The clerk and stenographer sit up front with Judge Volpe. Blum and I take seats in the middle.

"Bold move, not giving an opening," I say to Blum as the bus starts up and we pull out into the traffic. "Have you even decided on your defense?"

"I'm leaving my options open. It's your burden. I think I'll just sit back and watch the show—let's see if you can make good on your promises." He takes out a box of orange Tic Tacs, shakes one out, and pops it in his mouth.

Two police cars lead the bus, guiding us through the streets of the city. When we get to Belmont Street, we park in front of the porch where my victims sat. I look out the window and think about Tim, wishing that he were here.

Chapter Twenty-five

After we resume the trial, I stand at my table and turn to Kevin, who is seated on the aisle of the front row next to Jackie Reed. He nods, giving me the signal that Jemald is waiting outside in the hallway. Predictably, Jemald wouldn't talk to Nestor when he picked him up and drove him to court this morning.

"Ms. Endicott, call your first witness," Judge Volpe says.

I take a breath. "The Commonwealth calls Jemald Clements."

Sal steps out into the hallway and shouts Jemald's name. After a minute, Jemald shuffles in, hands in pockets, shoulders hunched. Sal commands him to take off his baseball hat and spit out his gum.

He scans the packed gallery, sees the North Street Posse in the back row, and tilts his head in recognition. All the players, including the gold-toothed man, echo his gesture.

Sal directs him to the front of the courtroom, staying two paces behind, in case he decides to bolt. After the clerk swears him in, he takes a seat in the witness box. Sal pours him a cup of water and adjusts the microphone.

Jemald settles in, looks at Orlando, and smiles. I plant myself midway between them, blocking their line of vision.

I take a formal, weighty tone. "Good morning, sir. Please

introduce yourself by spelling your name and stating your address."

He guzzles some water, puts the cup down, and sighs. "Lady, you know my name."

I turn to the judge. "Your Honor, may the witness be instructed to answer the question?"

"What's your name?" Judge Volpe says.

"Jemald Clements."

I pick up the ball. "And your address?"

"That's my own private business."

I pause and stare at him. "Sir, the way it works in a court of law is I ask questions and you answer them."

Jemald shrugs.

"Your answers have to be verbal. The court reporter can't record body language," I say.

He shifts in his chair. "I live in Mattapan."

"North Street?"

"Yes."

"Do you know the defendant, Orlando Jones?"

"Yup."

He's as warmed up as he's going to get. Time to cut to the chase.

"On August 8, last year, there was a shooting out on Belmont Street."

"Okay."

Jemald pours himself another cup of water, downs it, and then crushes the empty cup in his fist. He doesn't look at me and doesn't answer my question, so I ask another one.

"You reported that you witnessed the murder?"

Jemald shrugs. "If you say so."

"What *I* say isn't relevant. It's what *you* say." I pick up his statement and read part of it out loud. "'I heard four or five shots. I looked up and saw a man in a beige Toyota. I believe this was the shooter.' Those were your words, correct?"

"I can't recall."

"Where were you located when you made these observations?"

He starts to squirm and looks down. "Where was I located?"

"That's the question, sir."

"I'm gonna have to take the Fifth on that."

His taps his foot. His knee bobs up and down. I struck a nerve. He's not just protecting his friend, he's protecting himself. I'm finally getting somewhere.

"You were there, weren't you?"

"Say what?"

"You were in the beige Toyota, in the passenger seat, right next to Orlando Jones when he blasted off those rounds. Isn't that true?"

"Objection!" Blum says.

Judge Volpe signals us up to sidebar. Jemald looks out into the audience, at the man with the gold teeth. They exchange smirks. I nod at Sal, directing him with my eyes. He moves in front of Jemald.

As we huddle at sidebar, I keep an eye on the North Street Posse.

"Clearly, this witness needs the advice of counsel," Blum says. "Ms. Endicott has accused him of being an accomplice to murder."

"I haven't accused him of anything. I asked where he was when the shots were fired. If he admits he was there, that wouldn't necessarily implicate him in the murder. Mere presence is not enough to charge him with a crime." I do my best to sound convincing, although even I don't fully buy into what I'm saying.

"We're wandering into a potential minefield. I'm going to appoint him counsel." Judge Volpe scans the gallery for defense attorneys.

"Ms. Streleski," Volpe calls out. "Please join us up here."

Kit Streleski perks up, thrilled that she's been invited to the party. She tugs at the gap between the front buttons of her purple-and-white floral blouse, maybe wishing she'd chosen to wear something more flattering. Clutching a legal pad, she practically skips to the front of the courtroom.

Judge Volpe calls a recess and meets with Streleski and Jemald in his chambers. He'll conduct a *Martin* hearing, where Jemald will have to reveal why he's entitled to assert the Fifth Amendment, by detailing his incriminating activity. Judge Volpe will determine whether his explanation is legitimate or if it's a pretense to avoid testifying. I'm kept totally in the dark about everything—before, during, and after the hearing.

As soon as court breaks, Harold waves his cane, eager to catch my ear. We walk out into the hallway together.

"Buck up," he says in his pseudo British accent.

I picture him wearing a monocle and decide that I like the image. I'll give him my great-grandfather's opera glasses after the trial is over.

"Everyone can see Jemald is lying, right?" I say.

"Sure as fate. He looks like a gangster. Observe how he's come to court—his trousers are torn, his work boots are muddy, and there's grime under his fingernails."

Harold doesn't miss much, especially when it comes to personal hygiene. Jemald does look like he just walked off a construction site. I remember the steel-toed work boots in his apartment. I hope Judge Volpe orders him to testify—I want to ask him about his job.

When Kit and Jemald exit the judge's chambers, Sal calls order. Judge Volpe takes the bench, and Blum and I join him at sidebar. I look at Melvin, who is leaning forward, trying to make out what we're saying.

"This witness has a valid claim," Judge Volpe says. "I'm not going to order him to testify unless you plan to grant him immunity. "

He's not getting a free ride on my watch. "That's not going to happen."

"In that case, Mr. Clements should be excused," Streleski says.

"I object," I say. "I have a couple of questions that don't relate directly to the murder."

"Let's go," Judge Volpe says.

We retake our positions in the courtroom. Streleski stands up front by Jemald's side and faces out into the gallery. She looks directly into the cameras, savoring her fifteen minutes.

"What do you do for a living?" I say. "Do you work construction?"

Jemald turns to Streleski. She leans in as though she's going to whisper, but practically shouts at him loud enough for all to hear.

"You have to answer," she says.

"I install drywall," he says to her.

"You have to tell the prosecutor," she says.

"She heard me." He turns to me. "I install drywall."

"Who do you work for?" I say.

Jermald, unlike most people in the room, understands the significance of the question and doesn't respond.

"Do you work for Melvin Jones, Orlando's father?"

No response.

I point at Melvin. "This man seated in the front row, does he pay you?"

I glance at the jurors, and most of them look back at me, encouraging me to hang in there. Except number two, whose eyes are closed, his head bobbing up and down. He's dozed off. Seriously? The guy has fallen asleep in the middle of a murder trial. I walk past the jury box and slam a heavy book on the railing. His head shoots up; he opens his eyes and looks around.

I turn back to my witness. "Does Orlando's father, Melvin Jones, pay you?"

"Say what?" Jemald says.

"Objection," Blum says. "Asked and answered."

"It's been asked, but it hasn't been answered."

"Answer the question," Judge Volpe says.

"He pays me for an honest day's work. Something wrong with that?"

"Possibly," I say. "Did he also pay you to create a false suspect? Did he hire you to give police a bogus description of the shooter?"

"Objection."

This time, rather than wait for a ruling, I push on.

"Is he now paying for your silence?"

"Objection."

"Sustained."

"How much did he give you to come forward last summer and lie to the police?"

Blum starts to rise, but Judge Volpe cuts him off.

"Mr. Clements, I am instructing you not to answer. Anything else from the Commonwealth?"

Two jurors look at each other and raise their eyebrows.

"Nothing further," I say.

Chapter Twenty-six

On my way back to the office, I pass Carl Ostroff, who is setting up a live shot in front of the courthouse. When the light flicks on, he looks at the camera and speaks into his microphone, unaware of my presence. He's also oblivious to the buffoons in the background, photobombing him, waving green foam fingers that proclaim *We're #1*.

As Carl delivers his report, I listen and cringe.

"The high-stakes trial did not start out well for the prosecution. The prosecutor was forced to take the unusual tack of impeaching her own witness. She didn't gain substantive ground from the maneuver, but she managed to score points by sending a signal to the jury that Orlando Jones is a threatening figure, whose reach extends far beyond the prison walls."

At least he understood what I was trying to accomplish—hopefully the jurors did too.

The cameraman packs up and heads back to the news truck. Carl calls out my name. I ignore him, not breaking stride, but he catches up with me and tags along. We descend the steep concrete steps.

"Who's on deck for tomorrow?" he says.

"A bunch of experts—blood, medical, DNA."

"Sounds like you're tap-dancing. Are you having trouble corralling your witnesses?"

"Sorry if it bores you, but I have to prove the elements of the crime. The identity of the victims, type of weapon, cause of death."

"You also have to prove that Orlando Jones pulled the trigger. Who's going to ID him?"

I stop walking, look around, and whisper. "Off the record?"

He leans in, eager. "Absolutely," he says.

"I don't have a clue. If you have any thoughts, I'm all ears."

He tries to keep pace as I continue down the stairs.

"I'm supposed to be objective, but it's tough. Orlando Jones is one scary dude." Carl is sincere, but he's also trying to gain my confidence by using the *I feel your pain* approach to cultivating a source.

I don't bite. "Yup, he's a dangerous guy."

Knowing that his shtick isn't working and I'm about to walk away, he steps in front of me and touches my arm.

"Is it true that Orlando killed your best friend?"

I wince. I should have expected this. Someone, probably Blum, tipped him off.

"Those records were sealed."

"Does that mean it's true?" He's excited to have caught me off guard.

"Please don't make the story about me. It will detract from the trial."

"You made yourself part of the story when you took it on. You could have assigned it to anyone."

"Case assignment decisions aren't news."

"It's news when the prosecutor, in a high-profile murder trial, has a personal vendetta against the defendant."

"Do me a solid. Keep it under wraps for now."

"We all have a job to do."

"I'll owe you one."

Carl considers the proposition. "Deal, but I plan to collect," he says.

"I have no doubt."

We walk along Cambridge Street. The sidewalk is crowded, and the street is jammed with traffic as government workers head home for the night.

Just as I'm about to step into the crosswalk, Carl throws another curveball. "What do you think about the gun?"

"What gun?"

He pauses, keeps me waiting as he checks his phone, and scrolls through his e-mail. He's messing with me and I want to shake the answer out of him.

Finally he says, "The ATF ran the shell casings from Tim's murder scene through their system."

"Did they get a hit?"

"Yes, the murder weapon was used in another shooting."

My mind races. This could be the break that we've been looking for.

"Which shooting did it connect back to?"

"That's not what's important." He pauses and looks at me. "The gun was stolen out of the police evidence locker last month."

I rush back to the office and go directly to the executive suite. It's close to seven, and Owen and Max are the only ones still here. They're in Owen's office lounging, ties loosened. Every bit of wall space is covered with Boston sports memorabilia. Autographed baseballs from the 2004 and 2013 World Series. A Patriots jersey, signed by Tom Brady. The obligatory Boston sports fan poster of Bobby Orr, flying through the air. There are also a dozen photos of Owen's three children, dressed in various sports uniforms.

Max is guzzling an Amstel Light. Owen is wrestling with a bag of Doritos. He rips it open, stuffs a handful of chips in his mouth, and then licks the orange dust off his fingers. He gave up alcohol after his oldest, Patricia, was born, and he's packed on the pounds, which is an accomplishment considering the hours he spends running around baseball diamonds and soccer fields, coaching his kids.

They're talking about Tim's pension. Owen managed to find a loophole in the system; he qualified Tim's family to get benefits that go only to people with twenty years of service. Owen took Tim's death hard, and—unlike me—he's been there for Julia.

Max offers me a beer, Owen holds up the bag of chips, and I decline both.

I drop my files on the table and sit in a chair. "Did you hear about the gun trace?"

They shake their heads.

"What do you know?" Max asks.

"Remember the guns that were stolen out of the evidence locker last month? One of them was used to kill Tim."

"Holy shit." Max twists the cap off another beer and snaps his fingers, sending the bottle cap spinning across the room.

"I spoke with Dermot this morning and he didn't mention a word about it," Owen says.

"I can see why. The murder weapon was stolen from Boston police custody," I say.

"There's no way a cop killed Tim," Owen says, crumpling up the Doritos bag and tossing it basketball-style into the trash can.

"Where are you getting this from?" Max says. "I hope you're not trading information."

"Don't worry." I stand, gather my things, and move toward the door.

"The commissioner called," Max says. "BPD found a burner phone in some brush, fifty yards from where Tim's body was found."

Burners are inexpensive prepaid disposable phones. The

owners don't have to sign contracts or give personal information in order to buy one, making them nearly impossible to trace.

"Tim's prints and DNA are on it," Owen says.

I sit back down. "Did they do a phone dump?"

Owen nods. "Tim got two incomings, both from the same number. One of the calls came in right before he was killed."

"Do we know who it was from?"

"It came from another burner and lasted less than a minute," Owen says.

"It was probably to arrange the meet-up," Max says. "Bottom line—Tim planned the meeting. He went there voluntarily, which means he probably trusted the guy."

"On second thought," I say, "I'll take one of those beers."

Chapter Twenty-seven

After a few days of testimony from medical experts, forensic analysts, and first responders, Tiffany Reed takes the stand—her mascara is smudged, her eyes red. Judge Volpe allowed my request to ban the media from filming her—microphones are set up to record her voice, but the cameras are all pointed at me.

The courtroom is quiet as I press the start button on my laptop. Everyone in the gallery leans in to listen.

"*Nine-one-one, please state your emergency,*" a dispatcher says.

"*Oh my God. People have been shot. My sister, she's bleeding. Please send an ambulance. There's three of them. Please, hurry. Oh my God.*"

Tiffany closes her eyes and stifles a gasp. Her hands tremble as she relives the horror. I usually sit with my witnesses and listen to the 911 recording as part of trial prep, but knowing it would make for more dramatic testimony, I didn't play the tape for Tiffany ahead of time. She's lost in the memory of the night her sister died in her arms.

My mind travels back to the night that I saw Tim in the tow lot. I don't think that I'd ever be able to do what I'm putting Tiffany through—sit on the witness stand and describe what I saw, heard, felt. Looking at Tiffany, I try to convince myself that I'm not a bad person.

"Okay, stay with me, help is on the way," the dispatcher says calmly. *"Can you tell if anyone is still alive?"*

"I don't know. Please, hurry."

"Can you give me a description of the shooter?"

"No. I don't know. Hurry, please."

I turn off the recorder. "You arrived on the scene in the immediate aftermath of the shooting?"

Tiffany looks down at her lap, shreds a tissue. "Yes, I heard some popping noises when I was coming down the street. I think there were four of them."

Both Tiffany and I are speaking quietly, almost whispering, giving jurors the impression that they're privy to a private conversation.

"What happened when you arrived at the house?"

"I saw her." She suppresses one hiccup and then releases two more.

"You saw Jasmine?"

"Yes."

"Your twin sister?"

"Yes."

The crime scene photos are on my table, sorted and labeled. Tiffany is supposed to identify them, so I can offer them into evidence and project them onto a screen. Tiffany's identification of the crime scene photos will be compelling. It'll make for one of the most emotional moments of the trial. She takes another tissue from the box in front of her, and blows her nose. She bites her lip, and tears pool in her eyes.

"No more questions," I say.

"Mr. Blum, any questions?"

Blum rises, but remains at his table to telegraph that he'll be brief. His jacket has a rip in the right-hand pocket, an interesting changeup from the stains and smudges. The wool fabric even looks a little frayed. Maybe he has a special instrument, specifically for this purpose.

"You didn't see the shooter, did you?" Blum is gentle but firm.

"No," Tiffany says.

"So you can't prove that Orlando Jones had any involvement in this crime whatsoever, can you?"

"Objection. Ms. Reed doesn't carry the burden of proof."

"Sustained."

Blum smiles with sympathy. "That's all I have for this witness. Thank you. We're all sorry for your pain."

I fight the urge to roll my eyes.

Judge Volpe calls the midday recess. Out in the hallway, Harold grabs my elbow and whispers in my ear, "Am I sensing a crack in your veneer?"

"Don't worry," I say, worried that I'm losing my edge.

Kevin joins me, and we avoid the crowd by ducking down the back stairway. In an empty conference room on the fifth floor, I take a small plastic container from my tote.

"Your boyfriend packed your lunch again?"

"Seared ahi on a bed of field greens."

"This guy is spoiling you."

"You might be onto something with this protein thing." I put down my fork. "Where are we on Ezekiel?"

"Three squads are out looking for him." Kevin unwraps a protein bar and shovels it down in two bites.

"You sure he's still alive?"

"Yesterday, he made a withdrawal from an ATM in Dorchester."

"That gives us a shred of hope."

I finish my lunch and search my tote for a bottle of Poland Springs. I always keep two bottles of water with me. I open one, give the other to Kevin.

"If you can keep it going until the end of the day, I'm sure I'll catch up with him this weekend."

"I'll kill time by putting Denny's boss on the stand. I

wasn't planning to call him, but I asked him to be here, just in case."

"What's he going to give you?"

"He can establish a timeline. More importantly, he can help me rally more sympathy."

When court starts back up, Sal summonses the manager of the Chinese restaurant, Doug Huang, who takes the oath. He looks nervous in an ill-fitting suit jacket; the sleeves are too long and the shoulders tight. On the stand, he's a perfect witness, presenting as sincere and unrehearsed, even though we spent hours together.

"Denny was an excellent worker, the best." Doug looks directly at the jury. "He was responsible and reliable, and the customers loved him."

"Did he ever return to the restaurant, after the delivery on Belmont Street?" I say.

"No."

"Did you ever see Denny Mebane again?"

"I saw him at the hospital, when he was in intensive care." Doug scans the gallery and fixes on Adele. "I still go to see him in the rehab sometimes."

"Does he recognize you?"

"I hope so."

"But you're not sure."

"No."

"Thank you. Nothing further."

I take my papers from the podium and return to my table. Blum stands in place at his table.

"Just one question," he says. "Did you see who fired the shots?"

"No, sir, I didn't see that," Doug says.

"That's all I have for this witness."

I end the day here. When the jurors are home with their families this weekend, walking their dogs or listening to their kids practice the piano, I want them to think about Orlando Jones and the damage that he has done. I know that I will.

Judge Volpe excuses the jury, Orlando is taken away in shackles, and the courtroom empties. I pack up my papers, file them in my trial box, and look for my phone. When I reach into my tote, I feel a piece of paper that wasn't in there earlier. I pull it out; it's folded in half, and *ADA Endicott* is written on the front in block letters. That rules out a love note.

The message is short and to the point: *Die Bitch*.

My heart races, my chest tightens. The door to the courtroom slams open and bounces off the back wall. I hold my breath and whip my head around to see who it is.

"Sorry, I didn't mean to scare you," Sal says. "I didn't know anyone was still here."

"No problem," I say.

I fold the note and stuff it back in my bag. It's already dark outside, and I don't want to walk to my office alone. My hands tremble as I text Kevin: *Are you around? Meet me on the Plaza?* He responds right away: *I'm in Eastie checking on a lead. Ok if we meet up later?* I hear someone in the judge's chambers, probably Sal. I'll ask him to escort me to my office. I write Kevin back: *Sure. Catch you later.*

I pick up my trial box and hold it close to my chest, wishing it were made out of Kevlar. I push the door open with my elbow and look around for Sal. The hallway is empty and feels darker than usual—maybe a lightbulb burned out.

"Sal, are you still here? Sal?" My voice echoes in the hallway.

Pushing the button for the elevator, I hear footsteps. Before I can turn my head to see who is behind me, the elevator doors open. I shiver when I see who is in the car. He's looking at me, smiling broadly: the man with the gold teeth.

Chapter Twenty-eight

I stand in the hallway, my arms wrapped tightly around the trial box, staring at the gold-toothed North Street Posse member. He is alone in the car.

"You going down?" he says.

I remain frozen in place without responding and wait for the doors to close. I watch as the floor indicator light gives proof of the car's descent. *Six, five, four, three, two, lobby.* Footsteps behind me grow closer. I twist around and see a shadow. A man rounds the corner.

"Can I carry something for you?" Sal says.

I shake my head and force a smile.

"Long week," he says.

I nod.

"You okay?"

I weigh my options, whether to report what happened. Legally, the guy from North Street didn't do anything. If he really wanted to hurt me, he'd have done it by now. I don't want to make a big deal about it and draw attention to my history with Orlando.

"I'm fine," I say, "but do you mind walking me back to the office?"

"No problem," he says. "Let me carry that box for you."

I surrender the box to Sal, and he escorts me across the plaza. The area is dark and deserted. I look around. There's no sign of the gold-toothed man. Even Rodney Quirk has abandoned his post in the coffee shop and gone home for the night. Sal walks me to the lobby of Bulfinch and hands me the trial box, and I go upstairs to my office.

I spend an hour working on my closing argument. I read it to myself out loud, editing and rewriting as I go. I avoid reflecting on what happened earlier in the hallway, preferring to tuck it away, deep in my subconscious, until after the trial.

When my eyelids start to grow heavy, I call it a night. I decide to use extra precautions on my walk home by taking a new path. I choose a route that's circuitous but will keep me on well-traveled streets.

Passing the construction zone in front of City Hall, I stick close to other pedestrians. Parts of the sidewalk are closed, requiring us to traverse narrow paths marked by black arrows and orange-and-white blockades. The Government Center T stop is closed for renovations, and some of the surrounding buildings are boarded up.

I look up at the enormous copper kettle that hangs from the building on the corner of Cambridge and Court Streets. The shiny metal teapot spouts delicate puffs of steam into the cold, still night air. An engraving on the front of the kettle declares that it has the capacity to hold *227 gallons, 2 quarts, 1 pint, and 3 gills of tea*. The artifact is reminiscent of the city's history of rebellious tea tossing. It's uniquely Boston, quaint and charming. A few years ago, the building that it hangs from was renovated and converted into a Starbucks.

The Downtown Crossing area, usually bustling with shoppers and tourists, is desolate and creepy. There are a couple sketchy-looking men lurking in the doorway of E. B. Horn Jewelers. A rat the size of my brother's Yorkie darts by. I regret my decision to take this route, but I'm well past the point of no return. I think my brother was right: my judgment isn't the best these days.

Near Temple Place, I grow increasingly aware of a shadowy figure. He's too far away for me to make out his features, eye color, hair color, or facial hair, but it looks like he's wearing a light-colored overcoat. From this vantage point, he looks taller than Rodney Quirk and shorter than my new friend from the North Street Posse. As I pick up the pace, so does he.

There are a few people within earshot, but most of them appear homeless and as helpless as I feel. I reach into my tote and grab hold of the Mace that Ty gave me last month. I was hesitant to accept it, but now I'm glad I did. I cradle the canister in my palm, keeping my hand inside my purse, and flip off the safety switch. I feel around for the spray nozzle, my finger at the ready.

Around the corner, in front of the Ritz-Carlton hotel, there are two bellmen, wearing crimson uniforms with gold epaulets. They're hailing cabs and unloading pieces of luggage from the backs of limos. A doorman opens the heavy glass door, and I walk inside the hotel lobby and take a seat in one of the plush leather chairs, relieved to be surrounded by activity.

The concierge gives a group of German tourists restaurant recommendations. A bellman passes by, wheeling a brass luggage cart. A woman takes a seat at the bar and orders a glass of Cabernet. I'm tempted to do the same, but alcohol will only make things worse. I think about walking up to the reservation desk, checking in under an alias, and hiding from the world.

After a few minutes, I pry myself from the chair and head outside, and the bellman puts me in the back of a cab. The ride home takes about four minutes, and I spend the time convincing myself that no one was following me. By the time we reach Berkeley Street, I come to the conclusion that I'm narcissistic, maybe even paranoid.

When we arrive at my building, I give the driver an extra five and ask him to wait until I'm safely inside. Manny is at his desk in the lobby. He stands and greets me with enthusiasm.

"You slayed him today," he says.

"Slayed?"

"The news station live-streamed from the courtroom. You're taking no prisoners."

I do my best to muster up a smile. "Is Ty upstairs?"

"I haven't seen him. But I just got on duty an hour ago."

Gabe, the maintenance guy, sees me in the lobby, comes over, and hands me the key to my apartment.

"You're all set with the sink," he says.

"Was there a problem with my sink?"

"The guy from the fixture place came by. He said that you ordered a new faucet. He was here to install it."

"I didn't order a new sink—my sink is fine." My stomach drops. "You let a stranger in my apartment?"

"I'm sorry—I thought that's why your boyfriend left the key."

"Ty left the key for my housekeeper, Lilia." My mind races as I try to figure out who it could have been. "What time was he here?"

"He came in at around noon."

That rules out anyone from North Street, or at least my friend with the gold teeth, since he was busy sitting around the back of the courtroom all day, glaring at me.

"I'm sorry," Manny says. "I'll talk to the day guy when he comes in for his shift."

I want to ream them both out but yelling won't help, and it'll make me more agitated.

"I'll call the police," Manny says.

"No, I'll do it," I say.

Chapter Twenty-nine

I wait in the lobby for Kevin, who arrives in a matter of minutes. Soon there are a dozen police officers inside my apartment. Detectives search to make sure no one is hiding in a closet or under my bed. The bomb squad sweeps for explosives and checks for hazardous materials. Technicians dust for prints and search for stray hairs. Once they give the all clear, Kevin and I go inside.

"Nice digs," he says. "I knew you were hoity-toity, but this place is above and beyond. Like by a mile."

"Please—it was hard enough to get you and the rest of Boston PD to take me seriously."

"I'll keep it under my hat."

Kevin may not recognize the Kenneth Noland hanging over the sofa, but he's got a discerning eye. He can tell that it's an original and that it's expensive. He zeroes in on a handcrafted cherry-red Murano table lamp and smiles.

"This light looks like it cost more than my car," he says.

"I don't want to hear about it." My voice cracks. "Seriously, not tonight."

"You could probably work anywhere. Hell, looks like you don't have to work at all. But here you are, fighting the fight."

He puts his arm around my shoulder and squeezes. "You're crazier than I thought."

I fight tears. "You sure know how to make a girl feel special."

"Crazy in a good way, like jumping out of planes or swimming with sharks."

I walk around the apartment, hoping to find that something is missing, that this was a run-of-the-mill breaking and entering. I'm disappointed to find that my jewelry and silver are in the wall safe. I open my desk drawers and see that my checks are all there, untouched. Nothing is missing.

"What do you think they wanted?" I say.

"They probably grabbed something small, and you won't notice it's not there until later. Or maybe they didn't take anything and just wanted to scare you."

We hear someone come in the door and call out, "Hello?"

Kevin puts one hand on the small of his back, where he keeps his gun. He uses his other to nudge me behind him.

"It's Ty," I say before Kevin fires off a round, "my boyfriend."

Ty sees us in the living room. Kevin slowly returns his Glock to his waistband. The two men check each other out with interest and suspicion.

"Ty, this is Kevin. Kevin, this is Ty."

They shake hands, each with his own misgivings about the other's presence.

"What's going on?" Ty takes off his coat and hangs it in the closet.

"Someone may have come in here this afternoon," I say.

"Broke in is more like it," Kevin says.

I smile and try to downplay it. "It was probably nothing—a repairman with the wrong address."

"We checked. Restoration Hardware doesn't make house calls," Kevin says.

"Nothing was taken. Nothing is broken. Let's not blow it out of proportion."

"I think you should move out for a few days," Kevin says.

"No way."

I look to Ty for support, but he seems to be siding with Kevin.

"We can stay at my place," he says.

"I'm in the middle of trial. I'm not moving—it's too disruptive."

"Then I'll arrange for protection," Kevin says.

"Closing your eyes isn't going to make it go away," Ty says.

Both men aren't backing down. I put up my hands, not in surrender but in annoyance.

"Enough," I say. "Don't patronize me."

Kevin surveys the living room and checks the sliding glass door to be sure it's secure.

Ty points to Melvin Jones's Big Dig files on the floor. "That box was on the dining table when I left this morning."

"Are you sure?" I say.

"Positive. I ate a bowl of cereal on the couch. I didn't want to move your stuff. I figured you had some kind of system going."

There's a knock on the door. Kevin goes to answer it and lets Manny and Gabe back in.

"We watched the security video, but it isn't much help," Manny says.

"Do you remember what the guy looked like?" Kevin says.

Gabe does his best, but he would be a lousy witness. "He had a baseball cap on."

"Did you see if it had a logo? Something that might give us a gang affiliation?"

"I wasn't paying attention," Gabe says. "He asked for the key, I handed it to him, and he left it on the desk when he was done."

"All the same, I'm going to have you come by the station and look at mug shots."

After Gabe gives his contact information to Kevin, he and Manny leave.

"Is Abby going to be okay staying here?" Ty says.

"I don't want a security detail, and I'm not carrying a gun." I take a breath and think about Tim. As much as I want to convict Orlando, I don't want to end up with a hole in my head. "But I do have to tell you something."

"What's up?" Kevin says.

"Did something happen to you, babe?" Ty says.

I take a breath and show Kevin the note.

"You know the guy from North Street, the one with the gold teeth?" I say.

"Darrius Palmer," Kevin says.

Kevin is good, but I'm surprised he has this guy's name on the tip of his tongue. "You know him?"

"I don't like the way he's been eyeing you in court."

"What's his deal?"

"Darrius and Orlando met in juvie, bonded over being the youngest killers there. They've been running buddies ever since," Kevin says. "Why? Do you think he's the guy who wrote the note?"

"I don't know who did it."

I tell him about the elevator incident and what happened after I left the office tonight. I reiterate that I don't want to give in. And that I refuse to live like a prisoner.

"Can't you arrest him?" Ty says.

I shake my head. "Any dim-witted defense attorney will have the charges tossed and he'll be out before lunch, smirking and planning his next move."

"If you won't take a security detail, and we can't lock him up, then I'm going over to his place and have a little chat," Kevin says. "And then I'm going to arrange a surveillance team."

I start to protest, but he stops me.

"We won't put the tail on you—they'll be following him."

Chapter Thirty

Max is hosting a fund-raiser for Tim's family today at Doyle's. In a moment of weakness, I invited Ty to join me. I've never taken him to anything work related, which hasn't been an issue since most nights he's with his band, rehearsing, traveling, or performing. Today's get-together is on a Saturday afternoon, and he's not booked.

Ty and I are in the bedroom, getting dressed. I make a mental note to avoid allowing him to be photographed anywhere near my boss. An image of Max standing with a convicted drug dealer could come back to haunt him when he seeks reelection or announces his run for mayor.

"It's weird, holding a party at the place where the guy was last seen alive," Ty says.

I slip into a black leather shell and turn my back to him. He picks up on my cue and zips me in.

"The pub's owner is a big contributor to Max's campaign. Money trumps decorum."

"I hate politics."

That's my opening. I pounce on it.

"I won't be offended if you don't want to come."

"I'm coming. I want to."

I sort through my bureau and select a pair of skinny black jeans.

"We can go out to lunch instead. There's a new place in the seaport that I want to try," I say.

"You guys were good friends. You have to show up."

"No one will notice if I'm not there. I gave a donation to the scholarship fund. That's all they care about."

Ty looks in the mirror and buttons his white shirt. "Cutting a check is great, but you should still show your face. Besides, I'm kind of curious to meet your friends."

"Owen and Max are my friends. The rest of them are just colleagues."

Ty steps into his cowboy boots and looks at me. "I've been wondering—have you been keeping me from them or them from me?"

Both, I think. "Neither," I say.

I feel bad. I don't want him to think I'm embarrassed about our relationship—I'm not.

"You've never introduced me to anyone in your office," he says.

"I guess it's a habit, or a neurosis. I compartmentalize—work, home, family. I'm sorry."

Ty doesn't say anything. He forces a quick smile but I know that he's looking for a better explanation—and he deserves one—but that's as deep as I can dig right now.

I kiss him, hoping this will punctuate the discussion, and move into the bathroom to look for my hairbrush. I check the cabinets and under the sink, and then settle for a comb. The downside to paying someone to clean and organize my apartment is that I can never find my stuff.

When we get outside, the air is frigid and the sky bright and cloudless. I linger on the sidewalk, tilting my pale, sun-starved face up to the sun. During my last checkup, I was diagnosed with a severe vitamin D deficiency—a result of my unhealthy lifestyle.

The only time I'm outside during daylight hours is walking
back and forth between the courthouse and my office, or getting in and out of a police car. My diet doesn't help—most of
the time, the only calcium I ingest comes from the foam in my
lattes.

On Dartmouth Street, I slip my arm into Ty's and lean my
head on his shoulder. He pulls me closer and gives me a kiss. We
seem to be back on track.

"The sun feels good," I say. "Maybe we should take a vacation, someplace exotic."

"Sounds great. Like where?"

"Fiji or Bali."

"Let's aim for a couple of days in Ogunquit this summer. You
talk a good game, but I don't see you leaving your murderers
long enough to take a cruise around the world."

We take Ty's Civic. As he drives along Tremont Street, we pass
the Piano Craft Guild, a factory that was converted into artist
studios and loft-style apartments. Around the corner is where
number eleven, Theo McDaniel, shot and killed a fifteen-year-
old boy and stole his bicycle. I look out the window.

"You're quiet. What are you thinking about?" Ty says.

I consider sharing my thoughts. The sorrow I experienced the
first time I met the victim's mother. How I almost cried when
she came to the arraignment wearing a large metal button im-
printed with a picture of her son at his middle school spelling
bee. How lonely I felt watching her sit by herself in the audience.
How she hugged me, told me that she appreciated me, after the
guilty verdict came in.

"Nothing," I say.

"Are you freaked out about seeing Julia?"

I don't meet his eyes, unsure of where he's going with the
question.

"I mean, it might be kind of awkward," he says.

"Awkward?" I look straight ahead.

"Well, you were sleeping with her husband."

I guess we weren't done with the argument that started in my apartment. I thought he was hurt or annoyed that I've never introduced him to Max or Owen, but that's not it. This is about Tim. I'm shocked that he knows and that he's decided to casually drop it into the conversation, today of all days. I look at him without responding.

"I thought you should know that I know," he says.

"Okay." I take a breath. "Is there anything that you want to ask?"

"You were seeing each other before we met."

"Right."

"And after we met."

"For a little while."

"When did it stop?"

"I don't know, like six months ago. When you and I started to get serious. I don't remember the exact date."

I do remember the exact date. Tim phoned me on July 1, at 10:00 P.M. and said we had to talk. He sounded tense, formal, distant. *Abby, I have to break things off for good. I can't see you anymore. This time I mean it. I need you to respect me and my family.*

I sensed that he was acting under Julia's strict supervision. I pictured him making sure he uttered the words precisely as rehearsed. I wanted to argue with him, plead with him, but I could tell that she was sitting next to him, close enough to hear my reaction. I told him I understood and would respect his wishes.

After we hung up, alone in my apartment, I opened a bottle of wine and got extremely intoxicated. Ty and I weren't spending a lot of weeknights together yet, but I called and invited him over. After that, we started seeing each other more regularly.

"Anything else?"

"The rest can wait. I wanted to clear the air, since I'm about to meet his widow."

"I'm glad you brought it up. I don't want to lie anymore," I say, knowing that I'll likely lie to him many more times.

"No worries, I mean people in glass houses, right?"

"Right." *Wait. What?* "You've been sleeping with other women?"

"Would that surprise you?" He tries to gauge my reaction.

"Who are you sleeping with? Groupies?" I am fully cognizant of the fact that I'm more upset than I have a right to be.

Still several blocks away from Doyle's, Ty pulls the car over and puts it in park.

"I'm not going to be the only monogamous one in the relationship. If you've decided that you want to be exclusive, then let's talk about it. But from where I sit, it seems like the only reason we're even having this conversation is because Tim is dead."

"That's not true."

"Sure it is. You miss him and you don't want to be alone."

I look at him and tear up. "I'm not alone, I'm with you."

"Not really."

"What's that supposed to mean?"

"You always have one foot out the door. It's been almost a year, and you still haven't decided if you can trust me, or if you even want to trust me." He stops, considers his words. "When are you going to let me in? When are you going to let yourself be vulnerable?"

He waits for a response but the truth is, I don't know.

"I can't sit around and watch you self-destruct," he says.

"Then don't." I sound angry, but feel hurt.

Ty pulls back onto the road, and we ride in silence. He stops in front of Doyle's and lets the car idle. We watch a few police officers and prosecutors walk in the front door. It becomes clear that Ty isn't coming inside with me. I guess I got what I wanted, after all. I step out and slam the door shut.

He sits in the car and watches, making sure I get inside safely. Even in the heat of battle, Ty is a gentleman.

Chapter Thirty-one

The back room at Doyle's is jam-packed, noisy and hot, and it's difficult to breathe. There is a blur of familiar faces—people talking, drinking, and stuffing their faces with ham sandwiches and sugar cookies. I move to a spot in a corner and make myself as invisible as possible, trying to formulate a strategy.

Max is in the middle of the room, surrounded by a half-dozen young, eager ADAs all vying for his attention, trying to think of something clever and memorable to say. They're wasting their time. Max is nodding, but his expression is vacant—he's not listening to a word.

Max's wife, Cindy, and their twelve-year-old, Maxie, are standing off to the side with Julia. An arm's length away is Max's majordomo, Owen, and Chris Sarsfield. The men are talking, looking down at the floor, probably sharing a memory of Tim. Owen's hand is resting proudly on the shoulder of his eight-year-old, Patsy, who is chomping on a blueberry muffin, shedding crumbs on the floor. Owen's wife, Megan, is working the crowd, shaking hands, and extending sympathies. Owen and Megan were high school sweethearts. She's a natural beauty. Her shiny black hair is pulled into a loose ponytail. She's wearing jeans and an old green-and-white "Lombardo for DA" T-shirt.

Owen steps up to the podium and taps on the microphone.

"We have a great crowd, and I know Julia appreciates it. Our district attorney would like to say a few words."

Max puts down his pint and picks up the microphone.

"Thanks for your generous contributions to the scholarship fund, which we've established at Tim's alma mater, Boston College Law School. The award will be given to a student, selected by Tim's family, who has exhibited excellence in academics as well as a proven commitment to public service. We want to capture the essence of Tim's love for his job, his fellow citizens, and his community."

Max pauses for applause. After a minute, Owen raises his hands, signaling everyone to let him continue.

"I also want to recognize Tim's family. His parents couldn't be here, but they send their heartfelt thanks. His wife is with us. Julia, you have been a rock throughout this horrific time. We salute your courage and support your determination. Please, know that you are not alone."

Julia moves slowly up to the podium, and everyone applauds, myself included. She's nervous, soft-spoken. A wave of compassion and empathy hits me.

"Tim would be both pleased and embarrassed by the love that you've shown us. Emma and I are blessed to have you as part of our extended family. I'm so grateful."

Max gives her a hug. An Irish band starts to play and I make my way to the coffee urn and grab a cup. Pushing through the crowd in search of the milk pitcher, I see Julia and reverse course. I look around for a safe harbor and am relieved to see Owen a few feet away, but Julia taps my shoulder before I get to him. Turning around to face her, I feel too ashamed to look her directly in the eyes.

"Abby, I want to thank you," she says.

I don't know her well and can't tell if she's being sincere or setting a trap.

My hand shakes. "Thank me?" Coffee sloshes over the rim of the cup and pools on the saucer.

"The scholarship money you donated to BC will pay the first recipient's tuition for a full year. And the fund you set up for Emma, that was so unexpected and generous."

"The donations were supposed to be anonymous. But you're welcome. If you ever need anything, please don't hesitate."

"I know you miss him too." She exhales and pauses. "But you really screwed up our marriage."

I wish I could find a rock to crawl under. I miss Tim, but Julia was his wife and the mother of his child. My face is flush with shame.

"It was over," I say, as though that's going to make it better.

"Only because I threatened to leave and take the baby with me. If we didn't have Emma, who knows what he would have done. It's the only reason he married me. I was pregnant."

My heart pounds. That's why he chose her. I thought that they had planned to get married before Julia discovered she was pregnant. I wish she hadn't told me—it just revives the fantasy that Tim and I might have ended up together, after all.

"I'm thirty-three years old. I can't believe I'm a widow." She starts to cry. "I promised myself I wouldn't fall apart." She wipes her eyes and shakes her head.

"If I could go back and change things, I would."

I'd like to end it here and walk away, but I can't turn my back and leave her standing alone. People are looking at us, trying not to gawk, but staring nonetheless. My coffee is cold, but I drink it anyway so I have something to do with my hands and mouth.

"How could this have happened?" she says. "People are saying he was doing something wrong. Was he?"

"I don't know. Did he talk to you about what he was working on?"

"He didn't say, but I grew up in a police family. I could tell it was sensitive."

Some of the gossipmongers are still keeping watch. I turn my back to the room.

"Is there anything you know that could help the investigation?"

"If I knew anything, I would have told Middlesex."

"Did he ever talk about a federal investigation?"

"An FBI agent came by the house a few times."

"Josh McNamara?"

Julia stops talking, as though she's considering whether to continue.

"Please, tell me. We have our differences, but we also have a mutual interest in finding Tim's killer," I say.

I turn to look over my shoulder and scan the room until I see Max, who is downing a pint and talking to Chris Sarsfield.

"Do you know what they talked about?" I say.

"Whatever it was, I assumed they didn't want people in the office to know that they were meeting."

"Do you know how long they'd been working together?"

"I don't think that they were exactly working together. It seemed more like Tim was working *for* the feds."

"You mean as a special prosecutor?"

"No, I don't think so. Josh was . . . what do you call the guy you give information to?"

"A handler."

"Right. I think that Josh was his handler. Tim was going to wear a wire."

My mind races. "Are you sure?"

"Yes."

Tim was working as an FBI informant. Shocked, I excuse myself, take out my phone, and call Agent Josh McNamara.

Chapter Thirty-two

As the crowd inside Doyle's dwindles, I locate a quiet corner table and deposit my coat and bag in the extra chair to discourage stragglers from joining me. Josh hasn't returned my call, and after a ten-minute staring contest with my phone, I send him a text. *Call Abby Endicott.* I wait a few seconds and send another, with a *911* for emphasis. I don't reveal what I want or why it's urgent—Josh won't rush to call me back if he learns that the exigency is purely one-sided. My discovery that Tim was a federal informant is hardly breaking news for him.

A few minutes later, Josh calls and agrees to pick me up. We decide to meet around the corner to stave off potential gossip and speculation. If anyone sees us together, they'll question what I'm doing with an FBI agent on the weekend. By Monday morning, everyone will surmise that we're either working a case or having an affair.

By the time I arrive at our meeting place, Josh is already there, waiting in a black SUV. We make small talk; he's in no rush to find out why I called, probably because he's figured it out.

"I saw you," he says as we drive past the dead-end street where Tim's body was discovered.

"When?"

"The night Tim was killed."

I turn and look out the window, remembering the scene at the tow lot. The yellow tape. The press gathered at the perimeter. The pavement where Tim's Yankees cap landed. The white tent shielding the horror of Tim's body.

Josh's voice pulls me back. "I heard the calls come over the scanner, so I drove over. I didn't stay long."

"Why were you there?"

"Tim and I had business together." He pauses. "He told me about the two of you."

Josh is trying to disarm me by catching me off guard, and he's succeeded.

"What did he say?"

"That you were involved, romantically."

Tim never would have disclosed this, least of all to a fed. I struggle to stay on point.

"The case that you and Tim were working, did it have anything to do with his murder?"

"I'm not sure yet."

"Are the feds running their own investigation?"

"Not officially."

Josh is giving me more information than I would have expected.

"Meaning you are but you'll deny it if anyone asks."

The sun is setting, and the glare is making it difficult to see. Josh pulls a pair of Ray-Bans from his pocket. There's something familiar about his overcoat, something that makes me uncomfortable. Trying not to be obvious, I look it over, searching my memory.

The day I chased him down on Cambridge Street and spilled coffee on myself, it was warm outside—Josh was wearing a suit jacket. Then I remember—it looks like the coat on the man who followed me home from work on the night my apartment was broken into. The man had the same build as Josh.

It was him. Josh was the guy I saw in Downtown Crossing,

the one who scared me and made me seek refuge in the Ritz. He was either tailing me or stalking me. I fear it's the latter.

My mouth is dry, my heart pounds. No one knows where I am or who I'm with. As an FBI agent, Josh must have a gun strapped to his ankle or hidden in the small of his back.

I subtly rest my hand on the door handle. I consider pulling it open it and jumping out of the car, but we're going at least fifty, and I'd probably get killed by oncoming traffic. My Mace is back in my apartment. I thought I was going to be with Ty all afternoon, surrounded by law enforcement, not alone in a speeding car with an armed psychopath.

We approach the busy intersection near the Forest Hills T station. There's traffic ahead at the red light, which should give me an opportunity to escape. As we near the line of cars, the signal turns green. We zoom through the intersection as the light turns from yellow to red.

Having little to lose, I decide to put it on him and see how he reacts.

"Why were you at Downtown Crossing the other night?"

"Why were you there?" he says without hesitation.

"I was walking home."

"You might want to consult a map. That's not the most direct route from Bulfinch to the Back Bay."

"You're following me."

He looks at me as though he were talking to an insane person. "Believe me, if I was following you, I would have caught you."

Realizing how ridiculous I sound, I backpedal. "Never mind."

He smiles, not looking like a guy who's going to put a bullet in my head.

"If I were you, I'd be looking over my shoulder too," he says.

We drive past Jamaica Pond, where a group of children are rolling snowballs and piling them atop one another to form a snowman. One of the kids takes a bite out of a carrot and then pushes it into the snowman's face, giving him a stubby orange nose.

"I know that Tim was your informant."

Josh doesn't say anything.

"What about Orlando Jones?" I say.

"Why do you ask?"

Josh is deflecting, but I'm not easily deterred.

"He had a gun case that was dismissed—he was working for someone."

"Interesting."

"Do you have any idea how Orlando got his case tossed?"

He shuts me down. "Where do you want me to drop you off, home or office?"

When I open the door to my apartment, it's dark and empty inside. Ty has a gig—I hope he's planning to come by later. He was pretty angry when he dropped me off at Doyle's.

I check the bathroom and see that his toothbrush and razor are here, but since he doesn't leave anything of substance, there's no way to tell if he plans to return. I promise myself that when he comes back, I'll clean out a couple of drawers and make space for him in one of the closets.

I pour myself a glass of Sangiovese and decide to call him, be direct, confident. I'll ask him about his plans, try to get a read on where we stand, and encourage him to come over.

When the call goes straight to voice mail, I grow anxious, and my mind races. I have only a couple of seconds to decide what kind of message to leave. Conciliatory, angry, matter-of-fact? I don't want to sound too pushy or desperate. I try to imagine what I would say to a reluctant witness, how I would coax him into doing what I want.

When Ty's voice directs me to leave a message and I hear the beep, I do the only thing I can think of—I hang up and grab my coat.

Chapter Thirty-three

The traffic on Storrow Drive is light, eliminating any time to second-guess my decision to go to Cambridge. Chances are nothing good will come from surprising Ty at a performance, especially when we're in the middle of a fight, but I keep driving. If I screwed up at work, I wouldn't hesitate to fix things. Maybe it's time to use this strategy at home.

The car rattles as I cross over the bumpy steel grates of the Charles River drawbridge. When I reach Inman Square, the street is lined with hip coffee shops, restaurants, and traffic. I circle around twice, looking a for parking spot. Not finding any empty meters, I pull into the lot behind Olé. Luckily, a couple exits the restaurant, freeing up a space.

It's a short walk to Ryles, but when I arrive, there's a line out front, twenty people deep. I reach in my tote, fully prepared to do what I haven't done in years—badge my way in. A familiar-looking goateed bouncer is guarding the door. I rack my brain, trying to recall if he's friend or foe.

"Miss Endicott?" he says.

"Albert?" I say.

Albert Knowles was my star witness in the trial against number nineteen, Jerome Percival, who drove his Subaru into a crowd of Christmas carolers.

Albert unhitches the red velvet rope and waves me through.

"You came here on a great night," he says. "Close your eyes and you'll think the dude on the sax is Coleman Hawkins. You gotta hear him jam. He's awesome."

The club is filled to capacity, dark and loud. Ty's band is on break, and I debate whether to look for him backstage. Then I see him, bellied up to the bar, chatting up a woman who is hanging on his every word. She's sitting on a backless bar stool, her left leg touching his knee. She has close-cropped jet-black hair, ripped jeans, and a suede jacket with fringe on the sleeves. I rub my fingers over my front teeth, in case I have a lipstick smear, and approach the cozy couple.

Ty is midsentence when he sees me. He does a double take. "Abby, what are you doing here?"

"I got off work early and thought I'd surprise you." I suppress my jealousy and turn to his new friend. "Hi, I'm Abby."

"Oh, sorry. Abby, this is Vera," he says, noticeably failing to claim me as his girlfriend.

"Nice to meet you." She extends her hand.

"Vera writes for *The Village Voice.*"

"You're from New York?" I say, trying to suss out information.

"I freelance. I live here, in Cambridge."

"Vera wrote that article about my band last summer. She's a great writer." Ty sounds a little too proud of his friend Vera's accomplishments.

I do the math and calculate that they've known each other for at least seven months, which is a long time, considering he's never mentioned a word about her.

"I had a great subject." Vera smiles and touches his biceps for emphasis.

She takes a swig from her bottle of Rolling Rock, looks at Ty, and fiddles with her silver skull earring. Albert comes by to tell Ty it's time to start the next set. As he and Vera wrap up their conversation, Albert whispers in my ear.

"Between us, I think you stand a shot with this guy."

"You think?"

Albert returns to his post at the door, and I catch up with Ty near the stage.

"How many more sets do you have?"

"Two," he says. "I'm going to be here late. And I'm sure that you've got to get up early."

"I don't mind waiting."

"I'm going to crash at my place tonight."

I try not to react. "Okay, but I'd still like to hear you play."

He looks around the room and sees that the pianist and drummer are ready to perform. "Go home, Abby. Everything will work itself out."

"I could meet you at your apartment later," I say.

"Be sure you have Albert walk you to the car."

As I make my way to the door, Vera is settled in at the bar. The bartender hands her another beer.

"Did you get his number?" Albert says.

"He didn't really seem interested."

"You want me to walk you to your car?"

"No, I'll be fine."

When I get outside, the temperature has dropped, and I can see my breath. Hampshire Street has quieted, but there is still some foot traffic. I round the corner. Olé is closed for the night. My Prius is one of the few cars left in the lot.

I take my key fob out of my tote, and as I'm about to hit the unlock button, someone approaches me from behind and presses something sharp and pointy against my throat. I don't have time to react. I can't see the blade, but I know that it's there.

"Don't say a word," a man says. "And don't turn around."

I try not to faint as the man's other arm wraps around my chest and yanks me in. His breath smells of cigarettes and beer. Out of the corner of my eye, the handle of the knife looks red. I hope it's not blood.

"Unlock your car."

I've handled enough kidnappings to know that the worst thing I could possibly do is get in a car with a knife-wielding assailant. I stand still, listening to his demands.

"Give me your key. Where the fuck is your key?" He rummages through my bag.

When he notices that my fist is clenched, he grabs my hand and peels open my fingers, uncovering the fob. I hit the red panic button, triggering the blare of the car alarm. As we struggle, he loosens his grip on me, giving me enough space to elbow him in the face. He slams me into the hood of the car. I throw the key fob under my car. He hesitates. We both hear footsteps.

Someone is behind us.

"Hey, what are you doing?" a man says.

"Get the fuck out of here."

"Leave her alone."

The knife pricks the side of my neck and slices into my skin, and blood trickles out. He throws me to the ground, kicks me in the gut, and takes off.

A man with shoulder-length gray dreadlocks sprints to my side.

"Are you okay?" He helps me back on my feet. "You're bleeding."

The man uses his cell phone as a flashlight and inspects my wound.

"Is it bad?" I touch my throat and feel the wetness.

"It looks like he just nicked you. Good thing—that's a dangerous place for a cut."

He takes off one of his leather gloves and presses it to my throat.

"You may want to go by the emergency room. You should have that looked at."

"I will," I say.

"The hospital is a few blocks away."

"Sure, I'll go over there."

The man shrugs. He can tell that I don't have any intention of going to the ER.

"Thanks for your help," I say.

"Want me to call the police? I can stay with you until they get here."

"I'll never be able to identify him."

He helps me search until we spot my key fob, and uses a tree branch to drag it out from under my car. I get in my car and he watches until I pull out of the lot.

Turning onto Hampshire Street, I consider calling 911 or Kevin. I didn't get a good look at the guy, but it couldn't have been Darrius, because he's got a police detail following him. Reporting what happened would draw attention away from Orlando and Tim, which would only hurt the case.

I slow down as I pass Ryles. Albert is out front, smoking a cigarette. He sees me, waves, and shouts out, "Have a good night, Ms. Endicott!"

"You too."

"Drive carefully—there's a lot of crazies out at this hour."

Chapter Thirty-four

The next morning, Kevin is waiting for me in the lobby of my apartment building, sitting in a leather chair, holding two cups of coffee. He hands me my latte and inspects the Band-Aid on my throat.

"You nicked yourself shaving?"

"Very funny." Unable to muster up a smile, I sip my coffee.

As we walk to his car, I consider telling him about what happened last night, but decide against it, promising myself that I'll tell him as soon as the trial is over. Until then, I'll be careful not to be alone.

"It's nothing." I toss my tote in the backseat, get in the car, and close the door.

"Don't tell me it's nothing. You're hiding something under that bandage."

"I tried to cut off a price tag. Next time, I'll remember to take the sweater off first."

He doesn't laugh. "You should ask one of our witnesses to give you some lessons in how to sell a convincing lie."

We drive through the South End, into Mattapan.

"Do you have a line on what Darrius has been up to?" I say.

"A couple of guys from the gang unit have been keeping an

eye on him. There was a little mix-up last night, but they're on it."

I rub my fingers over the bandage. Darrius managed to elude surveillance last night. He probably knows that he's being watched. I cover my mouth and turn to look out the side window. Any more information will only make me panic. I turn my attention to the trial.

"What are we going to do if we can't find Ezekiel?"

"We'll find him," Kevin says.

"I'm used to being blown off, but never when so much is at stake. All our eggs are in Ezekiel's basket."

"We'll see if we can shake some information from his boss."

We pull into the gas station and find Ezekiel's manager, Freddy Stafford, in the garage, under the hood of a Honda, working a ratchet. This time I'm dressed for the occasion, in jeans and boots.

"I'm Detective Farnsworth, we spoke earlier," Kevin says. "This is Abby Endicott, with the DA's office."

Freddy extends his greasy paw. "Good to know you."

It would be rude to just stand there, so I accept the handshake, making a mental note to wipe myself down with Purell as soon as I get back to the car.

"You're wasting your time coming all this way. Like I told you on the phone, Ezekiel isn't here."

"We need to ask a favor," I say.

"No offense, but I don't want to step in the middle of that murder. It sounds like a snake pit."

"Can you tell us where Ezekiel is living?"

"I don't have any idea."

A mechanic working on a car in the next bay turns on a hydraulic jack. Competing with the hiss of the machine, I raise my voice.

"It's crucial that we talk to him. If you don't want to tell us where he is, maybe you could talk with him about cooperating."

Kevin steps in. "We can park a marked police cruiser outside your garage 24-7 for however long it takes. It could be there for days, maybe weeks, waiting for him to come back to work. We might even ask Inspectional Services to have a look around, see if there are any environmental code violations. Who knows, maybe Immigration would be interested in checking out your employee roster."

The whir of a power drill drones nearby. Freddy stops what he's doing and looks up.

"I'm telling the truth. I have no way of getting in touch with him."

"You must have some idea."

"All I know is that he called in sick a couple of days. Then he asked me for a week off, probably to avoid you all. Can't say as I blame him."

I hand him my card. "Please call if you hear anything."

We head over to Ezekiel's last known address, his mother's house. Renée Hogan answers the door, wearing pink slippers and an orange waitress uniform, with sweat stains under the armpits. She stands in the doorway, looking exhausted.

"Hi, Ms. Hogan, I know you met the other prosecutor, Tim. I'm Abby Endicott. I've taken over the case."

"Ezekiel's not here," she says without inflection.

"It's important that we speak with him."

"I haven't seen him all week."

While I talk to Renée, Kevin shifts his body to get a peek inside the house, through the front windows.

"Do you know where he is?"

"No, but in all honesty, I wouldn't tell you if I did."

"I appreciate your candor."

"Mind if I have a look around inside?" Kevin says.

"Go ahead."

Kevin walks into the apartment. I stay on the porch with Renée and try to keep her engaged.

"I'm sure this has been a nightmare for your whole family," I say.

"My son has been through a lot, the shooting and all those surgeries. It's been almost a year, and he's still going to physical therapy. I swear he jumps out of his chair every time he hears a door shut."

"I've offered to refer him to a counselor. I'm sure he could benefit from having someone to talk to."

Renée looks in the doorway and watches Kevin push back coats in the front closet. "My son could benefit from being left alone," she says. "Can't you let him be? Let him heal. That man ruined his health and his peace of mind. Now you're coming here, harassing us, making everything worse."

"It doesn't seem like it right now, but I'm on your side."

"No, it doesn't seem like that at all."

Kevin comes outside, shaking his head in defeat. We thank Renée, and she goes back in the house.

Once we're inside the car, Kevin says, "The room was stripped bare."

"Did it look like he just packed up today?"

"Hard to tell. Did you get anything out of the mother?"

"She made me feel guilty for hounding him and talked about how bad his health has been." I pause. "She got me thinking."

"Don't go soft on me."

I look at him and roll my eyes. *As if.* "She gave me an idea," I say. "Let's go over to the BMC."

Kevin's wife is a nurse at the hospital. I've met her over the years, mostly for work-related reasons—she's always been pleasant enough. She invited me to Kevin's surprise fortieth birthday party, and after a few glasses of white wine, she let her feelings show when she referred to me as Kevin's "work wife."

It could have been the word *wife* that set me off, or it could have been her pejorative tone. Either way, I hope we don't run into her.

We park in front of the hospital and stop in the records department. There's one clerk on duty, and she pulls Ezekiel's file. It's Sunday, and his doctor isn't in her office. We have her paged, and she calls us back immediately.

"I've treated a lot of patients with gunshot wounds, but few as serious as Ezekiel's," she says. "He's lucky to be alive."

"When did you see him last?"

"He was in on Friday."

"Can you check to see when he's due back?"

I wait as she logs on to her home computer.

"He has an appointment next month."

The trial will be over by then, and without Ezekiel's testimony, Orlando will be free to kill again.

"Ezekiel lists his mother's house as his home address, but we know he's not living there. Do you happen to know where he might be staying?"

"He mentioned that he has two children by different mothers. You might want to talk to them."

"Do you know their names?"

"Not offhand."

After I get off the phone with the doctor, I ask the clerk to search for Ezekiel's emergency contact form.

"Marie St. Pierre," he says. "She has an address in Lower Mills."

When we get back in the car, Kevin and I agree that knocking on Marie's door would tip them off and drive him deeper underground. Kevin dispatches someone to sit on Marie's house to try to catch Ezekiel coming or going. We still have to find out the name of the second woman.

It's after eight when Kevin drops me off at home. We make plans to reconvene in the morning. Monday is Martin Luther

King Day, and court will be closed. Inside my apartment, I check for a sign that Ty has been here since I left this morning.

In the kitchen, I forage for food. I open the refrigerator and pull out a block of Manchego cheese, grab a box of rosemary crackers from a cabinet, and open a bottle of Merlot. I take my dinner into the living room, plop down on the couch, and wonder how to make things right.

Chapter Thirty-five

Pretrial detainees are held at the Nashua Street Jail, a modern building on the fringes of Boston's West End. Orlando, along with about 450 other upstanding citizens, reside there while they await the outcome of their cases. There are far worse places to be locked up—some of the cells have water views.

Prisoners' phone calls are automatically recorded and we routinely subpoena the audiotapes. The conversations can provide a treasure trove of information.

"I pulled Orlando's jail calls and e-mailed them to you," Kevin says, looking up from his laptop.

"What's he got to say?"

"Listen for yourself—you're going to love it."

While I log on to my e-mail, Kevin walks around and surveys my apartment, inspecting the artwork and books. The last time he was here was the night of the break-in, and he didn't have a chance to do a lot of snooping. He was busy making sure a crazed killer wasn't hiding in my linen closet.

"Is this a first edition?" he says, carefully taking my copy of Poe's *Tales* off a shelf.

He's good. It is a first edition, first state, and it cost more than a Hyundai.

"No, it's just old," I say.

I open the e-mail and hit play. A female voice issues a warning. *This call is being recorded.* It's the advisory that all prisoners hear, and couldn't be any clearer. Fortunately, inmates often ignore the message, call their friends, and brag about their crimes. They ask their fellow gang members to hide evidence or threaten witnesses. Sometimes they speak a foreign language, thinking we won't know what they're saying. They're right—we won't. But our certified interpreters will, and they'll translate every syllable for us.

Some Einsteins think they're clever by speaking in code. They seem surprised when we play their calls for jurors, who know exactly what they mean when they say, "Hide the puppies in the basement ceiling." Especially when police get a search warrant and go into the basement, remove the ceiling tiles, and find not a littler of newborn labradoodles but a stash of fully loaded AK-47s.

I listen to the call on my laptop.

"That federal dude came to see to me," a man says.

"That's Orlando," Kevin says.

"Yeah, what's he want from you?" another man says.

"Who is that?" I say to Kevin.

"Orlando's father, Melvin."

"I don't know. But my lawyer says if he don't put it in writing, then I shouldn't talk to him," Orlando says.

"Your lawyer's costing me a fortune. Listen to him," Melvin says.

"Blum says the feds can't tell the DA what to do. It's up to her," Orlando says.

"That bitch?" Melvin says. *"She's got it in for you."*

"No shit. She's been after me since I was in juvie. Did you see her up in my face, waving her finger? I'm gonna fuck her up when I get out of here," Orlando says.

The call ends. I ignore the part where Melvin calls me a bitch and Orlando says he wants to inflict bodily harm.

"They're talking about Josh McNamara," I say. "It would have been nice if he'd have told us what he's been up to."

"He's a feeb—they're all the same," Kevin says. "Sounds like he wants to flip Melvin and Orlando. I wonder what they have to offer."

"He should have told us. Feds and their 'need to know' nonsense."

A few years ago, between the first and second days of trial, federal marshals showed up at the jail in the middle of the night and swooped up my defendant. They didn't ask permission—they didn't even give me a heads-up. I found out about it the next day, when my defendant failed to show up at trial. I'm still waiting for them to tell me where he is and when they're bringing him back.

"What's the federal interest here? Why is McNamara sticking his schnoz in our case?" Kevin says.

"Tim's murder may be connected to an investigation they've been working."

"Who's the target?"

"I don't know."

My front door lock clicks and we hear footsteps. Kevin bolts up, whips his gun out, and signals me to stay seated.

"Wait," I say.

Ty comes in the living room and throws up his hands in exasperation. Kevin tucks his gun into the small of his back and pulls his shirt over it. Ty looks at me and then back at Kevin as though he's caught us in the act.

"Hey, you remember Kevin. We were working." I offer the information a little too eagerly. "But I'm glad you're here—Kevin and I could use a break."

"Oh, yeah, right," Kevin says, picking up on the tension. "I have to make a few calls. I'll go in the other room."

"Don't stop what you're doing on my account," Ty says. "I came over to pick up my phone charger. Have you seen it?"

"It's on the bureau," I say.

He goes in the bedroom, and I follow.

"We should probably talk, don't you think?" I say.

"It can wait." He pockets the charger.

"There's nothing going on between me and Kevin. You know that, right?"

"Sure," he says.

"I'm sorry about what happened yesterday."

"It's all good."

He's calm, emotionless, which makes me more anxious. He moves toward the door, but I block his path.

"Don't be mad," I say.

"I'm not." He sees a book on a chair, a biography of Beethoven, and tucks it under his arm.

"Want to go get coffee or something?" I say.

"Let's give each other a breather. You need to chill."

He walks around me, back through the living room. On his way out the door, he speaks to no one in particular.

"See you," he says.

"Nice talking to you," Kevin says after he's gone. "You have a little spat?"

"I don't want to talk about it."

I pretend to focus on my computer screen. He seems to let it drop, and we work in silence for a couple of minutes.

"Nothing like a woman scorned," he says.

"Seriously, Kevin, I'm not in the mood."

I whip my head around, ready to launch into a lecture on the importance of boundaries and respecting my privacy.

"Before you go all 'I am woman, hear me roar' on me, don't. I wasn't talking about the situation with your boyfriend. Believe it or not, everything's not all about you." He smiles and points to his computer screen. "Look what I found."

"What?"

"Ezekiel Hogan's bachelorette number two."

Chapter Thirty-six

The Tobin Bridge sits high above the industrial-waste-filled Mystic River. As Kevin zigzags in and out of traffic, I look out the window and think about number twenty, Clyde Ellis, who took out an insurance policy on his business partner and then laced her iced coffee with antifreeze. A month after the murder, just as we were closing in, Clyde jumped off the bridge to his death. I was really upset—I had been looking forward to convicting him.

Kevin reaches around to the backseat, grabs a folder and hands it to me. It's a restraining order, prohibiting Ezekiel Hogan from having contact with a woman named Helena Marshall or her daughter, Zara. *He put me in fear. I believe that he may try to hurt me.*

"Her statement is pretty generic," I say. "She says she's scared but doesn't allege any actual abuse."

"Probably because there wasn't any," Kevin says. "He's got two girlfriends and two kids, both about the same age. Marie is his main squeeze—"

I throw him a look. *Puleeze.* "Main squeeze?"

"Primary partner. That sound better?"

"Not really."

"And he's got this other woman, Helena. Both think she's his special lady."

"Seriously, *special lady*?"

He smiles and continues. "Helena finds out about Marie, realizes that she's not Ezekiel's one and only. She punishes him by taking out a restraining order and hauling his ass into court."

Restraining orders can be a lifeline for victims of domestic violence. It takes courage and resolve to get one. Victims have to stand in a public courtroom and tell the judge, a complete stranger, about the most intimate and embarrassing details of their relationships. Sometimes, however, women apply not out of fear but spite. Looks like Helena is one of those women.

Helena lives in a massive public housing complex built in the 1960s. We get out of the car and navigate a maze of cement footpaths until we locate her apartment. We can hear a cartoon playing on the TV from outside the building. *Th-th-th-that's all, folks.*

We knock on the reinforced metal door, and within seconds, Helena pulls it open. She steps aside and lets us in. Rail thin, with a lot of energy, she talks a mile a minute, making me wonder what she's on. Her three-year-old daughter, Zara, is planted in front of the television, watching *Looney Tunes*, sipping from a juice box.

Unlike most people we visit, Helena is an over-sharer. We have no problem extracting information from her.

"Zeke told me that he was going to dump that slut," she says while folding pillowcases from a bottomless pit of laundry. "I actually believed him. What a fool I was."

"Let me guess, you ran into her in the hospital?" I say.

"My cousin Tanya called, said she heard that Zeke got shot. I took the bus over to BMC to see him. That bitch was there, standing next to his bed, acting like she was his wife or something. I totally busted his ass."

A hospital emergency room is a cheater's purgatory. Spouses

and girlfriends rush to be by their man's side, only to discover that he has another significant other—or others. There's nothing that a bed-bound patient can do to prevent the encounters. Especially if he's in a medically induced coma.

"Do you know where we can find Zeke?" I say.

"Who cares," she says.

Time is short, so I hit the note that's guaranteed to elicit a response. "How much does he owe you in child support?"

"A lot," she says, rolling her eyes and releasing an exaggerated exhale. "Do you know how much a box of Pampers costs?"

I have no idea, and at the rate I'm going in the dating department, I'll never have the need to find out.

"How does Zeke get money to you? Does he mail it or deliver it in person?"

"He brings it by when he feels like it."

"Call him. Tell him that you'll call the cops if he doesn't give you some money."

"You want me to threaten him?"

"That's not what I said. I just think you should let him know his options."

Helena is more than happy to comply, and she makes the call that will smoke Ezekiel out of wherever he's holed up. She hangs up and smiles, pleased with her performance.

"He said he'd meet me at the burger place and give me fifty bucks. Like that's gonna make up for everything he owes me."

"Better than nothing," I say, rushing her to grab her purse.

She insists on changing her clothes and comes out of the bedroom all sexed up, wearing a low-cut tight T-shirt and leggings. She combs Zara's hair and wipes juice from her face.

We drive over to the Burger Bonanza on State Boulevard, Kevin and I wait in the parking lot while they go inside. I wish I had used the bathroom at Helena's. My bladder is about to burst, but I have an aversion to public restrooms, especially at fast-food joints.

"They're not supposed to be within a hundred feet of each other, which means we're aiding and abetting in the violation of a restraining order," Kevin says.

"Arrest us," I say.

When we get inside the restaurant, it's dinnertime, and there's a line at the counter. A dirty mop and bucket are in the corner, next to an overflowing trash barrel. The odor of grease is so strong that I feel like I need to go to Elizabeth Grady and have my pores extracted. I was hungry when I walked in here. I'd planned to get a burger and a bag of fries for the road. Now I'm seriously considering becoming a vegetarian.

A twentysomething woman with smeared lipstick exits the ladies' room. A fiftysomething man who forgot to zip his pants follows behind. I'm definitely going to wait to pee.

When we approach Exekiel, he turns to Helena. "You set me up," he says.

"Break up with that bitch, then you get to complain," she says. "Until then, I don't want to hear you flapping your gums."

I take a seat next to Ezekiel on a plastic chair the color of Bozo the Clown's hair. Kevin remains standing.

"Told you we weren't going away," Kevin says.

"Look, we need you for a couple of hours tomorrow, that's it. You'll never have to talk to us again."

"That's what that other dude said after I testified in the grand jury."

"I know you've been through a lot and that you're scared."

"Don't try to play me," he says.

Kevin pretends to stretch his arms but twists his body in a way that shifts his jacket and exposes the handcuffs that are clipped to his belt. Ezekiel gets the point and says uncle.

We take him to the Parker House, where we stash our most reluctant witnesses. The hotel rooms are pricey, but it's in a great location, a couple of blocks from the courthouse. After we get him checked in at the front desk, Kevin escorts him to his room. I stay behind to talk to the manager.

"No charges to Mr. Hogan's room," I say. "If he wants anything from room service, he'll have to pay for it with the cash we gave him."

"Don't want to get burned again?" she says.

"Not if I can help it."

A couple of months ago, one of my witnesses invited six buddies up to his room to eat steak dinners, drink bottles of booze, and watch porn. He charged everything to the room, which we didn't discover until after he checked out. Owen wasn't pleased when he got the bill. Worse, I had to disclose it to the defense attorney, who argued that I was bribing my witness with food and drink.

We make arrangements to come by and get Ezekiel in the morning and escort him over to the courthouse. Kevin arranges for a uniform to stand watch for the night outside his room, in case he has second thoughts.

Chapter Thirty-seven

Court resumes for the day, and the jurors file into the court-room and take their seats. I glance over at Orlando, and he looks back at me, his eyes landing on the side of my neck. This morning, I removed the Band-Aid and a small scab has formed. Orlando smirks and snorts a little air out of his nose, as though laughing at his own inside joke. I turn to the back of the room. Darrius doesn't flash his gold-toothed smile. He just gives me a vacant stare. He's too smart to threaten me in public.

Sal goes into the corridor to summons my next witness. In what feels like an hour, but is actually about a minute, Ezekiel comes hurtling through the courtroom doors. It's hard to tell who is more surprised to see him, Orlando or his lawyer.

Ezekiel looks like a new man, wearing the oxford shirt and green tie that I had Kevin drop off at the Parker House this morning. I keep a pretty extensive supply of clothing in my office. There are shirts and pants in a variety of colors and sizes for both men and women. I also have an assortment of toiletries that I've acquired from the cosmetic counters of Saks and Neimans—soap, shampoo, combs, brushes, and makeup. It's good to be prepared—left to their own devices, witnesses frequently show up for court wearing tattered T-shirts and dirty jeans, looking like they haven't showered in weeks.

Ezekiel wastes no time stepping into the witness box. He sits and leans forward, eager to begin, making it clear that he wants to get out of here as soon as possible. He keeps his gaze on the floor as the clerk swears him in.

"Mr. Hogan, are you in court today under protest?" I say.

I want to give him a chance to let the audience, especially the gangsters, know that this is on me. That it's my fault. He seems to appreciate the gesture and responds by lifting his head and glaring at me.

"I'm here because you threatened to lock me up. I don't want nothing to do with this trial."

"The record shall reflect that you are an unwilling witness," I say. "I'd like to draw your attention to last August, the evening that you were shot."

Under different circumstances, I would work up to this point slowly, milking Ezekiel's testimony for all it's worth, evoking every painful detail about the suffering he's endured and how deeply this crime has impacted his life. I'd ask about his education, work history, family and, most importantly, the severity of his injuries. But I can get this information in through a number of other avenues: witnesses, medical records, and photographs. I want to limit the questions and minimize his exposure. It's the least I can do.

"What had you been doing around the time that you were shot?"

"Partying with friends."

"One of those friends was the deceased, Jasmine Reed?"

"Objection. Leading." Blum wants to drag this out, make it as painful as possible.

"I find that the prosecution has laid the foundation," Judge Volpe says. "Mr. Hogan is a hostile witness and I will permit the use of leading questions."

Judge Volpe could have made me jump through a few more

hoops, but he's cutting me slack. I'm not the only one who wants to get this over with.

"Was Jasmine, the deceased, your friend?"

Ezekiel nods. "Yes."

"Tell us what happened."

He sits for a minute, looks at me, and then looks away. Open-ended questions aren't going to work—I have to feed him ones that he can answer with a yes or no.

"A man pulled up in a beige Toyota?"

"Yes."

"This man had a sawed-off shotgun?"

"Yes."

"You had never seen him before?"

"Never."

"You had no axe to grind with him?"

"None."

After setting the scene, I slow down and take a breath. "The man who shot you and Jasmine and Denny, is he present in this courtroom?"

He drops his head and looks at his feet.

"Yes," he says.

At this juncture, I need to get him to make the ID, and I can't do it by spoon-feeding him leading questions.

"Please tell us where he's seated and describe an article of clothing that he's wearing."

I move to the witness box and stand next to Ezekiel, facing out into the audience. I look over at Orlando, daring him to look back at me. Orlando takes the bait and glares at me, shooting venom in my direction. This gives Ezekiel a moment to breathe and do what he has to.

"He's at the table, wearing the purple tie, sitting next to his lawyer," he says.

I turn to the judge and say as quickly as I can get the words out of my mouth, "Your Honor, may the record reflect that the witness has identified the defendant, Orlando Jones."

"Yes," Judge Volpe says. "I find that the witness has made a positive identification."

Suddenly and without warning, Orlando shouts, "Mother-fucker!"

Judge Volpe scans the courtroom, making sure that the court officers are at the ready, and then pounds his gavel. *Bang. Bang. Bang.*

"Mr. Jones, settle down. Outbursts like that will not be tolerated—"

Orlando doesn't wait for Judge Volpe to finish his admonition. He jumps out of his chair, extends his arms high in the air, and yells, "This is bullshit. Punk-ass snitch!"

Court officers run to Orlando, but before they reach him, he takes hold of the heavy oak table in front of him, hoists it off the ground, and hurls it in my direction. I'm stunned motionless.

A few pencils fly by, narrowly missing my eye. A cup of water hits my shoulder. I try to duck but the table strikes me head-on, knocking me to the ground. I whack the back of my skull against the floor so hard that I see a flash of light. I think I lose consciousness.

After a few seconds, I pick up my head, lean on my elbows, and open my eyes. Court officers pile onto Orlando and tackle him. Sal races Judge Volpe off the bench and into his chambers and locks the door behind him. A deputy radios for backup. Dotty gets down on her hands and knees and crawls under her stenographer's table. Blum jumps out of the way and hysterically yells at Orlando to calm down. The clerk bolts out a side door and into the stairwell, followed closely by Ezekiel. Reporters snap pictures. Bystanders turn on their cell phone cameras. Harold waves his cane in the air. Jackie Reed starts to pray.

Darrius rushes from the back row and joins the fray. Police

officers and two random men from the audience come forward to help. Some struggle to intercept and capture Darrius and others fight to hold Orlando down. Court watchers jockey to get out of the courtroom as more police officers charge in from the hallway.

Finally, Orlando is subdued and dragged out of the courtroom in shackles. Darrius is yanked to his feet and frisked for weapons. A police officer discovers a small folding knife with a red handle tucked in his shoe.

I become aware of Kevin, who is kneeling at my side. I'm not sure how long he's been there. He offers his hand and helps me to my feet. My head is throbbing. My back is sore. A bump is starting to form behind my right ear, and there's a welt on my forearm.

I turn to the jurors, who are frozen in place—still seated in their assigned chairs, clutching their notebooks. They're staring at me, stunned, looking for guidance. They've now experienced, firsthand, Orlando Jones's propensity for violence and the lengths to which he'll go in order to get what he wants.

I take a breath, trying not to throw up or pass out. Looking around the courtroom, I take it all in. I want to savor the moment. This is unequivocally the best thing that has ever happened to me.

Chapter Thirty-eight

The court takes a recess, giving everyone a chance to decompress and check for broken bones. Sal directs the jurors to stay together in their deliberations room, behind locked doors. He orders lunch, a couple of platters of turkey sandwiches and chocolate-chip cookies from a nearby deli, and tries to keep them calm by cracking jokes, telling them that the lunch is their combat pay. What he doesn't tell them is that the free lunch was intended to address Judge Volpe's concern that they might walk out of the courthouse and never return.

Kevin insists that I see the court doctor and has him paged. I don't put up a fight, knowing that Dr. Finn will give me a clean bill of health. He routinely examines defendants and witnesses who claim that they're too sick to testify. Nine times out of ten, Dr. Finn concludes that they're malingering and sends them back to the judge. He's a hard-ass, a doctor after my own heart. I'd make him my primary-care physician if he took private patients.

Kevin and I take the elevator to the seventh floor and wait for him to arrive. When Dr. Lantigua, the court psychiatrist, shows up instead, I try to make for the elevator, but Kevin grabs my tote and holds it hostage.

"I'm feeling fine," I say.

Dr. Lantigua is about sixty, easily identifiable by her standard female shrink uniform: elastic-waist slacks and a shapeless tunic, both in neutral colors, and a bold, chunky necklace. She's insightful, curious, and thorough, which puts her at the bottom of the list of people I want to talk to right now.

"Where's Dr. Finn?" I ask.

"He's on a personal day," she says. "Can I help you?"

I turn to Kevin, who is hovering. "A lady needs her privacy," I say.

He parks himself on a bench and keeps my tote with him. "No problem—I'll wait here."

We go into the office. I hear Kevin outside the door, clearing his throat. He's not going to let me out of here without the doctor's approval.

"I came in contact with a flying table," I say. "My detective wants to be sure that I don't have a brain hemorrhage."

"It's been a while since I've done a physical, but I can check your blood pressure."

She pulls a cuff out of her medical bag. Reluctantly, I extend my left arm. Dr. Lantigua senses my misgivings about the checkup.

"We don't have to do this," she says.

"No, go ahead."

"'No, go ahead.' That sends kind of a mixed signal. I'm detecting some misplaced anger."

"Sorry, I don't mean to be rude."

"Is there something you want to talk about?"

Yes, there are a million things I want to talk about: Tim, Crystal, Ty, my family, my career choice, my anxiety, my migraines, my list.

"No, thanks. I'm fine."

She wraps the cuff tightly around my arm, and we both watch it inflate.

"Your pulse is high. You may want to cut down on the caffeine. I can write you a script for Ativan," she says, ripping apart the Velcro.

"Maybe another time."

"You're probably going to feel worse tomorrow. You might have a concussion. I strongly recommend that you go over to Mass General and get a CT scan."

"I'll call my physician as soon as I get out of here and schedule an appointment."

I thank Dr. Lantigua and dash out of her office before she changes her mind and decides that I'm not healthy enough to return to court. Outside her office, Kevin is waiting for me on the bench in the hallway, exactly where I left him.

"Everything copacetic?" he says.

"All good," I say. "She told me I have nothing to fear but fear itself."

We go back down to the courtroom, and Judge Volpe calls me and Blum in for a lobby conference. Dotty is by his side, her face buried in the black cone.

"Judge, I move for a mistrial," Blum says.

"You've got to be kidding," I say.

"Careful, Ms. Endicott," Judge Volpe says. "I know you've been through a lot, but let's try to remain professional."

My attention shifts to a partially eaten chocolate-chip cookie on top of his desk. Feeling like I could use a sugar boost, I'm tempted to ask for a bite. He notices me eyeing his dessert and pulls the cookie closer. *Don't even think about it.*

"My client can't possibly receive a fair trial. The jury has been irreparably prejudiced. I'd like to be heard on my motion," Blum says.

"Where is he now?" Judge Volpe says.

"He was taken by ambulance to Mass General," Blum says, adding, "on a stretcher," as though that will garner sympathy.

"For the record, I find that you have zealously represented your client and argued forcefully and articulately on his behalf, which is admirable given the circumstances. Your motion for a mistrial has been heard and duly considered. It is denied," Judge Volpe says. "Mr. Blum, go to the hospital and talk to your client. Tell him that if he can't behave, I'll rule that he's waived his right to be present in the courtroom and he can watch the remainder of the trial on a closed-circuit screen in his jail cell. Got it?"

Blum nods. "I'll pass it on. For the record, I don't endorse his actions."

"I'm going to explain what's happening to the jury, and I'll see you all back here tomorrow morning," Judge Volpe says.

Kevin catches me coming out of the courtroom. Without saying a word, he puts his hand on my back and whisks me down a side staircase.

"What's up?" I say.

He starts to speak and then stops and looks at me. This can't be good.

"He escaped."

"What? Who?"

"Orlando, he got out."

"When? How?"

"The deputies had to uncuff him for an MRI. He broke a glass tube, made it into a weapon, and took a nurse hostage."

"Is she okay?"

"Yeah, there was a brief standoff. The guards subdued him, but he got a burst of energy, knocked out a deputy, and injured two others."

"And he got out of the room?"

"And out of the building. He's one tough bastard."

"Orlando is on the street. There's no telling what he'll do."

My head throbs and I feel dizzy. I grip the banister to prevent myself from falling, but my palm is sweaty and I start to lose my footing. Kevin holds on to my elbow.

"Can you take me over to Mass General?" I say.

"With pleasure. Give me your doc's number, and I'll call ahead and let him know we're on the way."

"No, not *my* doctor. I want to talk to Orlando's doctors and the technicians and EMTs who treated him. We have to retrace his steps, see if he said anything, and find out how bad his injuries were."

"Let's leave that to the sheriffs and the fugitive squad. Right now, I'm worried about you. We're arranging security for your apartment and an officer to watch out for you 24-7 until we find him."

I start to protest but Kevin cuts me off.

"Don't even think about fighting me on this."

He walks me back to Bulfinch, and while he arranges for my bodyguard, I sit at my desk and scan the Internet. Word about Orlando is all over the news: his outburst in the courtroom, his escape, his potential involvement in Tim's murder. And there's speculation that I could be his next target.

There are a ton of missed calls on my cell.

From Max: "*Abby, I want you to know that you have my full support. Whatever you need, you let me know. I'll check in on you later.*"

From my father: "*Enough is enough. I've spoken with the mayor and the governor. I want you off this case. Let someone else risk their life. I want you to call me as soon as you get this message. I mean it, muffin.*"

From my brother: "*Everyone is freaking out. Are you okay? Can you at least call us and let us know what's going on?*"

From Crystal's mother: "*Abby, honey, I saw you on the TV. I'm so proud of you. But, please, take care of yourself. This man has caused enough heartache.*"

From Owen: "*Hang in there, buddy. We have your back. You need anything, a hotel room, a safe house, let me know. Oh, I left a picture for you, on your shelf.*"

I look over at the bookcase and see a framed photograph of

me, Tim, and Owen. The photo was taken at the Kinsale a couple of years ago, after I won a conviction against a serial rapist. We're smiling, beer mugs hoisted in the air. The three of us made some good memories.

There are about a dozen more messages from an assortment of people—my high school Latin coach, my college suite mate, my law school torts professor. Everyone has lodged a call. Except Ty.

Less than an hour later, Kevin comes in and introduces me to my security detail, Detective Sandra Holmes, who drives me home in her unmarked Taurus. She's the girliest cop on the force, chock-full of extensions—hair, nails, eyelashes. If cops were allowed to wear stilettos, she'd be chasing down felons in four-inch spikes. Still, I wouldn't want to mess with her. She's got a reputation for being a kick-ass cop.

"Awesome earrings," she says as we get off the elevator. "Are they real or cubic?"

"Cubic," I say. "An old boyfriend gave them to me. He got them at Old Navy." Adding a couple of specific details to a story always makes it sound more believable.

"Old Navy doesn't sell earrings," she says.

I unlock the door to my apartment. Sandra goes inside to do a security check. From where I'm standing, I can see that the living room is lit by the glare of the TV set.

"Down, asshole!" she says.

I rush into the apartment and see Sandra holding Ty at gunpoint. He has a Rolling Rock in his right hand, his left raised in the air.

"No, Sandra," I say. "Stop. That's my boyfriend."

She returns her gun back to her waistband. "Sorry about that," she says.

Ty sits on the couch. "I'm glad you got security, but I didn't think it would be at my expense."

Sandra looks around the apartment, makes sure it's secure, and then takes in the leather chairs and the wide-screen plasma.

"Those earrings are definitely real. What I don't get is why you'd lie about it." She doesn't wait for a response. "I'll be right outside the door if you need anything."

"Don't you want something to sit on?"

She grabs one of my glossy white Eero Saarinen tulip chairs from the dining table and drags it to the door.

"Someone will relieve me in an hour. They'll be outside all night if you need anything. I'll be back in the morning to take you to court."

Sandra steps out into the hallway and closes the door.

"One of these days, my luck is going to run out, and someone will actually pull the trigger." Ty kills off his beer, goes into the kitchen, and returns with another bottle for himself and a glass of wine for me.

"I'm really sorry. Are you okay?" I say.

"I'm fine. How are you doing?"

"Not great. Thanks for coming over."

I sit on the sofa, and Ty sits across from me.

"Does this mean you're not mad anymore?" I say.

"No, I'm still pretty pissed off."

I take a sip of wine and relax my neck and shoulders. "I don't get it. Why are you so angry?"

"I'm done with all the head games."

"We were both wrong. I wasn't honest with you about Tim, but you weren't straight with me, either. For all I know, you and that Vera chick have been sleeping together since last summer."

"Abby, I'm not sleeping with Vera. I never was. She wrote an article about me and that's it. And there were no other women."

My phone rings. I ignore it. "So you lied to me?"

"Yup, I lied."

Ty puts down his beer, leans in, and looks at me for a minute. Nervous about what he's going to say, I put my wineglass down.

"I'm tired of being taken for granted," he says.

"Then why are you here?"

"I care about you. But you need to decide what you want. Either you're all in or we need to stop seeing each other."

My phone rings again, and I silence it.

"This is a bad time to issue an ultimatum," I say.

"There's never a good time with you."

We look over at the TV—Orlando Jones's mug shot flashes on the screen. Carl Ostroff is standing in front of Mass General. Ty ups the volume.

"There is a statewide manhunt on for accused killer Orlando Jones. In a maneuver that would impress Houdini, Jones escaped custody at Mass General. Police are warning residents that he has a history of violence and is presumed to be armed and dangerous. He's facing a mandatory life sentence for the murder of Jasmine Reed, and sources are saying he could face additional charges in connection with the death of ADA Tim Mooney. At this point, he has little to lose."

Ty gets out of his chair and sits next to me on the sofa. As he wraps me in his arms, I tremble.

"I'm scared." My voice cracks.

He kisses me softly on the cheek, tilts his head back, and looks at the cut on the side of my neck.

"What happened here?" he says. "It looks like a cut."

My phone vibrates, and I see it's Chris Sarsfield. The other two missed calls are from him too.

"This is the head of the gang unit," I say to Ty. "It could be about Orlando."

I answer the phone and listen to Chris.

"Sounds like a bad scene in court today," he says. "I thought you'd want to know Darrius Palmer is going to be arraigned tomorrow."

"Good. Who's handling it?"

"I'm going to keep it."

I'm glad Chris is holding on to the case. "What are you charging him with?"

"He was booked on disorderly and affray."

My stomach drops. "Those are only misdemeanors. He'll be back on the street before lunch."

"It's the best I could do."

"Did you run it by Max?"

"Yes, he knows."

Ty sees me getting worked up and rubs my back.

"But they found a knife."

"He didn't do anything illegal with it."

I think about telling Chris about the parking lot incident, but there's no point. I can't pin it on Darrius. Besides, I'm not sure I even trust Chris anymore. I don't know who I can trust.

Chapter Thirty-nine

I'm prepared to continue with the trial, but Judge Volpe hasn't made a ruling on whether he plans to keep going. Some judges would proceed without the defendant; others would adjourn for a couple of days to see how things shake out with the search. Calling my next witness without Orlando seated at the table would be easier on everyone, especially me. But it would be like hosting a party without the guest of honor.

Sandra is superglued to my hip as we make our way to the courthouse. We pass the coffee shop; Rodney Quirk is seated in his usual spot, staring at me as I pass by. Even though I've grown accustomed to seeing him there, I still feel a jolt of anxiety every time we lock eyes. I consider telling Sandra about him but decide to keep moving forward.

We're the first to arrive in the courtroom. Sandra helps me unpack boxes of files and unwrap exhibits, and we spread everything out on my table. The door swings open; Sandra and I spin around to see my victim witness advocate, Winnie Hanlon. Advocates are assigned to every trial team in our office. They start in district courts and climb through the ranks, like the lawyers.

Winnie and I have been working together since our days in Roxbury District Court. She wears a lot of different hats, including social worker, therapist, travel coordinator, investigator, paralegal, babysitter, and real estate agent.

"I found an apartment for Ezekiel," she says. "It'll get him out of the city and away from North Street's reach."

"Where is it?"

"In Canton."

"That's far. Did he agree to go?"

"He said he's tired of the Parker House."

"That's a first."

Usually we have to drag our victims out of there, kicking and screaming. But before they check out of their rooms, Winnie inspects luggage to be sure they haven't stolen anything—towels or pillows, or the television.

"I'm not going to question it. I'll drive him there myself—anything to get him out of harm's way."

The door opens again. It's Blum. This time he has a bloodred ink spot on the breast pocket of his light gray jacket. He looks the way I feel, like someone stabbed him in the heart with a tiny paring knife. Every time the door swings open, my heart skips a beat. I'm still hoping to see Tim walk in, carrying his canvas briefcase, ready to reclaim his trial.

The gallery fills with spectators, family members, the media, and gangsters—minus Darrius. Everyone assumes their place in the pews. Sal escorts Blum and me into Judge Volpe's chambers, where he is seated behind his desk, Dotty at his side.

"We have a number of issues to resolve." He gestures for us to sit. "Your client has done himself a great disservice. The entire county is afraid of him, including the panel. Juror number nine has decided not to join us today."

"Move for a mistrial," Blum says.

"You're going to have to find a new theme song," Judge Volpe says.

"Has anyone been able to make contact with the juror?" I say.

"Sal called her house, and she refused to get on the phone. Her daughter said she's sick and faxed over a so-called doctor's note."

Judge Volpe shows us a copy of a handwritten note, declaring that juror number nine is suffering from "a cute" anxiety attack. Get in line, sister.

"I think she means an *acute* attack," Blum says.

"We can all agree that the note is a forgery," Judge Volpe says.

I don't want a juror who doesn't want me. "I suggest that we excuse her. We have alternates."

"That's what I intend to do," Judge Volpe says. "Next, I want to give you both an opportunity to state your position on how to proceed in light of Mr. Jones's flight from the hospital yesterday and his intentional absence from court today."

"The Fifth, Sixth, and Fourteenth Amendments to the United States Constitution require that my client be present in court and that he be given an opportunity to confront his accusers," Blum says.

"He certainly exercised that right yesterday," I say. "He's given the confrontation clause a whole new dimension."

Blum ignores the comment. "The Supreme Court has consistently held that the defendant's right to be present at trial is one of the most basic and fundamental of rights of all."

"The right is not absolute." I try to sound more lawyerly, less emotional. "There are exceptions, particularly when the defendant knowingly, voluntarily, and violently absents himself from the proceedings, as he has done in this instance."

"I agree with the prosecution," Judge Volpe says.

"I request that you instruct the jury that Mr. Jones's flight can be considered consciousness of guilt, evidence of his guilty mind," I say, pushing the envelope.

"I'm not going to do that, at least not at this juncture."

"How about we recess for a couple of days, and give him a chance to turn himself in?" Blum says.

"Not going to happen. This train is moving forward."

When the trial resumes, the number of court officers in the room increases to ten. Uniformed and plainclothes police officers line the perimeter of the courtroom. The jurors seem reluctant as they file in and take their seats. Juror number one scans the room, taking careful inventory of the location of both emergency exits. Number three has dark circles under her eyes and looks like she's been up all night. Number six has developed a twitch. They all look at the empty seat at the defense table, where Orlando had been sitting. Two jurors glance at each other, lifting their eyebrows.

"All rise," Sal says.

"Be seated." Judge Volpe takes the bench. "Ladies and gentlemen, I'm sure you've noticed by now that the defendant is not present in court today. I am instructing you that, as a matter of law, you are not to speculate as to where he is or why he's not here. We are going to proceed with the trial. Mr. Jones may at some point rejoin us. Ms. Endicott, you may call your next witness."

Since Ezekiel has already ID'd Orlando as the shooter, there's no longer any reason to drag things out. The rest of the day flies by. I zip through Denny's doctor, Ezekiel's nurse, and Jasmine's mother. They're brief but impactful, delivering a steady stream of suffering and heartache.

Just before we recess for the night, juror number three, a fortysomething woman with a bouffant hairdo, raises her hand. Dozens of metallic bracelets on her right arm clatter as they slide down her forearm and cluster at her elbow. Sal escorts her to the sidebar, and we follow.

"I can't do this anymore, Judge," she says. "My nerves are shot."

"Unless you have a documented medical condition, I can't excuse you from service." Judge Volpe knows our numbers are dwindling.

She scrunches her face and returns to her seat.

The day moves quickly, a race to the finish line. When we break for the evening, I see Sandra in the back of the courtroom. She escorts me back to my office.

"Any sign of Orlando?" I say.

"Not yet," she says. "The feds think he may have crossed state lines and fled to New Hampshire."

"Of course the FBI is going to say that, whether or not they believe it. It gives them jurisdiction. They're chomping at the bit for a legitimate reason to join the hunt."

When I get to Bulfinch, I'm surprised to see Josh McNamara seated in the reception area, his hand cupped over his mouth, talking on the phone. He hangs up when I get off the elevator and follows me into my office.

"Did you find Orlando?" I say.

He shakes his head and turns to Sandra. "Can you excuse us? We need the room."

"No" is all she says.

Boston police and state police dislike the feds even more than local prosecutors do.

"I'll be okay," I say. "Give us a minute."

Begrudgingly, Sandra steps into the hallway, and Josh closes the door.

"I need you to come to the federal courthouse with me," he says.

"What for?"

"Let's talk about it when we get there."

"I'm not in the mood for games today. I'm kind of in the mid-dle of a high-stakes trial." I take off my coat and hang it on the back of my door.

"This is something you're going to want to know about."

"Whatever it is, I'm sure there's more in it for you than there is for me." I sit at my desk and log on to my computer, hoping he'll take the hint and go away.

"I think you'll find it mutually beneficial."

Curious, I look up. "Fine. Let me tell Sandra. We'll meet you there."

"She can't come—that's nonnegotiable. Let her know that I'll give you a ride home and see you safely inside your building. She can take over from there."

Against my better judgment, I agree to the terms. Sandra puts up a little protest, but she gives in pretty quickly. She's probably getting tired of babysitting and could use some alone time. There's a nail salon on Newbury Street that she looks at longingly every time we drive by.

"I'm going to call Kevin," I say when we get into Josh's car, "let him know where I'm going."

"No," he says. "He doesn't have clearance."

I underwent the federal background check years ago, when I was assigned a joint state-federal investigation. I peed in a cup to prove I didn't have drugs in my system. My neighbors were interviewed to be sure I wasn't running a human trafficking ring out of my apartment. My passport was checked to verify that I wasn't canoodling with foreign dictators. I filled out endless forms and I was interviewed by an agent who seemed to disbelieve everything I said.

Once the FBI determined that I wasn't a threat to national security, I was sworn in as a special assistant United States attorney. I became part of a joint state-federal prosecution of a terror suspect who had been involved in a horrific bombing. Predictably, in the midst of a national tragedy, Max and the U.S. attorney were duking it out over jurisdiction.

"Kevin doesn't have federal clearance," I say, "but that's not why you want to keep him out of the conversation. You're using national security as a pretense to get me alone. What's going on?"

He looks at me and grins. "You'll see."

The office buildings in the Financial District are dark and the area is deserted. When we approach the Moakley Courthouse, we drive around to the side of the building. Josh uses his pass to open the garage door and drives down the ramp into the parking lot beneath the building.

Everything about the federal justice system appears newer and shinier than ours. Josh's car is a black SUV, like Kevin's, but it's a later model with hands-free navigation and bulletproof glass. The new federal courthouse is in the fashionable Seaport District, near the Institute of Contemporary Art. Inside, the building is clean and airy, with sweeping views of the harbor and art lining the walls. Federal judges have cushier assignments and shorter days. Federal prosecutors have grander offices and bigger paychecks. And federal defendants who have been convicted of murder can be sentenced to death by lethal injection.

The courthouse is closed for business. Josh shows his badge to a marshal, who is seated at the front door, holding the *Herald*, working on a sudoku puzzle. We take an elevator to a floor I've never visited, and are buzzed in by someone I can't see. We enter a secure area with closed-circuit cameras everywhere.

As we pass through another security station, Josh nods at a marshal, who leads us into the lockup area where the prisoners are held. There is a long, narrow line of empty holding cells.

Josh stops in front of a door that has a small window. He looks at me, tilts his head, and shifts his eyes, indicating that I should look inside the room. I step in front of the window and see a black man in an orange prison jumpsuit handcuffed to a metal bar on the wall. He is hunched over, head down, arms covering his face.

"Who is it?" I say.

Josh raps his knuckles on the window, causing the man to stir. He lifts his head and looks up at us. I wasn't sure who to expect, but it definitely wasn't Melvin Jones.

Chapter Forty

Josh and I take seats in the oxblood leather chairs across the table from Melvin. There's no need for introductions. Josh pulls a laminated Miranda card from a compartment in his badge and reads from it, out loud.

"You have the right to remain silent. Anything you say can and will be used against you in a court of law. You have the right to speak to an attorney and to have an attorney present during any questioning. If you cannot afford a lawyer, one will be provided for you at government expense."

Melvin Jones is a savvy guy with a boatload of resources. He should know it's in his best interest to hit the pause button and call a lawyer. We may be in a rush to speak with him, but that's not his problem. He should be worried that he might incriminate himself. Anyone who has read the news or watched an episode of *Law & Order* knows that what happens post-Miranda rarely turns out well for the guy on the hot seat. It couldn't be more obvious that we're not here to help. There may as well be a bare lightbulb dangling from the ceiling, shining in his face, blinding him.

"Do you wish to waive these rights and speak with us?" Josh says.

"Sure." Melvin starts to scratch his head, but the cuffs stop him short. "What do you want to know?"

"First you have to sign the waiver."

Josh uncuffs him and hands him a pen. Melvin scans the paper briefly and signs on the dotted line.

"I'd be more comfortable if we recorded the conversation," I say.

Josh ignores me and there's nothing I can do about it. Local prosecutors have the ultimate authority over local homicide investigations but Melvin is in federal custody. I could get up and leave but decide to stay. Nothing illegal is going on, at least not yet.

"Do you know why you're here?" Josh says.

"You tell me." Melvin is finally showing some brains. "Why am I here?"

"Where were you yesterday?"

"I was at the trial—she knows that," he says, acknowledging my presence for the first time.

I nod but remain neutral. I don't want Melvin to think I'm here to support his cause.

"I can confirm that you were at the courthouse," I say.

"What about after? Did you visit your son in the hospital?" Josh says.

"No."

Josh opens a folder, takes out a photograph, and slides it across the table. It's time-stamped, dated yesterday at 1:00 P.M., and it shows a silver Lexus in what looks like a parking garage. Next he displays another picture, a close-up of a Massachusetts license plate.

"Careful not to walk yourself into an obstruction charge. Lying to a federal official is a crime," Josh says.

"You got me—that's my car. I'm guilty of driving a Lexus."

"We pulled that off the security video in the Mass General

parking garage yesterday afternoon. Do you want to revise your response?"

Josh just revealed that FBI agents have been surreptitiously following Melvin. I wonder who else they've been tailing.

"You asked me if I visited my son. I tried to visit him, but they wouldn't let me."

Melvin is cagier than I would have expected.

"Who did you talk to at the hospital?" Josh says.

He looks at the ceiling, pretending to rack his brain. "I don't recall talking to anyone."

Josh takes out another photograph that shows Melvin standing in the lobby of the hospital, talking to a woman who is wearing scrubs.

"Who is she?"

"Rosalee, my wife's cousin. She's a nurse at the hospital." Caught in a lie, Melvin doesn't miss a beat. "I said hello to Rosie. That's a crime now?"

"It's a crime if you're conspiring to aid and abet in the escape of a prisoner."

As much as I want to grab paper and a pen from my tote and jot down notes, to get an accurate record of this interview, I don't want to interrupt the flow. I sit still and listen to Melvin inculpate himself.

"Your only evidence against me is a picture of my car in a public parking lot, and two people standing next to each other in a public building. I didn't go to law school, but I can tell the difference between a conspiracy and a conversation."

Josh stands and reaches across the table as though he's going to smack Melvin in the face. Melvin looks at him but doesn't flinch.

"Don't bullshit me, Melvin. Who else was involved in helping Orlando escape?"

Melvin tries to stand, but his feet are shackled. "You should have been able to control him better."

Now we're getting somewhere. Melvin has revealed that the feds were working with Orlando.

"What are you talking about?" I say, hoping to explore the subject.

"Get a clue, lady. What do you think?" Melvin says.

Josh cuts us off and zeroes in on his reason for the meeting. "Did Max Lombardo help you arrange Orlando's escape?" he says.

"I want to talk to a lawyer," Melvin says.

Melvin has uttered the magic word: *lawyer*. He's invoked his right to counsel, which means that I have to leave. I'd rather stay and listen, but I can't be a party to a Miranda violation. I stand and push in my chair. Josh doesn't move a muscle.

Alone in the hallway, I can hear bits of their conversation as they go back and forth. Melvin: "Check . . . facts . . . don't try to pin this . . . me." Josh: "I'm . . . playing . . . you'll . . . federal time."

After a few minutes, Josh leaves the room and joins me in the hallway. Marshals come and take Melvin back to the lockup.

"I've charged him with obstruction," Josh says.

Obstruction of justice is an all-encompassing offense, used when officers are frustrated because they can't get someone on a substantive charge. Like Martha Stewart or Barry Bonds.

"What is the extent of your relationship with the Jones family?" I say.

He looks around to make sure no one is in the area and speaks quietly. "What do you mean?"

"You know exactly what I mean. It seems like you have a history with both Orlando and Melvin."

"Keep your voice down," he says. "Melvin has been on our radar for a while."

Josh sees my surprise and starts to walk away, down the hallway. I follow close behind.

"Why have you been looking at Melvin?"

He leads me into an office and closes the door. We stand face-to-face.

"This is about the Big Dig," he says.

"But the investigation was closed out last year," I say.

"Max shut down the local part of the case. The federal investigation is still open."

"If Tim was working as your informant, and you were trying to squeeze Melvin for information, then who was the ultimate target?"

"Your boss."

He stops, tries to read my reaction. At this point, I don't want to acknowledge what I'm feeling—shock and skepticism.

"You think that Max was on the take?"

"Melvin was slated to testify in the grand jury."

"What was he going to say?"

Josh shrugs. "He refused to give a proffer. He said that he'd only talk directly to the grand jurors. We think he was going to testify that he paid off Max."

I try to picture Max and Melvin in cahoots, meeting up in the back booth of a bar, drinking and exchanging money.

"Melvin bribed Max?"

"Yes—and so did a lot of others."

This is about more than the Big Dig. "Who else?"

"Dozens of people who wanted to get their cases dismissed. Tommy Glenn and Paul Priestly, to name two."

I remember both cases. The first was a nasty domestic. The charges were dropped, the defendant was released from jail, and he went home and almost killed his girlfriend—broke her jaw and took out one of her eyes. The other was a drunk-driving case that was broomed. The next day the guy got behind the wheel of a Subaru and plowed over a troop of Cub Scouts in a crosswalk.

"How many were there?"

"A lot. Some people paid to avoid prosecution, others wanted to get their kids jobs. He was running a full-service operation."

I'm not sure what to believe. The FBI's public corruption unit isn't exactly batting a thousand, the poorly investigated and prosecuted case against Senator Ted Stevens being one of the most glaring examples.

"You feds get it wrong all the time."

"Not me, not this time."

Josh and I take the elevator down to the garage. He drives through Chinatown, past Kneeland Seafood, where Tim and I used to go after hours for peking duck and "cold tea," which was code for beer. A couple stumbles out of the restaurant, laughing, holding on to each other. I choke back the memory of late-night dinners with Tim. The flirting and the romance leading up to lust and passion. We drifted apart sexually but never emotionally and never for long, always picking up where we left off. I thought we'd end up with each other, up until the night he died.

"What do you want from me?" I say.

"You asked if you could step in where Tim left off. I want to take you up on your offer."

"You're asking me to help you take down my boss?"

He nods. "That's what Tim was doing."

"What if I don't believe he's dirty?"

"Then you can help prove his innocence."

"I've known Max a long time—he's all about power. He's not in it for money."

"Maybe he didn't start out that way. They never do. But once they get in office, they change. I've seen it time and time again. They think they're invincible and entitled, a lethal combination."

"Do you think Max had something to do with Tim's murder?"

"I hope not."

"What exactly are you asking me to do?"

Josh pulls up in front of my apartment building, and turns off the headlights and cuts the engine.

"I want you to wear a wire. If Max hasn't done anything wrong, then you can walk away and no one has to know. If he's guilty, then he has to be held accountable."

Tim may have been an informant against Max, but I'm not ready to turn on him.

"Can it wait until I'm done with my trial?"

"We think Max has been talking to Melvin about your case, and there's a good chance that they tried to help Orlando escape. We want you to be prepared, in case he approaches you, asks you about it, or tells you to do something."

Josh takes out a large circle pin adorned with red stones posing as rubies and hands it to me.

I inspect the cheap-looking jewelry. "This is the listening device?"

"It's both audio and video. I need you to stick it on your lapel whenever you meet with him."

I hold the pin up so it catches a glint of light from the street. No one will ever believe I'd wear something this tacky. They'll make me in a second.

"Look, I don't think I can do this. I've known Max for a decade. He's got issues, but he's always been a loyal friend and a good boss."

"Do him a solid—prove his innocence."

He grabs a file from the backseat and shows me the contents. It's a one-party consent form. After I read it, he hands me a pen. I've asked people to sign all sorts of consent forms over the years. I've persuaded them to allow us to search their cars, their apartments, their body cavities. Now it's my turn to consent— to being a rat against my boss. I hope that Max will prove me right. I don't believe he did what Josh is alleging, but if I'm wrong, he's going to have to face the music.

My hand shakes as I sign the form. "Now what?" I say.

"I'll be in touch. In the meantime, do your job, go on with your trial. Keep up your normal routine."

"I don't have a normal routine."

"Don't let anyone know what's going on."

I unlock the car door. "Don't worry. I'm not going to advertise that I'm spying on my boss."

Once inside the lobby of my building, I examine the faux-ruby recorder and then slip it in my pocket. I'll do what Josh is asking, I don't really have a choice. I'll just have to hope for the best. I gave my word that I won't tell anyone that Max is a target—and I won't. But I never promised to stay quiet about Melvin. Walking towards the elevator, I take out my phone and call Carl Ostroff.

Chapter Forty-one

I t's Friday afternoon, and I'm down to my last witness. My trials always start with the most emotionally compelling witnesses and end with the most disturbing visuals. In this case, the medical examiner will give me a chance to display Jasmine Reed's autopsy photos. I want the jurors to spend their weekend with images of Jasmine sprawled out on that cold slab.

"The Commonwealth calls Dr. Lisa Frongello," I say.

While Sal goes into the hallway to summons the ME, I turn to Winnie and nod. She knows that this is the signal that it's time to escort Jackie, Tiffany, and Adele out of the courtroom. I want to shield them from what is about to happen.

As soon as they're gone, I rip the brown paper wrapping from a twenty-four-by-thirty-six photograph that is mounted onto a foam board. I position the picture on a rickety wooden easel. It's horrific. A full-body shot of Jasmine, eyes open, a piece of her head missing, a portion of her brain exposed. The Y-shaped incision in her naked torso is partially open. Half of the jurors look at the floor, repulsed, and the rest stare at the photo, riveted.

"Objection," Blum says.

"Overruled," Judge Volpe says. "We've gone over this in our motions in limine. You know my position."

After Dr. Frongello is sworn in and introduced, I take out my laser pointer, but before I get a chance to ask my first question, I hear a loud gagging sound coming from the front row of the jury box. Juror number three drops her head, so all I can see is the top of her bouffant hairdo. Then she takes out her pink patent leather purse, unzips it, and vomits. At least she was paying attention.

She looks up and glares at me. "I told you all that this was more than I could take."

Judge Volpe calls a recess, and the courtroom empties, giving maintenance time to come in to spray air freshener. Luckily, juror number three had good aim, and there's not a lot to clean up. When she comes out of the bathroom, she joins us at sidebar. Judge Volpe thanks her for her service and promptly dismisses her. We're running low on bodies. There's only two alternates remaining, but the trial is winding down, so I think we'll be okay.

Court reconvenes, and Dr. Frongello resumes her testimony. I proceed as though nothing out of the ordinary just transpired, the only notable differences being now there are two vacant seats in the jury box and the autopsy photograph is gone.

"Dr. Frongello, did you conduct Jasmine Reed's autopsy?"

"I did."

"What did you determine to be the cause of death?"

"She died of a gunshot wound to the head."

I don't want to risk another medical incident, so I won't show the rest of the pictures.

"Were there any defensive wounds?"

"No."

"Did you test her system for drugs or alcohol?"

"I did a toxicology screening, yes."

"And what were your findings?"

"There was no evidence of drugs or alcohol."

"Thank you. That's all I have."

I return to the prosecutor's table.

"Cross-examination, Mr. Blum?" Judge Volpe says.

"One question." Blum doesn't even bother to stand. "Did you witness the murder of Jasmine Reed?"

"No, I did not."

At least Blum is consistent.

"Anything else, Ms. Endicott?" Judge Volpe says.

"No." I take a breath and turn to face the jurors, looking each one in the eyes. "The Commonwealth rests."

"This is a good time to break," Judge Volpe says, getting off the bench.

When I head toward the gallery, I notice a distinguished older man in the pews. He's sandwiched between a North Street Posse member and Harold, sitting ramrod straight, clutching his leather briefcase to his chest, as though he's worried someone might steal it. He's wearing a navy suit and the burgundy Charvet tie I gave him last year, on Father's Day.

"You bear a striking resemblance to one another," Harold says.

"Daddy, this is Harold."

Harold extends his hand. "Pleasure to make your acquaintance."

My father accepts the handshake and nods but doesn't speak. I lead him into the hallway.

"You made your juror regurgitate her lunch," he says. "I'm not a legal scholar, but I would imagine that is not a positive development."

"It wasn't that big a deal."

"Maybe not in your world, but most people would find it disturbing."

I want to cut this off before goes any further and distracts me from the trial.

"Why are you here, Daddy?"

"I saw that you got banged up pretty badly." He faces me and puts his hands on my shoulders as though he's going to shake some sense into me. "We're all worried about you, muffin."

I shrug him off. "I'm fine."

"You might want to have your head examined," he says, without apparent irony.

"Thanks for coming to see me, but you can save the speech. I'm not quitting my job. We can talk about this another time, but right now, I have to prepare my jury instructions and closing argument."

"I can't watch my daughter being assaulted by a murderer on MSNBC."

My father was watching MSNBC? Talk about burying the headline. Once, in a moment of weakness, and after a few gin and tonics, he admitted to me that he'd voted for Obama over McCain. He confessed that he thought it would be good for the country, making me swear never to tell my mother or my brother. It became our secret and we never spoke of it again.

"You have to leave this job," he says. "I'm not going to support it any longer."

"You've never supported it."

"I mean literally, financially."

"You're cutting me off?"

"You're going to have to make a choice, your job or your lifestyle. You won't be able to afford both."

I take a step back and look at him. "You're serious?"

"I believe it's called tough love."

We both hear the clattering of chains and a man's voice, muttering and swearing. *Motherfucker. Fuck you. Asshole.* Orlando, shackled and cuffed, is surrounded by guards. He's sporting a black eye and a cut on his forehead. His leg-irons clink as he shuffles toward me.

"There she is, that bitch lawyer who's persecuting me!" Orlando yells, his voice echoing up and down the hallway so my father can hear every word twice.

Orlando passes by, close enough to wrap his chains around my neck and strangle me. My father is stunned. So am I.

"I'll leave you to your friends." He turns and walks away. "Let me know when you change your mind."

I'm relieved when my father gets on the elevator and the doors close. I'll figure out the money thing later.

Kevin rounds the corner. "You might want to check your phone every now and then," he says.

"I've been kind of busy. Where did they find him?"

"He broke into someone's beach house in Hull."

"You got a tip?"

"Believe it or not, the feds found him."

Sal calls me back into the courtroom, and Blum comes up a couple of minutes later. When Judge Volpe exits his chambers and takes the bench, Sal remains by his side.

"You want us to uncuff him?" Sal says.

"No," Judge Volpe says. "Mr. Jones, I am removing your default. You will continue to be held without bail. Are you going to be able to comport yourself in a respectful manner during the remainder of this trial?"

"Mr. Jones informs me that he will behave," Blum says.

"I want to hear it from you directly, Mr. Jones."

"I'm sorry, Judge." Orlando sounds almost like he means it. "I apologize for saying this, but I think I'm a scapegoat. I didn't do any of those things they're accusing me of. I didn't know what else to do but run."

"That's what the jury is here to decide. You're going to have to control yourself. We'll proceed with the trial on Monday. Do you plan to present any evidence, Mr. Blum?"

"Yes, we have an alibi witness."

This is a total blind side.

"Objection! I haven't been given notice of alibi. I'm not prepared to cross-examine someone."

"I informed Mr. Mooney weeks ago," Blum says.

"There's nothing in the file, no letter, no discovery notice."

"I told him in person. He said there was no need to put it in writing."

Tim wasn't a stickler for documentation, and unlike most of the defense attorneys I deal with, Blum isn't a bald-faced liar. He exaggerates every now and then, but who doesn't? It's possible that Blum told Tim about the alibi, and if he did, that knowledge is imputed to me. I'm screwed.

"I'm going to have to take you at your word, Counselor," Judge Volpe says. "I can't deny Mr. Jones an opportunity to present his defense. The Appeals Court would reverse me in a second, and we'd be back here in a year, relitigating this case, which is the last thing any of us wants."

"Agreed," I say.

"You have until Monday to prepare, Ms. Endicott. Have a pleasant weekend."

Chapter Forty-two

Carl Ostroff stops me on the plaza as I exit the courthouse for the night. I ask Sandra to give us a minute, and she stands off to the side within eyesight but out of earshot.

"Thanks for the heads-up on Melvin," Carl says. "I was the only reporter in the federal courthouse when he was arraigned."

"I make good on my promises. That makes us square."

I start to walk toward the stairs, Carl in tow, Sandra only a few steps behind.

"Why is Melvin charged with obstruction?"

I shrug and keep going. "You'll have to ask Josh McNamara."

Carl persists. "If Melvin was part of Orlando's escape plan, he should have been charged with aiding and abetting or harboring a fugitive."

"Take it up with the feds."

"I think the FBI is after something else, a bigger fish. Or a wider tunnel, as the case may be."

Carl has shown his cards; he knows that Max is under investigation. He needs two sources in order to report on it, and I'm not going to be one of them. I roll my eyes, feigning disbelief, trying to downplay the significance of the disclosure.

Unsure of what to say, I echo what Josh said to me when I

asked him about it. "The Big Dig investigation was closed out a long time ago."

"Max never explained his decision to end the inquest. He hid behind the curtain of grand jury secrecy."

"That's not true. He issued a statement."

"His flack sent out a halfhearted one-paragraph press release. 'We followed the facts and applied the law and found there wasn't ample proof to issue indictments, blah, blah, blah,' " Carl says. "Max didn't hold a press conference or make himself available for interviews. Ducking out on reporters is definitely not Max's MO."

I don't want to let Carl accuse my boss of impropriety without speaking up on his behalf, but I'm not going to put my reputation on the line by lying for him.

"Legal analysts were divided on what the office should have done, but everyone agreed that it was a close call. I didn't hear you complaining at the time," I say.

"I thought he was being overly cautious, political. But in retrospect, it seems like there was more to it."

"I wasn't involved in the investigation. I don't know the specifics."

We stand on the sidewalk. Sandra is nearby. I look at Carl but remain silent.

"Don't play Mickey the Dunce with me," he says.

I'm growing uncomfortable, but my curiosity hasn't dissipated. Not wanting Carl to read my apprehension, I smile and wave at a colleague who is walking by.

Carl lowers his voice. "Melvin owned Zelco. I hear that he was a target—they considered charging him with manslaughter. And, coincidentally, around the same time, he donated big to Max's campaign."

We cross Cambridge Street, dodging a car that is making an illegal U-turn, and I stop at the sidewalk near my office.

"Every businessman in the city maxed out and ponied up the

$500. The savvy ones hedged their bets and gave to all three candidates."

"Melvin went above and beyond, hosted a bunch of fund-raisers, raked in a couple of hundred grand, and gave it Max."

"You'll have to take it up with his campaign manager. All I know is that Max doesn't accept money from employees. And he chose Tim and me to investigate and prosecute the Jones family. He could have tanked their cases outright or assigned them to newbies, but he didn't. He gave them to his most experienced incorruptible lawyers."

I look at Sandra, signaling that I'm done with Carl, and we head inside Bulfinch. I'm surprised to find Owen and his daughter in my office, sitting in front of my desk, waiting for me. Sandra takes up her post in the hallway.

"You remember Patsy," Owen says.

"Sure! Hi, sweetie." I take off my coat and give her a hug. "Happy belated birthday."

"We had a skating party. You were invited," she says, "but Daddy said you had to work."

"Patsy heard you're having a hard time and wanted to give you something," Owens says.

Patsy reaches into her pocket and pulls out a clunky red, white, and blue charm bracelet.

"It's a good-luck charm. It helped me win the school spelling bee last month," she says.

"Impressive," I say. "Thank you."

I hold out my arm, and Patsy clasps the bracelet around my wrist.

"We want you to know that we're in your corner," Owen says. "We've only loaned it outside the family once before."

"To Uncle Tim, when he got married," Patsy says.

I had forgotten that Patsy was a flower girl at Tim and Julia's wedding. She was adorable, tripping on her dress as she walked down the aisle tossing clumps of rose petals.

"Honey, why don't you go back down and say hi to Uncle Max," Owen says.

She steps out into the hallway. Owen stays behind.

"I saw you outside, talking to Carl Ostroff. He looked like he was pumping you for information."

"You know Carl," I say. "He loves to stir the pot."

"He's been running around, spreading rumors about Max."

"I heard."

"Max has been good to you, to all of us. I hope you have his back."

Owen puts up a good front, but he must have doubts too. I fiddle with the bracelet, a symbol of Owen's friendship and an exemplar of the type of jewelry I'll be able to afford from now on, since my father cut off my cash supply.

"Actually, while we're on the subject of loyalty," I say, "I'd like to talk about my salary."

"Let's schedule a meeting after your trial is over."

He stands, hoping to make a quick exit. I'm not going to let him off the hook this easily.

"I haven't had a raise in years. I make less than all the guys on my team, even though I'm their supervisor. Men in this office are making more than their female superiors."

Owen opens the door.

"A record of gender inequality won't bode well for Max, come election time," I say.

He closes the door and sits back down. "How much are you asking for?"

I hesitate, unsure what to say.

"You don't even know how much you make, do you?" Owen says.

"I make sixty thousand-ish."

"You make seventy-two-five."

"You probably make twice that."

"Aren't you like a billionaire?"

"My financial status isn't relevant. Need-based salaries went out in the 1950s. Earnings are supposed to be value based, merit based, both of which qualify me for a bump."

"You have no idea what I have to contend with. The legislature doesn't give us half of what we need to run this office."

"When Patsy grows up, do you want her to make less than her male colleagues?"

"I'll take a look at the financials," he says, regretting that he came in to talk with me.

Chapter Forty-three

In my office, I prepare for cross-examination on the off chance that Orlando takes the stand. After a couple hours, I take a break and go downstairs to see if I can catch Max before he heads home for the weekend. That way, I won't have to spend the next two days stressing about how to approach him. I stick on my fake ruby pin, pick up the phone, and call Josh.

"I'm ready to talk to Max. What exactly do you want me to say?"

"Wing it—see if you can get him to talk about Melvin."

"Max isn't stupid. He'll figure out that something is up."

"Be casual, don't push too hard. Try to introduce the topic. Talk about Orlando, your trial, see where it goes."

I start toward the stairs but remember that the stairwell locks from the inside and my badge won't work on Max's floor. I take the elevator and get off on the executive floor. Owen buzzes me in and follows me into Max's office, where we find him behind his desk, finishing a beer.

"You look like you could use a drink," Max says. "Let's all head over to the Red Hat. It'll be like old times."

Back in the day, Max, Tim, Owen, and I would go out after work on Friday nights. Various others would join us, but we were the constants, and we all enjoyed the ritual. Tim was still single, Owen was still drinking, and Max's alcoholism hadn't yet fully blossomed. We'd walk across the street to the Kinsale and trade war stories from the past week. These days, going to bars with Max is a chore. His drinking got worse after he was elected into office, and it has been escalating in the past year.

"Stevie's got a hockey tournament," Owen says, putting on his coat and grabbing his briefcase. "He made bantam. Can't miss it. Call if you need anything."

"I've still got a lot of work to do on my closing," I say after Owen is gone.

"Come on—I'm buying. Your old man told me you're a little short on cash these days."

It's not like my father to talk about family business, least of all money, with an outsider.

"My father called you?"

"Actually, I called him. I'm thinking about running for mayor, and I formed an exploratory committee. I asked if he'd be my finance chair."

"What did he say?"

"He said that he'd love to help, but only under one condition."

"You switch to Republican?"

He laughs. "I'd never survive as a Republican in this city. Besides, it's not my party affiliation that concerns him."

"Then what is it?"

"He wants me to fire you."

I knew my father wouldn't give up on his mission to get me out of this office, but I didn't think he'd recruit Max.

"What did you say?"

"I told him you're my strongest player and I'm not letting you go. But if I'm elected mayor, I'll get you out of here by taking you with me to City Hall."

"Clever. That'll light a fire under him."

"It did. He agreed to host a fund-raiser at the Liberty Hotel next month," he says, putting on his coat. "Come on—one drink."

"Just one," I say.

When we get outside Bulfinch, Carl is doing a live shot. We stand in the background and eavesdrop.

"A spokesman for the district attorney declined comment, but insiders have confirmed that Melvin Jones has close ties to this administration, both financially and politically. Jones has been a loyal donor and field organizer for the past three years. Also, reliable sources informed us that there is a link between Melvin Jones and his son's escape from the hospital. Some speculate that this will tie back to the district attorney."

Max looks at me. "This is bad."

I nod.

"Where did he get that bullshit?"

"I don't know," I say. "Maybe Josh McNamara."

"Fuck those feebs."

I glance over at Carl, trying to hide my discomfort. Max knows a lot of people, and it wouldn't surprise me if someone told him they saw me with Josh over at the federal courthouse last night. I decide to say something about it in the bar.

It takes us about an hour to walk the few blocks to the Red Hat. Max stops every few feet to shake hands, answer questions about Tim's murder, and accept condolences. Both Sandra and Max's police detail, Detective Mark Jackson, walk a short distance behind us.

When we finally arrive, we take seats in a back booth. Sandra and Mark sit at the bar, where they can keep an eye on us as well as the front door. They're both armed and ready to pounce— they'd make a cute couple. It looks like Sandra thinks so too. She's flipping back her ombré hair extensions in between sips of Diet Coke, laughing enthusiastically at whatever Mark says.

Max orders a bourbon, and I ask for a Rolling Rock. The red wine here is always either sour or watered down.

Max waits until we're alone before speaking. "This isn't the first time a reporter has gone after me, but it's always been case related. This time it feels personal. Carl Ostroff is out for blood," he says.

"He cornered me out on the street tonight." I get this out up front to cover my bases in case Owen has already told him that he saw us talking. "He asked about a connection between you and Melvin Jones."

I lean in to be sure my fake ruby camera captures his response. Max downs his drink and signals the waitress for another round. I've barely had a sip from my beer bottle.

"Ostroff created those rumors just so he could have something to report," Max says. "What did you say to him?"

"I told him the truth."

"Which is?"

"I don't know anything about it."

"Here's everything you need to know—there's absolutely nothing to his bullshit."

I shift in my seat and watch beads of sweat drip down the beer bottle and pool on the table.

"Does that mean what he's saying isn't true?"

"How can you even ask me that?"

I look away, ashamed of myself, but when I look back at Max, for a second, it seems like he's talking directly into the microphone on my jacket. The waitress brings over his second drink, and he downs it like medicine, in three quick gulps.

"Abby, we've known each other for over a decade. I've trusted you with the most sensitive cases in the office. Why the hell are you talking to the FBI behind my back?"

"That's the reason I stopped down to see you." I try not to seem too eager. "Josh had Melvin in custody. He brought me over to the courthouse to talk to him."

"What did he say?"

"He invoked."

Max tries to catch the waitress's eye.

"What's the thinking? What's Melvin hiding?" he says.

"Money."

"That's not a secret. Melvin gives big every election cycle, that's his game: the mayor, the council, the reps."

"And to you."

I nurse my beer. Max starts in on his third drink.

"They focused on what Melvin expects in return for his donation." I say.

"He wants access, and that's what he gets. I take his calls and listen to his opinion on high-profile cases, but that's as far as it goes."

"He didn't call you when Orlando was charged with murder?"

"No, I had no idea."

Feeling jittery, I clasp my hands in my lap and cut to the chase. "What about the Big Dig?"

"He never approached me about that, either."

"I think they've impaneled a federal grand jury to look into your dealings with him."

Max puts down his drink and looks at me. "Did they subpoena you to testify?"

"Not yet, but they might."

"Do you think I'm on the take?"

"Honestly, I don't know what to think." I take a breath and exhale. "Did you have something to do with Tim's murder?"

I know this will upset him. I don't expect him to confess, but I want to send a message. The idea of Max involved in bribery or extortion is no longer out of the realm of possibility, at least not to me.

"Jesus, I would never, ever orchestrate the murder of one of my own." He puts his head in his hands and looks like he's about to cry. "You know how things work. If word starts to get out that I'm under suspicion, I'll never recover. My reputation will be destroyed, my career will be over."

My phone vibrates, and I'm happy for the interruption. I check the screen.

"It's Blum, probably calling about the alibi witness. I have to take it."

I move to the back of the bar. Sandra swivels her bar stool so she can keep an eye on me.

"Orlando knows his back is up against the wall," Blum says.

"Meaning what?" I say.

"He wants to plead guilty."

I feel like I should pinch myself—this sounds too good to be real. It's noisy in the bar—maybe I didn't hear right.

"Orlando is agreeing to plea to murder and take a life sentence?"

"He won't plea to murder one, but he'll agree to a murder two."

If Orlando pleads guilty to second-degree murder, he'll get a life sentence, but he'll be parole eligible in fifteen years. That'd be a good resolution, but not a great one. The only way to guarantee life without any possibility of parole is with a first-degree murder conviction. Still, I don't want to dismiss it out of hand.

I look over at Max, who is focused on his next bourbon, swishing it around in his glass.

"I need a little time," I say.

"I figured you'd have to run it up the flagpole."

"I'm not sure where Max is right now. It'll probably take me a while to find him. I'll call you as soon as I do."

I hang up and return to our booth.

"Anything important?" Max says.

"No," I say.

Chapter Forty-four

Sandra double-parks in front of the Metropolis, a diner in the South End, a high-rent, high-crime Boston neighborhood. Kevin is visible through the window, seated in a booth, scanning his phone and drinking coffee.

"Kevin will give me a ride back to the office. I'll see you there in about an hour," I say, jumping out of the car.

Sandra watches me go inside and waits until I reach the booth and Kevin gives her the nod before pulling away.

I take off my coat and sit. "Orlando wants to plea to second."

"Wow, that's out of left field. What do you think?"

Our multipierced, magenta-haired waitress pours me a cup of coffee and refills Kevin's. I ask for a chocolate croissant. Kevin orders scrambled eggs and turkey bacon.

"I want him to rot in prison," I say.

"That's not nice," the waitress says before moving on to the next table.

"I wouldn't be so quick to turn down an offer on a murder plea," Kevin says.

"Second degree isn't enough. I want to hook him on a first."

"It's a crapshoot. You never know what a jury is going to do."

"I think they're going to do the right thing—convict his ass for first-degree murder and put him away for life."

"You know how it goes—there could be one nutcase who hangs the jury and makes us do it all over again. Or worse, they could acquit. There's something to be said for having that bird in the hand."

When the waitress delivers our food, we both dig in. I bite into the croissant, and powdered sugar snows all over my new black cardigan. Wiping at it with a paper napkin only makes it worse.

"I say we take the plea," Kevin says.

"I think we should turn it down. He's a scary guy, and I don't ever want to see him back out on the street."

"God forbid we lose, but if we do, people will think you rejected the plea because you've got an axe to grind."

"This isn't about protecting my image."

"What did Max say when you told him?"

I take a sip of coffee and then another. "I didn't tell him."

"I'm no expert in office politics, but I know something about chain of command. You don't have the authority to make a binding decision on a murder plea."

"I don't think Max can be objective."

"You have to ask someone. Or, at the very least, tell them that he approached you with an offer."

"I'm going to run it by Owen, but I want to get your blessing first."

I finish my pastry. Kevin scoops up a spoonful of eggs.

"I'd feel better about it if we knew who their alibi witness is," he says.

"I'm not sure Blum even has an alibi witness."

"You think he's bluffing?"

"Ever since Volpe ordered him to disclose the name and address of his so-called witness, he's been dragging his feet and avoiding me."

Kevin calls Nestor and asks him to go by Blum's office to lean on him and see what he can find out. Kevin picks up the tab, and we head over to Bulfinch, where Sandra is waiting. They've become quite a tag team.

After a few minutes of trying to figure out who the alibi witness could be, I come up empty. My phone rings, and I'm surprised to see that it's Owen calling from an inside line. It's a sunny Sunday afternoon, a time when he is usually running around a field with his kids.

He says he has an update on Tim's murder and asks me to come down to his office. Perfect timing—he's saved me the trouble of hunting him down to talk about the plea offer. I hope he's in a good mood, but in case he's not, I reach into my bottom desk drawer and dig under some papers, where I find Patsy's bracelet. Hopefully, it'll remind him of our friendship and grease the skids. I hook the bracelet around my wrist and push the sleeves of my sweater up to my elbows.

Owen is at his desk, sipping from a handmade "My Dad Rocks" coffee mug. The cup is misshapen and chipped, but he carries it around like a trophy. Owen's devotion to his kids and the pleasure that he derives from being a parent almost makes me want to have a couple of my own. Almost.

"How's the trial going?" he says.

"Blum is pulling some last-minute stunts."

He looks at the bracelet and smiles.

"Middlesex is no longer running Tim's murder investigation," he says.

I take a seat in an armchair with the Suffolk Law School seal laser-engraved on its crown.

"Who's handling it?" I say.

"The FBI is doing the investigation, and the U.S. attorney's office is taking over the prosecution."

Josh is sneaky, but I would have expected him to let me know that there's been an official shift in the handling of the case.

"Why would Middlesex hand it off so easily? It's the most significant trial they'll ever have."

"The feds are looking to impose the death penalty. You can't argue with lethal injection."

The U.S. attorney takes a case away from locals only when it's a guaranteed slam dunk, especially when it's this high profile.

"They must have a target," I say.

"They're holding it close to the vest, but I hear they're closing in on Orlando and Darrius."

Owen looks over my shoulder, and I turn to follow his gaze. Max is in the doorway, arm raised, waving a piece of paper.

"What the fuck is this?" He jams the paper in my face. "Someone came by the house this morning and left it with my wife."

I read the document—it's a subpoena. "You're Blum's alibi witness?"

"Apparently."

"How could you possibly help their case?"

"I have no idea."

His face is sweaty, his breathing heavy. It's hard to determine if he's angry, frightened, or intoxicated, but he's making me anxious.

"Did you see Orlando the night that Tim was killed?" I try to tread lightly.

"Don't be a moron—I would have told you if I'd seen him."

"Let's relax. Now's not the time to turn on each other," Owen says. "Can you give Abby anything that might help her prepare?"

"You know what I know. Melvin is a donor. I've been to his house. None of that is a secret." Max retreats slightly and takes out his iPhone. "I'll triple-check my schedule to be sure that I wasn't with Melvin at the same political event that night, but I'm positive I wasn't with Orlando."

"Let's circle back later," Owen says. "Abby, I can help you prepare a motion for an offer of proof and a motion to quash the subpoena. Let's do our best to keep Max off the stand."

Max leaves. I start to follow but remember that I have to tell Owen about Blum's offer.

"Orlando offered to plea to a second."

"That's fantastic." He's more enthusiastic than I had hoped. "We have him on the ropes. This alibi bullshit is posturing. He's trying to get me to fold."

"This isn't Texas Hold 'em. Take the plea. It's a win-win. We get a guaranteed conviction of life."

"A second-degree murder conviction will make him parole eligible when he's thirty-six. He'd still be young enough to pick up where he left off. He could do a lot of damage."

"We'll petition the board when he's up for parole. They won't release him."

"That's fifteen years away—who knows if any of us will still be here. Hooking him on a first is the only way to guarantee that he stays in for life."

Our voices are raised. I close the door so Max, or anyone else who might be in the office, can't hear.

"A piece of him is better than nothing."

"I don't want to give up because they're throwing out this bogus alibi defense."

"Look, Abby, I respect you, and I consider you a good friend." He stops talking, I look at him. "Are you about to pull rank?"

He nods. "Take the plea. It's not a suggestion, it's a directive," he says. "If I didn't know you better, I'd question your motives."

Before this gets uglier and Owen outright accuses me of misconduct, I turn toward the door. "I'll check in with you later," I say.

"Take the plea. It's a gift." Owen looks down at the bracelet on my wrist. "See? Patsy was right—your luck is changing."

I step into the elevator and then it occurs to me. I can't believe I missed it. The bracelet.

Chapter Forty-five

Sandra drives me to the Equal Exchange Café, a hippie-dippie coffee shop on the outskirts of Boston's North End. Inside, there are a few sleepy-looking tourists and a homeless woman who hits me up for money. I find a couple of bucks in my wallet and hand them to her. She inspects the bills, turns, and directs my attention to the price list on the chalkboard. I reach back into my wallet and give her a five. Organic fair-trade coffee doesn't come cheap.

Josh is sitting at one of the few tables, drinking tea. I walk past the counter, craving an espresso and a scone, but this isn't a social call, and I don't plan to be here long.

I unbutton my coat but don't take it off, and launch into him.

"You tell me to record Max, and then you tell Owen to plant a listening device on me. Am I a double agent or something?"

"We don't have double agents," he says. "That's CIA."

He tears open a packet of honey, and it squirts all over the cuff of his shirt.

"You feds are all the same."

I remove the charm bracelet from my coat pocket and slam it down on the table. He picks it up, looks around to be sure no one is watching, and slips it in his briefcase.

"I told them in D.C. that you'd figure it out," he says. "They thought it was worth a try."

"Main Justice is involved?"

He dabs water on his sticky shirt cuff and then gives up and sips his tea.

"This is a big one. They want to swoop in and take credit when it's done."

"Who else did you stick a bug on? My doorman? My boyfriend? My hair stylist?"

"If you don't have anything to hide, then what's the problem?"

"It's an abuse of power."

"Don't take it personally. We're looking at anyone with possible motive."

"Enlighten me. What's my motive? Why would I want to kill Tim?"

"One could argue that you were fighting to keep the relationship going. And he turned you down."

I laugh in disbelief. "So you're saying that Julia talked to you, and she thinks I killed Tim? Come on."

I wonder if Julia was wired up when I spoke with her at Doyle's. I try to remember if she was wearing anything that could have been doubling as a camera, but all I can picture is her prissy lace-collared blouse.

"Unrequited love is a powerful motivator," he says, smirking.

He's hit a nerve, and I try not to react but can't help myself.

"It was requited," I say. "More than you or Julia know."

He puts down his tea. "You had some pretty hefty withdrawals from your savings last month."

"So that makes you think I hired a hit man? Even you can't actually believe that."

"I'd be negligent if I didn't look into it."

Talking about money with anyone, never mind an FBI agent,

is crass, and it makes me uncomfortable, but now is not the time to be discreet about my spending habits.

"I had a lot of expenses in December. My brother got married, and I commissioned a painting for his gift. I think it cost like fifty grand."

"What about the other $15K?"

"The new spring collection came out."

"You spent $15,000 on clothes?"

"Suits, shoes, scarves. Oh, I also got a handbag."

He looks at me, incredulous.

"The bag was a Birkin." I throw this in to bolster my credibility, as if he knows the difference between Birkin and Birkenstock. I write down a name on a napkin. "This is my personal shopper. She's at Barneys—not the one in Boston, the one in New York. She'll vouch for me."

Josh gives me the once-over, trying to price my outfit, stopping to assess my maroon Balenciaga coat. Only the most discerning shopper would recognize the exquisite design and hand stitching. It cost about $4,500. Now that I'm cash poor and my condo fee is overdue, I wonder how much I can get for it if I take it to the high-end consignment shop on Charles Street.

"Our forensic accountant also checked into your November withdrawals."

"I bought some early Christmas gifts."

He reaches into his briefcase and pulls out a clear plastic evidence bag. My missing Mason Pearson hairbrush is inside.

"*You* did the B and E on my apartment?"

"We did a DNA comparison with the hair and fibers found in Tim's car. You were all over the front seat and the dash."

"Do you have any idea how many times I've been inside that car?"

"You intentionally blew the sit-down with Max," he says.

Josh couldn't possibly believe that I was involved in Tim's

murder. He thinks that I know something and I'm holding back to protect Max. He's trying to strong-arm me, get me to flip, so he can work his way up the office food chain. The problem for him is, I don't have information and I'm not holding back.

"I did everything I could to get him to talk. Has it occurred to you that he's not implicating himself because he didn't take bribes, that he's not involved in Tim's murder?"

"Don't go down with the ship, Abby."

"I get it—everyone is a suspect until proven otherwise. I'm telling you the truth, but if you don't believe me, there's nothing I can do about it. But don't try to play me and treat me like some mope. Find someone else to carry out your ridiculous fishing expedition."

"We already have."

I grab my tote and hold it up to taunt him. "See this bag? It's Bottega Veneta, and it cost about $3,000. You'll find it in next month's charges."

Sandra is waiting for me in the car. I'm obsessively private about my personal life, and having a permanent bodyguard, someone who knows my every move, is unsettling, but there's an upside. I never have to drive around in search of a parking space, worry about getting mugged, or worse. And Sandra never asks questions about who I'm meeting or what I'm doing. She waits patiently and quietly, off to the side, allowing me room to conduct my business in private. If only her eye shadow and lip gloss were as subtle as her surveillance techniques.

I slam my door and wrestle with the seat belt, telegraphing that I'm in a foul mood. At this point, Kevin would lecture me about how I should take up cycling or kickboxing to blow off steam. As much as I like working with him, he would want to know every detail of my meeting with Josh, and he'd have plenty to say about it. Sandra lets me stew in silence.

When we return home, there are papers taped to my apartment door. I think about Ezekiel, when he came home to find grand jury minutes stuck to his front door and the fear he must have experienced. Sandra untapes and unfolds the pages and inspects them. She hands them to me, raising her eyebrows.

"Notice to Vacate."

I hope Manny doesn't find out that I forgot to make good on my promise to settle my account. I guess the condo association takes this whole monthly maintenance fee thing pretty seriously.

Chapter Forty-six

Ty is a night owl who, until recently, never got up with me in the morning. Lately he's been waking up before me, cooking breakfast, and making sure that I'm ready to face the day. When I get out of the shower, he's in the kitchen, music is playing, and he's singing along with Bob Marley. *Don't worry about a thing, 'cause every little thing gonna be all right.*

"What are you making?" I say.

"Quinoa-and-coconut pancakes. I'm thinking about going vegan. You in?"

"Sure," I say, thinking about the tubes of beef jerky in my tote.

I have a couple of bites of the pancake, which isn't bad considering it's a disk of protein with a few stray shreds of coconut. I gulp down some freshly squeezed orange juice and grab my tote. Ty hands me the lunch that he prepared—chickpea quiche and chia seed cookies—and accompanies me downstairs, where Sandra is waiting.

She drops me off at the courthouse and goes to park the car. The security line is longer than usual, even for a Monday. It snakes out the door and twists around the corner. I wait at the elevator bank, keeping my eyes trained on the floor, and listen

for the ding of an arriving car. I tend to avoid eye contact with
people in the courthouse, especially when I'm on trial. The rules
dictate that we're not supposed to have any communication
with jurors, verbal or nonverbal.

A pair of black Nike Air sneakers are pointing in my direction, and I sense that their owner is staring at me. Not being
able to resist, I look up quickly. My neck stiffens, and my stomach drops. There he is in the courthouse, Rodney Quirk. I
haven't seen him in a couple of weeks, since I confronted him
out on Cambridge Street. I was hoping that Sandra's presence
had scared him off.

I consider calling out for a court officer, asking him to remove
Rodney, but it's a public building, and he's not doing anything
illegal. I don't want to have to explain our history. It's too con-
voluted to get into right now.

The courtroom is standing room only. Those without seats
will be asked to leave since, contrary to *To Kill a Mockingbird*,
fire regulations require that all aisles be kept clear. Even without
Darrius, the North Street gang has grown; they're occupying
their usual places in the back plus a few seats in the next row. I
walk past the bar and take a seat at my table. I can feel their
eyes drilling a hole in the back of my head. Carl Ostroff quietly
directs the cameraman to capture the image. If I were Carl, I'd
watch my back. These guys tend to be camera shy.

I've rested my case in chief, and now it's Blum's turn to present a defense. I'm eager to learn whether or not Judge Volpe is
going to allow him to put Max on the witness stand.

Sal announces that court is back in session.

Blum stands. "The defense calls Maxwell Lombardo."

People turn and whisper to each other. The press corps is ec-
static. Even the jurors seem to recognize Max's name and the
significance of what is happening.

I'm on my feet. "May we be heard?"

Judge Volpe signals us forward, and we huddle at sidebar.

"This is highly unusual and without precedent. I'm filing a motion to quash." I pass Blum and Judge Volpe the motion that Owen had helped prepare. "There's no compelling reason—in fact, there's no reason at all—to call the sitting district attorney to testify. I ask that he be excluded."

"Were you given notice of alibi as I had ordered on Friday?"

"We learned about the subpoena this weekend," I say, "but as far as I know, there isn't anything relevant that he could possibly offer. We haven't been provided any discovery."

"I don't have anything to give," Blum says. "There are no reports or images. I just plan to ask him some questions."

"I've warned you that I'm not going to allow this courtroom to be turned into a circus. I want an offer of proof. What's the purpose of his testimony?"

"I expect DA Lombardo to provide an alibi for my client."

"You're going to have to be more specific."

"I expect him to say that he saw Orlando Jones on the night of the murder, around the time of the murder, many miles away from where Jasmine Reed and her friends were located."

"Ms. Endicott, what do you say?"

I look down at my cuticles while I gather my thoughts, resisting the urge to bite a jagged piece of dead skin from my index finger.

"This is an absurd, baseless allegation. It's nothing but a thinly veiled attempt to distract the jury and impugn the integrity of the district attorney's office," I say.

"I believe that I can place him in the company of Orlando Jones, within minutes of the murder."

The courtroom door opens, and Josh slips in and squeezes into a seat on the aisle.

"I'll accept your assertion *de bene*. If it doesn't pan out, I'll strike it from the record. We'll take it question by question."

"Your Honor, I respectfully and strenuously object."

"Last time I checked the state and federal constitutions and the rules of procedure, the defendant had a right to call witnesses on his own behalf," Blum says.

"Ms. Endicott, your objection is overruled. Deputy, please summons the district attorney from the corridor."

Owen trails in after Max and looks around for an empty seat. Sal brings over a wooden folding chair for Owen. As he sits, he looks at me, shakes his head, and twists his mouth in disgust. He's furious that I didn't take the plea.

Max walks up to the clerk, who swears him in. I hope to God he's sober. It's ten in the morning, but you never know with him these days.

"Could you identify yourself for the members of the jury," Blum says.

"Maxwell Lombardo. That's L-O-M-B-A-R-D-O." Max is nervous, fidgety. "I am the district attorney for Suffolk County."

Blum sets the pace by asking short, rapid-fire questions.

"You were elected to that office?"

"Yes, for a four-year term."

"You are up for reelection next year?"

"Yes."

"Elections are expensive."

I could object to the form of the question, but I don't want to appear obstructionist.

"Unfortunately, yes, they are."

"Do you know Orlando Jones's father, Melvin Jones?"

"He was a supporter."

"By supporter, you mean donor? He gave money to your campaign?"

"Yes."

"And he was also what's known as a bundler?"

"He was a fund-raiser during the last election cycle."

"How much money did he raise for you?"

"I don't know the exact dollar amount. I'd have to see the records."

"Your Honor, may I approach the witness?"

Judge Volpe nods.

"I am placing before you the records from the Office of Campaign and Political Finance—"

That's as far as I can let this go on. "Objection," I say. "I was informed that there was no discovery in the defendant's possession."

"It's public record," Blum says.

"Overruled."

Blum moves to the witness box and hands over the reports. Max takes out his reading glasses, and there's a slight tremor in his hands.

"It looks like Mr. Jones added about $200,000 to your coffers," Blum says.

"That sounds about right," Max says.

"It also says that Melvin's wife raised about $75,000, his brother, $10,000, and his sister-in-law, $5,000."

I'm not the only lawyer on this case Carl Ostroff has been talking to; he must have been feeding his theory to Blum. I knew he'd turn on me at some point, but it would have been nice if he'd have waited until after the trial was over.

Blum presses on in his mission to taint Max. "That's a lot of money from one family."

"Objection," I say. "Argumentative—"

Max raises his hand to stop me from going further. "I'd like to answer," he says. "It is a lot of money. But if you look at the records in their entirety, instead of cherry-picking what serves your purpose, you will see that it's not unusual. I've raised more than $2 million over the past three years."

"Which brings me to my point: how many people have offered you bribes?"

I should object, but the question is out there, and I want Max to deny it. I don't want the jury to get the impression that I'm covering anything up. Besides, if Max is guilty, he's on his own.

"None."

"You didn't take money from people facing potential criminal charges? From lawyers who want favors, help with their cases?"

His face reddens. "No."

"Are you aware that you're under federal investigation for accepting bribes?"

"I have not been named as a suspect or a target, and I believe the investigation to be politically motivated. The United States attorney and the mayor are close friends, and they both know that many consider me a strong contender in the next mayoral election."

Max is holding his own, but all this talk about money and politics has wounded his credibility with the jury. By extension, it has wounded mine too, which can be fatal to the case. The jurors need to trust their prosecutor.

I rise from my chair. "Can we get to the point?"

Judge Volpe takes over from Blum and cuts to the chase. "Did you see the defendant on the evening of August 8?"

"No."

"Anything else, Mr. Blum?" Judge Volpe says.

"No."

Blum takes a seat. Even though the testimony was completely irrelevant, he managed to do some damage to me and my case.

"Anything from the Commonwealth?" Judge Volpe says.

Max looks at me. I'm tempted to cross-examine him about the timing of the donations, but that would open up a can of worms I'm not prepared to deal with. Josh can follow up on that later.

"You've never been charged with any crime," I say, rising.

"Correct."

"And you are not, in fact, able to provide an alibi for Orlando Jones, as promised by Mr. Blum."

"Correct."

"And this whole line of questioning has been a complete distraction."

"Objection."

"Sustained. We'll let the jury decide if there was evidentiary value in Mr. Lombardo's testimony. Anything else, Ms. Endicott?"

"Nothing further."

Max gets off the stand. On his way out of the courtroom, he glares at Orlando and then at Melvin.

It's time for Blum to either put up or shut up. He has to do something that will give credence to his alibi theory, like a photograph of Max, Melvin, and Orlando together at the time of the murder or an eyewitness to the crime.

Blum stands. "The defense calls Orlando Jones to the stand."

Chapter Forty-seven

Orlando walks to the witness stand, flanked by two guards. There are no empty seats in the gallery, but a few more people from my office come in from the hallway and manage to squeeze into the pews. Owen and Josh are seated on opposite sides of the door. Since Max became a witness, he's been sequestered and not allowed in for the rest of the trial.

The guards remain within arm's reach as Orlando is sworn in and sits in the witness box. Sal positions himself between Orlando and the jury. A new court officer, the largest of the bunch, stands next to Judge Volpe. The jurors lean away from Orlando, toward the exit signs, clutching their notepads and water bottles.

"Did you know Assistant District Attorney Timothy Mooney?" Blum says.

Orlando leans into the microphone and nods. "Yeah, I knew him."

"When did you first meet?"

"A while ago, after I got busted on a gun case, Mooney came to see me in the lockup."

Orlando has done me the favor of impeaching himself with the gun charge, but Blum is too smart to let this play out to my benefit.

"Was ADA Mooney alone when he came to talk to you?"

"No, he was with a guy from the FBI."

"Special Agent Joshua McNamara?"

"That's the one."

"Did Agent McNamara and ADA Mooney offer to help you with your firearms case?"

"They said they could help me, but I'd have to help them."

"What did they want you to do?"

It's encouraging to see that most of the jurors are not looking directly at Orlando; their eyes are on Adele and Jackie, who are seated in the front row.

"They wanted me to talk to my father."

"About what?"

"The FBI guy, McNamara, said that he thought the DA was dirty. That he was taking bribes."

"Did Agent McNamara tell you why he thought this?"

"Objection," I say. "Hearsay."

"Overruled."

"He said that some cases were getting dismissed for no reason."

"And they thought that your father was one of the people who had offered a bribe to District Attorney Lombardo?"

"Objection. Leading."

"Overruled."

Orlando looks at me. "They thought my father gave money to the DA so he wouldn't get charged in the Big Dig thing."

"So they wanted your father to cooperate and tell them what happened, that he had paid a bribe."

"They said that if my father helped them, and told the truth, then they wouldn't charge him. And they said they would help me with my gun case."

"Did you do what they asked?"

"Sure, I mean, what the fuck . . . excuse me . . . I mean, gun cases get you a year mandatory. I didn't want to do a year if I didn't have to."

I look back at Kevin and Owen, who are both leaning in, listening. Orlando is convincing.

"Do you know if they wanted your father to do anything, besides subject himself to an interview?" Blum says.

"They wanted him to testify in the grand jury."

"What happened?"

"I introduced them, like I said I would."

"And they let you out of jail."

"Yeah."

"Did your father cooperate?"

"You'll have to ask him."

"I'd like to, but he has a Fifth Amendment right against self-incrimination, which he will no doubt exercise."

The jurors are looking at him, writing things down, which is not a good sign. It means they think he's saying something they want to remember.

"Objection," I say.

"Sustained," Judge Volpe says. "Move on, Counselor."

"Sir, did you kill Jasmine Reed?"

"I was nowhere near that place when the shooting went down. I'm innocent."

"Why do you think you've been charged with a crime you didn't commit?"

"Objection. Calls for speculation."

"You may answer," Judge Volpe says.

"Payback," Orlando says. "The DA, Lombardo, is dirty. The whole office is bad if you ask me. Even this prosecutor, Endicott, she's had it in for me for years."

I take a sip of water, anxious to know what he's going to say and how I'm going to stop him.

"Because of an accident that happened when I was in middle school," Orlando says, looking at me.

"There was an incident when you were a juvenile?" Blum says.

I jump up. "Your Honor, please. This is irrelevant and inflammatory."

"Sit down. Your objection is overruled."

Orlando tries to look contrite. "Her friend got hit by a car, and she blamed it on me. Now she's out to get me. Aren't DAs supposed to be fair? How can she be fair?"

"Objection! No foundation, irrelevant, prejudicial."

Judge Volpe gestures me to sit. "You elected to venture into the deep end, Ms. Endicott. I warned you."

"Your Honor, may we approach sidebar?"

I start to move toward the judge's bench but he stops me.

"No, you may not. Ask your next question, Mr. Blum."

"But there's no evidence of misconduct."

"Your objection is overruled. We'll let the jury decide issues of credibility and misconduct."

I try to establish eye contact with some of the jurors, but no one wants to look at me.

"Your Honor, I see that end of the day is near. This might be an opportune time to recess," Blum says.

"It's only 4:15, and since we could keep going until 4:30, I'd like to start my cross-examination," I say.

I don't want to end the day with Orlando scoring all the points, but Judge Volpe is angry that I didn't recuse myself from the case. He bench-slaps me by adjourning for the day.

I trudge back to Bulfinch and find Owen, and we go into Max's office to debrief.

"Blum is leaving people with the impression that I'm on the take," Max says, between sips of scotch. "That I'm persecuting an innocent man."

"It's my fault," I say. "I never should have taken this case. I let my own ego cloud my judgment, and now we're all going to pay for it."

"You're not going to get an argument from me," Max says. "This case should have gone to Chris."

"It should have pled out," Owen says. "I told you to take the deal."

I reach for Max's bottle, pour myself two fingers of scotch, and take a long gulp. Orlando has a good shot at being acquitted, something I've risked my career and my life to avoid. Worse, it's on me—I'm responsible for the case, and I have no one to blame but myself.

"We have to do something," Max says.

"What do you propose?" I say.

"Subpoena Melvin. He's the only person who can corroborate my testimony," Max says.

"I'd love to, but he'll take the Fifth."

"Then force him to testify."

"You want me to immunize Melvin Jones?" I like the idea of forcing him to answer questions but am worried that it could backfire.

Always cautious, Owen says, "Let's keep our eye on the ultimate prize. What if he's involved in Tim's murder? We'll never be able to charge him."

"We know Melvin didn't kill Jasmine, so we're not giving up anything," Max says.

"What about your own exposure, Max?" Owen says.

"I have nothing to hide."

"I think it's a bad idea," Owen says.

In spite of Owen's misgivings, Max's suggestion and acquiescence in the plan bolsters my confidence in his innocence and Orlando's guilt. I return to my office and phone Kevin to make sure he's on board. After I write up a trial subpoena for Melvin, I call Josh to find out where Melvin is being held.

"Max was worked up," I say. "I don't think he'd be so adamant about calling Melvin to the stand if he had something to hide."

"We'll see."

"I need to get him on the transport list so he's in court tomorrow."

"He's not in federal custody anymore. He posted bail on our obstruction case this morning."

"Where is he?"

"Back home in Weston."

I spend the rest of the night working on an emergency immunity petition, e-mailing letters to all the district attorney's offices and the attorney general, notifying them of the proposal, and asking if they have any reason to oppose a grant of immunity. They all sign off and send the letters back.

Sandra drives me home. Walking into my apartment building, my cell phone rings. It's Kevin.

"Did you serve Melvin with the subpoena?" I say.

"Yup. He was in his living room, tossing back a frosty one. He's got a nice place out there in the burbs—huge swimming pool, tennis court, the whole nine yards. All gated and alarmed, totally secure. I wouldn't be surprised if there were snipers on the roof."

"Was he cooperative?"

"He agreed to meet us in your office tomorrow morning, before court."

"Was he surprised to see you?"

"Not really," Kevin says. "I kind of had the impression that he was expecting me."

Chapter Forty-eight

At a little after 5:00 A.M., Ty comes into the living room, wearing wool pants and a suit jacket. Not used to seeing him in anything other than jeans, I look up from my laptop and smile.

"Nice duds," I say.

"I'm going to cook us up some oatmeal, the old-fashioned kind, steel cut. I want to fortify you before you head off to war." He gives me a kiss. "I hear Melvin Jones is taking the stand today."

"How did you know?"

"It's all over the Internet. He looks like a mean son of a bitch."

"I have no idea what to expect. I'm prepared for hostile, would prefer cooperative, but will be happy if he doesn't throw a shoe at me."

Ty moves into the kitchen and grinds coffee beans. "Mind if I come?" he says.

"To court? Really?"

"You've seen me perform, so I figure it's only fair if I see you."

"I never knew you wanted to watch."

While Tim was alive, seeing Ty in court would have made me uncomfortable. Even though Julia came to see Tim a couple of times, I never wanted Ty to be there. Now I welcome his support and feel ashamed that I've never invited him.

We finish breakfast, and when we get outside, Sandra is waiting. At my request, she's loosened the reins a little. I don't think I need security anymore, since Orlando has been caught and Darrius was arrested, but Kevin and Owen insisted that I keep the detail until after the verdict comes in.

Sandra double-parks on Cambridge Street, where Ty and I hop out for a quick Starbucks run. I've downed a few cups of coffee already, but this is going to be a long day.

We walk under the copper teakettle into Starbucks. The barista looks sleepy, but the line is short. We get our drinks: Americano for Ty; grande latte for me; and caramel macchiato for Sandra. As Ty goes to the condiment counter and pours soy milk into his coffee, I grab a slice of pound cake. The oatmeal was good, but Ty's whole vegan kick has me craving processed carbs.

Heading back to the car, we cross paths with Rodney Quirk, who is likely en route to his post in the coffee shop. While Rodney and I play a round of who blinks first, a cyclist cuts in front of me, almost knocking me down. I drop my coffee. Ty grabs my arm and pulls me out of the way. Rodney passes us, continuing in the opposite direction.

"Do you know that guy?" Ty says.

"Who?"

"The guy you were just staring at."

I hesitate, weighing my options. I promised to be truthful with Ty, but that requires admitting weakness and possible paranoia. Lying allows me to cling to my precarious equilibrium and get through the day without being plagued with questions.

"I'm not sure. He looked kind of familiar. I may have prosecuted him years ago," I say.

"What did he do?"

"Huh?"

"What crime did he commit?"

"I don't know—stole a car or something. I can't remember. It was a long time ago."

While Ty goes back to Starbucks to replace my coffee, I wait in the car with Sandra.

"Kevin texted me," she says. "He's at your office with Melvin."

"I hope Melvin gives it up fast. I still have to prep for my cross of Orlando."

She drops us off at Bulfinch and goes to park the car. "Tell Kevin that I'll be up in five minutes," she says.

When Ty and I get off the elevator, I'm surprised to see Melvin, alone, in the reception area.

"Hello, Mr. Jones," I say. "Where is Detective Farnsworth?"

Melvin rises from his chair. He's got good manners—I gotta give him that. He may have raised a murderer and committed a host of felonies himself, but he knows to stand when a lady enters the room.

"He said he'll be back in a minute," Melvin says. "He told me that you'd be here with a female detective."

"Have you been waiting long?"

"No. Actually, I was going to run across the street for a bagel, but I couldn't get out of the building. The stairwell and elevator doors are locked from the inside. Farnsworth probably thought I'd sneak out when he wasn't looking. But the truth is, I wouldn't miss this for the world."

"Let's go get started."

Ty looks at me and whispers in my ear, "Are you sure you're going to be okay with him—alone?"

I nod. Melvin is the least of my concerns. He's an aider and abettor, not a violent offender. Besides, Kevin will be here in a minute.

"Holler if you need anything," Ty says.

"I'll do better than that—I'll whistle."

I escort Melvin around the corner and into my office and close the door.

Chapter Forty-nine

Melvin watches as I hang my coat on the back of my door and take a seat behind the desk. I gesture for him to sit.

"I'm surprised you want me to testify," he says.

"Why's that?"

"What I have to say isn't going to help your office or your case."

"I hope you're not going to waste time with this ridiculous alibi theory."

"That's not what I plan to talk about."

"You shouldn't have tried to help Orlando escape," I say.

"Do you want to give me a lecture, or do you want to listen to what I have to say?"

"Let's go over your testimony."

I take out a notepad and scan the questions that I've prepared.

"Before you start, I have something to say and I think you're going to want to hear it."

"I'm all ears."

"There are things you don't know about how the folks in your office do business."

I'm impatient but not disinterested. "Is this about Max?"

Melvin nods. "Yes, but it's not what you think."

He starts to talk but stops when my office door swings open. We both look to see Owen barge in. His face is flushed, and he's breathing heavily, as though he just ran up a couple of flights of stairs.

Assuming he's here to read me the riot act for not taking the plea, I try to cut him off at the pass.

"I'm sorry, Owen, but we're in the middle of prep. I'll call you when we're done."

He closes the door and leans against it. "Don't mind me. Pretend that I'm not even here."

Owen is stubborn, but he's usually discreet. I can't quite get a read on what he's up to.

"Can we talk later?" I say.

"I'd like to hear what Melvin has to say."

"I don't want to be rude, but we're pressed for time. I'll tell you about it later."

"It's not safe for you to be in here, alone, with him," Owen says.

"We're fine," I say, wondering if we are, in fact, fine.

"Let him stay." Melvin seems more clued in on what's going on than I am. "Owen, you should hear this. I was about to tell Ms. Endicott that someone in her office hasn't been playing by the rules."

"That's rich, coming from you," Owen says.

I'm confused and growing increasingly frustrated. Owen is loyal to Max, but Max authorized this meeting.

Melvin seems to be taunting Owen. "I got immunity, you know."

"You don't need immunity," Owen says. "You're not going to testify."

"Yeah, he is," I say. "I know you wanted me to take the plea, but I didn't. So I have to prepare."

"You know why he wanted you to take the plea?" Melvin says.

"Because your kid is guilty as sin," Owen says.

"Bullshit. He wanted you to take the plea because he doesn't want the truth to come out. He's worried about what I'm going to say."

I turn to Melvin. "What are you going to say?"

Owen interrupts. "Who cares? He's a sleazeball liar who obstructed justice and aided and abetted in the escape of a murderer."

My cell sounds. I let it go to voice mail. A second later, my office phone rings. I ignore that too.

"What's going on between you two?" I say.

"I paid bribes," Melvin says. "About a hundred grand in all."

"Shut up," Owen says.

Melvin keeps talking. "It was to shut down the Big Dig investigation."

My mind races as I try to process this. "So it's true. Max was taking bribes?"

"No—Max had nothing to do with it," Melvin says.

I'm relieved but ashamed that I made the accusation. I wish I could take it back.

"Then who did you pay?" As soon as I ask the question, I know the answer. Stunned, I look at Owen. "You?"

Owen meets my eyes but doesn't speak.

"Yup—your friend Owen has a side business," Melvin says.

"Shut the fuck up," Owen says.

"Tim was getting close to indicting his ass," Melvin says.

I catch a glimpse of the photo on my shelf—Owen, Tim, and me, smiling and hoisting our beer mugs. All these years, while we were working side by side, climbing the ranks of the DA's office, sharing moments of victory and defeat, Owen was taking bribes.

"I told Tim," Melvin says. "He was going to give me immunity, and I was going to testify. He promised me that he wouldn't tell anyone, not even the FBI, until after I got out of the grand jury."

That's why Tim didn't tell me what was going on. He was conducting an internal investigation of our colleague, our friend. I'm sure he wanted to talk about it, to get my input, and warn me, but he couldn't break confidentiality.

"Did you testify in the grand jury?" I say.

"I was supposed to, but I never got the chance."

Owen and I lock eyes. His hand reaches into his coat and pulls out a black semiautomatic handgun. I freeze.

"Put it away, man," Melvin says.

Owen isn't just an extortionist, he's a killer. Owen murdered Tim. I can hear my heartbeat as I picture the look in Tim's eyes as his friend stood in front of him, pressed a gun to his temple, and pulled the trigger.

The phones are ringing. Kevin is calling my cell. At the same time, Sandra is calling my office line.

"Don't think about answering." Owen grips the gun, racks the slide, and points the muzzle at me. "Both of you, don't say a word."

The gun looks like a .45 caliber, which means the magazine probably holds at least ten rounds of ammunition. I cling to the edge of my desk, my hands shaking.

"Owen, put the gun away," I say. "You're only going to make things worse."

Melvin bolts up out of his chair and tries to push Owen away from the door. Without hesitation, Owen turns and blasts off a round, striking Melvin in the thigh. He goes down, clutching his leg, moaning, grinding his teeth in pain.

"I should have done this months ago, but your house is like a fucking fortress."

"Okay, man, whatever you want," Melvin says.

Someone tries to push open the door, but Melvin is on the ground, blocking it. The door opens a few inches, slamming against his leg, and he shouts out in pain. Thank God. It has to be Kevin. Owen points the gun at the door.

"Kevin, we're in here. Be careful. He's going to shoot," I say.

Owen fires another round. The bullet rips through the door.

"Farnsworth, I know you're armed. Put your gun down and leave it in the hallway, or I'll kill them both." Owen walks to me, holds his gun at my head, and talks to Kevin. "Open the door, and come in with your hands over your head. Don't do anything stupid."

The door opens slowly. It's not Kevin.

"What the hell is going on in there? Abby, are you okay?"

I'm shocked as Ty steps into view. We exchange shared looks of dread.

"Put your fucking hands up," Owen says.

Ty raises his hands and locks his fingers behind his head. He looks down and sees Melvin, who is writhing on the floor.

"Owen, let us go," I say. "Kevin and Sandra are going to be here any minute."

"No, they're not. I put the building on lockdown. No one can get in or out. It'll take at least twenty minutes for the alarm company to get here and reset the code."

"You don't want to do this," I say.

"Let's go, everyone. Get up."

While Ty helps Melvin to his feet, Owen keeps the gun trained on me.

"You'll never get away with this," I say, trying to buy time. "Tell me what you want. Let's try to work something out before it gets any worse. Think about your wife, your kids."

He presses his gun to the side of my neck, an inch below my ear. The muzzle burns my skin.

"Open the door," he says. "Everyone out, single file, hands in the air."

I have no idea where Owen plans to take us, but I'm sure that

I don't want to go there. I look around for something to use as a weapon. A stapler, scissors, the fire extinguisher. Nothing will stand up to his pistol.

"Move," he says, propelling us forward, out of my office, into the hallway.

Chapter Fifty

Ty goes first, Melvin limps behind him, and then Owen and me. He directs us around the corner, in front of Tim's office. A small scrap of yellow crime scene tape is still stuck to the door and a withered bouquet of memorial flowers is on the floor. As we pass by, Owen kicks over the vase and then shoves me forward.

The door to the stairwell has been propped open with a chair. Owen motions us in. I slow down, hoping that someone was inside the building before it went into lockdown, that someone will see us.

The door lock clicks behind us, and Owen flicks off the light, leaving us standing in the pitch black. I hold on to the railing, try not to trip, and count the flights as we descend deeper into the darkness. Somewhere between the sixth- and fifth-floor landings, Melvin stumbles and tumbles down a flight of stairs.

"I'm bleeding bad," he says.

"Get up," Owen says. "I don't want to kill you here."

Ty helps Melvin to his feet, and we continue our march. When we reach the ground level, I hesitate and consider trying to make a run for it, but then remember that the doors are locked from the inside.

"Move," Owen says.

We continue down the next flight, into the basement. The

reinforced steel door to the storage room is open, ready to receive us. Owen presses the gun to my temple. It's still warm against my skin.

"Keep going," he says. "Inside."

He pushes Melvin into the unlit room and gestures for Ty and me to follow. I haven't been here in at least a year. I try to remember the layout. The door slams behind us. The sound echoes.

Owen flips on the light switch, activating row after row of long fluorescent light tubes attached to industrial ceiling fixtures. The room is cavernous, sterile, cold, like a vault. Or a tomb. There are hundreds of clear plastic storage tubs neatly stacked, dozens of metal filing cabinets, and no windows.

Under the glare of the artificial light, I can see that Owen's eyes are rimmed in red, bloodshot. It looks like he might have fallen off the wagon, or maybe he was never on it to begin with.

"Please, put the gun down," I say, trying to stave off a panic attack. "You'll never get away with this."

"Sure I will. I'll say Melvin came in here with a gun, kidnapped us all. He killed you and your boyfriend. I wrestled the gun away from him and shot him. I'll be a fucking hero."

He points the gun at Melvin, who sinks to the floor and covers his head with his hands. He blasts off a round, striking him in the gut. A little blood spurts out. Melvin utters a yelp and drops his head.

"Come on, man. There's got to be a better way," Ty says.

He turns and aims the gun in my direction. I hear a shrill, deafening scream, like a coyote—I realize that the noise is coming from me.

"You're scared?" Owen says. "Good. You walk around here with your nose in the air, thinking you're so fucking special."

I lunge forward and try to kick him but miss, knocking my shin into the corner of a metal filing cabinet. Sharp pain shoots up my leg. I think I fractured a bone. He stands there, looks at me, and laughs. I kick at him with my other leg. This time I make contact. Ty comes at him and takes a swing. The punch lands on the side of his head, but Owen, numb with manic adrenaline, barely flinches. He hits Ty in the face with the butt of the gun and knocks him off balance.

I look for cover, retreat, and duck behind a stack of boxes. Owen follows. I look up and see him standing over me. I've backed myself into a corner, stuck between a pile of boxes and the wall. He is blocking my only escape route.

"You're no better than the rest of us," he says.

"Leave her alone," Ty says, giving a sign of surrender by throwing his arms up in the air. "Shoot me."

We're all distracted by a noise. Melvin is moaning, on his hands and knees, dragging himself toward the door, desperate to escape.

"Where do you think you're going?" Owen says.

Melvin reaches the door handle and tries to move the lever, but it's stuck, locked from the inside. Owen fires another shot, hitting him in the back. Melvin grunts. This time he stops moving.

Ty charges at Owen and tries to grab his arms. They struggle and both go down. Owen falls on top of Ty, who lands on his back and whacks his head on the cement floor. Owen gets up and kicks Ty in the face. Something cracks. A piece of Ty's tooth falls from his mouth.

As Owen stands over Ty, deciding what to do, I can hear the ticking of his wristwatch. Kevin and Sandra must be frantic, looking for us since they began calling fifteen minutes ago. Maybe they're already inside the building, searching for us.

The basement is probably the last place anyone will check. Our only hope of getting out of this room alive is for someone to hear us before it's too late. Banging or screaming won't be loud enough to attract attention. The only sound that will make it out of this room is gunfire.

I push over a pile of boxes. Papers tumble out and fall to the floor. If I antagonize Owen, that might slow him down. I hurl a bunch of files at him. He turns and looks at me. I start to run and hide under the boxes. I can't see him, but I hear his gun go off.

The bullet barely misses my head. It careens off the wall and through a steel box inches from my nose. The spent cartridge casing drops, bounces on the floor, and comes to rest against my shoe.

"I'm going to kill you, but first I want you to watch me kill your boyfriend."

Owen pivots, points the gun at Ty, and pulls back on the trigger, striking him straight on in the chest. Ty puts his right hand over his heart. Blood seeps out and he falls to the floor.

I jump up and lunge at Owen, hang on to his back, stick my finger in his eye, and dig in until I think I feel the back of his eye socket. He pulls me off him, grabs my hand, and twists my arm back. He's unable to get a steady shot, so he uses the gun to pistol-whip the top of my skull. I drop to the ground.

Another gun goes off. Owen falls backward, and his head smashes into the wall. He goes down, landing inches away from me, close enough that his blood spatters onto my chin.

Kevin is standing in the doorway, aiming his gun at Melvin, who doesn't appear to be breathing.

While Kevin checks Melvin, I rush to Ty. He's been shot in the upper chest, below his left shoulder, near his heart. There's a spot in his jacket about the size of a plum. Dark-red blood is oozing out, starting to pool. He is quiet, in shock, eyes wide open, looking at me. I don't know what to do, how to help him.

"Stay with me, baby." I take off my jacket, press it to the wound, try to slow the bleeding, and cradle his head in my lap. "You're going to be okay." I take hold of his hand and kiss his forehead. "Try to stay awake."

I notice Sandra as she leans down to check on Owen, who hasn't moved since he hit the ground. One eye is open. Bloody pink spittle seeps from his mouth. He has an odd expression on his face, almost like he's grinning.

Chapter Fifty-one

Ty is hoisted onto a gurney, rolled out of Bulfinch, into the cold, and to the back of the ambulance. I sit with him, trying to stay out of the way as an EMT inserts an IV into the back of his hand and checks his vitals.

"How is he?" I say.

No one seems to hear me. They continue doing what they need to do, keeping my boyfriend alive. I hold the rest of my questions and watch Ty as he struggles to keep his eyes open.

"You're beautiful," he says, squinting, trying to focus on me.

We zoom down Cambridge Street and reach the emergency room in about three minutes. News crews, already assembled in front of the hospital, film the ambulance as we pull up. Guards are at the front door, ready to whisk Ty inside.

Cecil Gaultier, head of security, stops me at the door to the operating room and tells me that I'm not allowed in. Cecil, a retired Boston police officer, escorts me down the hall to an empty waiting room.

I've always thought of Cecil as the cheerful, extra tall, red-haired guy, the one with enormous hands, the one who's always in-your-face boisterous. Today he sits quietly and unobtrusively on a gray plastic chair while I try to gather my thoughts.

"I don't know what I'm supposed to do," I say.

"They've got the best of the best in there."

"I feel like I should call people, but I left my cell phone in my office."

"I'll get someone to pick it up," he says. "We're all here for you. You've been there for us all these years."

I think about who I should contact and what I'll say.

"I don't want Ty's parents to hear about it on the news."

"The public information officer got the media to agree to hold off releasing names for the time being," Cecil says.

Kevin comes in and nods to Cecil, who goes out into the hallway, giving us some privacy. He puts his arm around me. I let my head fall into the crook between his neck and his shoulder.

"How is Ty? Have you heard anything?" I say.

"The bullet cracked a rib and nicked his lung, but the docs don't think it did permanent damage to his vitals. They're removing the slug now. He should be out of the OR in a couple of hours."

"Did Melvin survive?"

"He's gone."

"And Owen?"

"He was pronounced at the scene."

Someone knocks on the door. Kevin gets up to see who it is. I can hear Cecil's voice from the hallway.

"Abby has a visitor."

"Who is it?" Kevin says.

"Says he's her father."

Kevin looks back at me, and I nod and start to cry. He steps aside, and my father comes in the room, gives me a hug, and sits down next to me.

Kevin and Cecil disappear.

"I'm sorry, muffin," he says. "Are you okay?"

"Do you know how Ty is?"

"I spoke with the chief of the ER. He says that you'll be able to see him soon."

"Can we get him a private room?"

"Already taken care of. I pulled some strings, got him into the Phillips House."

The Phillips House is like a five-star hotel, only better, with private rooms, pull-out sofa beds for overnight guests, and panoramic views. It also has state-of-the-art medical equipment and top-rate nursing care. Even though insurance doesn't cover the extra nightly fee of $500, getting into the Phillips House can be tougher than getting into the Gardner Club.

"I don't always understand your choices, but if Ty is important to you, then he's important to me."

When Cecil returns, he's accompanied by Ty's surgeon. She is a lanky woman in her fifties, with mousy gray hair and the weathered look of a long-distance runner.

"He's sedated," she says. "You can go up and see him in a little while. But first, I want to take a look at that wound on your leg."

My stockings are shredded, and there's a gash in my shin. She touches it, and I wince.

"I want to get an x-ray."

I sit on the table while a technician takes pictures of my leg. A few minutes later, the doctor comes in and tells me that my shin is okay but my ankle has a small fracture. She puts me in a walking cast.

I refuse the wheelchair and use a cane to make my way down the hallway to the elevator. My father rides up with me. We stop outside the locked entrance to the Phillips House, and I ring the buzzer.

"Charlie and Missy have cut their honeymoon short," my father says. "They're catching the next flight back from Saint Barths."

"I wish they hadn't. I'm not in the mood for their disapproval."

"I'll let you in on a family secret. Charlie has been lobbying me since the day we decided to stop giving you money."

"I thought he hated my job and Ty."

"He doesn't hate either. He says he doesn't agree with your decisions, but he doesn't think you should be punished for, well, being who you are. I think Missy put him up to it, but regardless, he's been championing your cause."

"So why are you punishing me? Are you that afraid to stand up to Mom?"

"It's not punishment, and don't assume that it's your mother's doing. It's about safety—I'm your father and, even though you're a grown woman, I still believe that my role is to protect you."

A security guard unlocks the door to the Phillips House, my father gives me a hug good-bye, and I hobble down the corridor. Ty is lying in his hospital bed, hooked up to all sorts of tubes and monitors. I sit by his bedside, take hold of his right hand, listen to the beeps and whooshing sounds coming from the machines, and watch him sleep.

When the anesthesia starts to wear off, he strains to open his eyes. He looks at me, groggy, using all his energy to focus.

"You're in the hospital." I squeeze his hand.

"Are you okay, baby?"

He musters up a smile and closes his eyes. I wipe his forehead with a cool cloth.

"Yes, I'm fine. We're both going to be fine."

Chapter Fifty-two

The trial is delayed for a week, and I spend the time working from home. I want to be close to Ty now that he's been released from the hospital. I'm happy and relieved that he's accepted my invitation to convalesce in my apartment.

The shooting, the corruption scandal, and the tie-in to Tim's murder are splashed across every media outlet from *The New York Times* to *Inside Edition*. Since the moment Ty got out of surgery, I've made numerous attempts to reach his parents and let them know what happened before they hear about it or see it on the news.

Ty's mother, Melody, is not easy to track down. I spend hours googling and calling various friends and relatives, trying to reach her, but I keep hitting dead ends. Finally I locate her at a sweat lodge in Taos. I dial the phone number for the better part of a day, using my phone's redial button, until someone finally picks up.

"I'd like to help you, but she's at a smudging ceremony," the lodge leader says as though that's a valid excuse. "It's a sacred rite, and I can't interrupt."

"Her son was shot. He almost died." I find it impossible to believe he heard me correctly the first time.

"I'll be sure to give her the message."

285

Ty's father is easier to find. He has two recent speeding tickets and one arrest for driving unregistered and uninsured out of Tampa, where he now lives with his twenty-three-year-old girlfriend. He returns my call immediately and tells me he's extremely concerned, but he doesn't offer to come up to Boston to see his son.

"Abby, honey, while I have you on the phone, do you think you could spare a couple of thou for my lawyer's fee? I'm a little short right now," he says. "I'll pay you back as soon as I get my tax refund. I swear."

"Let me talk to Ty about it," I say, knowing that I'll never mention a word about this phone call.

Charlie and Missy come directly to my apartment from the airport, with sun-kissed skin and an exquisite turquoise Hermès blanket. While Missy goes in to visit with Ty, Charlie sits with me on the sofa.

"Thanks for the blanket," I say.

"Missy thought Ty might want something soft."

"Should I take that as a dig?"

"Accept the gesture, don't analyze it," he says.

Missy comes out of the bedroom and makes a pot of ginger tea for everyone.

"Sorry we interrupted your honeymoon," I say as she hands me a cup.

"We've been to Saint Barths before." She sits across from me. "We'll have plenty of opportunities to go again."

"We're here for you," Charlie says.

"You always have been," I say.

"Do you need money?"

"I appreciate the offer, but I'm going to have to figure out how to make my own way."

"I wish you didn't always suffer in silence," Missy says.

"It's the Endicott way—we don't talk about money or feelings, and we don't complain. Welcome to the family."

When Missy smiles, I see that her bottom front teeth are slightly crooked, one of the few visible remnants of her impoverished past. She reaches into the pocket of her sweater and hands me a string of lavender glass beads.

"Worry beads. I got them from one of the nuns when I was a child. I take them out when I'm anxious, to pass the time."

"I'll keep them in my briefcase, for when I'm waiting for my jury verdict."

After Charlie and Missy leave, I find a roll of seven crisp hundred-dollar bills on my kitchen counter.

My mother calls every day to check on Ty's status. She sends vases from Winston Flowers, delicate anemones with papery white petals and bold black centers. She has platters of cold lobster salad and hearty beef bourguignonne delivered from Savenor's Market. She even stops by once, in the flesh, with my father.

She walks into my living room in a silk Valentino suit, looking like she has had her hair shellacked. She cases the joint with suspicion, examines the books on my coffee table. *Matisse,* a retrospective of his bright, cheerful cutouts. *The Nutshell Studies of Unexplained Death,* a macabre collection of dollhouses designed to re-create gory murder scenes.

She picks up the silver perpetual calendar on the mantelpiece, and as she puts it down, it looks like she's going to don a white glove and run her finger along the marble ledge, inspecting for dust.

"This is such a charming apartment," she says.

"I'll miss living here."

"You have options."

"I'm not quitting my job."

The door to my bedroom is closed, and I tell my mother that Ty is asleep, sparing us all what would surely be an awkward encounter.

She stays for about fifteen minutes and then begs off, claiming that she has to go to an event. She says she can't miss it; she's being honored by the Boston Ballet for her fund-raising accomplishments. After she leaves, I riffle through my desk and find my invitation to the party. The gala was last night.

Chapter Fifty-three

Court reassembles, and the jury is sent out to deliberate. In less than an hour, we hear a knock coming from inside the jury room. Sal pokes his head in and comes out with a piece of paper. I try to catch his eye, hoping he'll give me a clue about what's in the note. He goes directly to Judge Volpe's chambers, without glancing in my direction. A few minutes later, Judge Volpe calls us in to his chambers.

"The jurors have a question," he says, showing us a hand-written note signed by the foreman.

"What could they possibly want to know?" I say, worried that we have one lunatic who is going to hang the jury.

Volpe shows us the paper. *Which box do we check if we think he is guilty under both theories of murder in the first degree? Premeditation, Cruel and Atrocious, or both?*

"I plan to send this back to them in response," he says, jotting down his answer. *Both.*

The jurors file in, some taking note of the cast on my leg. The foreman announces the verdict.

"Guilty of the first degree murder of Jasmine Reed. Guilty of the attempted murders of Ezekiel Hogan and Denny Mebane."

As soon as the verdicts are recorded by the clerk, a mob of deputies swarm, cuff, and shackle Orlando. As they whisk him to the lockup, he turns and looks into the audience. No one is there for him—not his family, not his fellow gangsters.

Nestor walks up to the table and congratulates me. I give him a hug.

"You're a champ," he says.

"Thanks for putting up with me."

Out of the corner of my eye, I see Kevin in the back row of the gallery. He smiles, gives me a wink, and disappears. Jackie and Adele are seated in the front row. Behind them is Harold, along with a bunch of reporters, ADAs, defense attorneys, and people I don't recognize.

Out in the hallway, Jackie approaches with a basket of homemade gingersnaps.

"I saw what happened to your boyfriend. I hope he's okay," she says.

"He's going to be fine." I accept the basket and give her a hug.

"I can't wait to get back and tell Denny about the verdict," Adele says.

Winnie comes in the courtroom and hands me her phone. "Someone wants to talk to you."

"I wanted to thank you," Ezekiel says. "I'm sorry for giving you a hard time."

"Thanks for hanging in there with me," I say.

Max follows me into the elevator.

"I can't begin to express my appreciation."

"I wish it had turned out differently, for everyone."

"Me too."

"You and Owen had a long history."

"Thirty years. We were altar boys together at Holy Name. He was best man at my wedding. I'm Patsy's godfather. I should have seen it. Maybe I could have done something."

"We all missed it."

Kevin told me that Owen was deep in debt. When he gave up

drinking, he replaced it with another addiction—gambling. He was betting on everything, dogs, horses, scratch tickets, college football, even his kids' Little League games.

"Take some time off—you deserve it," Max says.

"I plan to."

"If I throw my hat in the ring for mayor, you should run for DA. You'd win by a landslide."

When we get out to the street, the media has assembled. They're holding cameras and microphones, waiting for an official statement about the verdict. Max walks toward the podium, but turns when he notices that I'm not following him.

"You should be up there with me. This is your win."

"I've had enough of the spotlight."

He puts his hand over his mouth. "Want to join me for a drink later?"

"I've got to get home to Ty."

I consider hailing a taxi but decide to walk. It's got to be at least forty degrees outside, warm for this time of year, and I need the fresh air. I'm not going to let a fractured ankle slow me down.

I head up Cambridge Street, toward the Boston Common, put my Bluetooth in my ear, and make a phone call.

"I wanted to be sure you heard the news," I say when Crystal's mother picks up

"I saw it on TV. Justice has been served, and Crystal can finally rest in peace. I hope you can find your peace too," she says.

I hang up and continue toward Park Street. I see a familiar figure standing at an ATM, collecting cash. I'm in no mood for Rodney Quirk tonight. I want this to end. I'm done living in fear. I reach into my bag, feel around for my Mace, and approach him.

"Why are you following me, Rodney?"

"Excuse me?"

"You beat your murder case—isn't that enough?"

"I don't want anything to do with you."

"I see you every morning at the coffee shop. Now you're out here following me. I should have reported you a long time ago."

"Following you? I work here. My public defender got me a job, I work at Legal Aid. The office is in Center Plaza."

"Bullshit."

"I'm assigned to the Innocence Project."

He reaches into his back pocket and pulls something out. I flinch and think about yelling or running or spraying him with Mace. He opens up his wallet and holds up his employee ID. *Rodney Quirk, Staff Assistant, Innocence Project.* I'm not sure what to do. Apparently, Rodney has a right to be in the area. He's a killer, but he's not a stalker, which at this point is as good as it gets.

When I get home, Ty is in bed, dozing. The curtains are drawn back, and I look out the window. I'll miss being in this apartment in the springtime, when the cherry blossom trees form a bright-pink umbrella over the Esplanade.

"You're late," he says. "Everything okay?"

"I ran into an old friend on my way home from work."

"Anyone I know?"

"No."

I kick off my shoes, sit down on the bed, and give him a kiss.

"Congratulations on your verdict," he says. "I'm glad it's finally over."

"I'm sorry you were one of the casualties."

"I'll heal."

"I'm going to take some time off, figure out where to go from here."

I kiss him again, careful not to bump or rub against his bandages.

"A real estate agent stopped by today. Are you sure you want to sell this place?"

"I don't have a choice. I can't afford this life anymore."

He shifts his weight and struggles to face me.

"I pay rent in Somerville. I could just as easily pay it here," he says.

"I can't charge you rent."

"I'm not looking to be your tenant. I know it's a new concept for you, but how about we work as a team, like a real couple."

"You're saying that you want to give up your apartment and move in?"

"I want to live with you, here—or anyplace else."

"You're on some pretty heavy-duty painkillers, I'm sure it's the meds talking. But you've tendered the offer, and I accept. That means we have a valid, binding contract."

"Okay, Counselor. But I have one condition."

"Name it."

"We have to be more open with each other. You have to let me know what's on your mind. Otherwise, this will never work."

"Deal."

Ty dozes off. I can hear his deep breathing and see his chest rising and falling. I lie down and nestle in next to him.

After a few minutes, he turns toward me, his eyes still closed. "Open, honest, full disclosure."

"I swear."

"No more secrets?"

"No more secrets."

"You have to tell me when you're afraid of something or someone."

"I'll tell you. I promise."

As Ty falls back to sleep, I look at him, and then close my eyes and begin to recite my list.

Acknowledgments

Victoria Skurnick, agent extraordinaire, thank you for your insight, expertise, and enthusiasm. And everyone at Minotaur Books, especially my fabulous editor, Kelley Ragland, for your discerning eye, and Elizabeth Lacks, for your patience and guidance.

I wrote the first draft of this book in a workshop at Grub Street. Thank you to my classmates and instructor, Sophie Powell, for the feedback and fellowship.

To my friends in Boston, New York, and Los Angeles: Joan Rater, Jenny Kane, Laurie Grotstein, Betsy Beale, Elizabeth White, Chris White, Ursula Knight, Mary Beth Long, and Sarah Ellis—I'm so grateful for your pep talks, notes, and guest rooms.

Billy Bob Thornton, thank you for listening to my stories and for sharing yours, for suggesting that I write this book, and for cheering me on along the way.

Thanks to my brother, Peter Wechsler, for your championship and counsel. And to my father, Henry Wechsler, for your unwavering encouragement, confidence, and support.